Kingdom of Scars

Eoin C Macken

WARD RIVER PRESS

This novel is entirely a work of fiction. The names, characters and incidents portrayed in it are the work of the author's imagination. Any resemblance to actual persons, living or dead, events or localities is entirely coincidental.

Published 2015
by Ward River Press
123 Grange Hill, Baldoyle
Dublin 13, Ireland
www.wardriverpress.com

© EOIN C MACKEN 2014

Copyright for typesetting, layout, design, ebook
© Poolbeg Press Ltd

The moral right of the author has been asserted.

A catalogue record for this book is available from the British Library.

1

ISBN 978-1-78199-946-2

All rights reserved. No part of this publication may be reproduced or transmitted in any form or by any means, electronic or mechanical, including photography, recording, or any information storage or retrieval system, without permission in writing from the publisher. The book is sold subject to the condition that it shall not, by way of trade or otherwise, be lent, resold or otherwise circulated without the publisher's prior consent in any form of binding or cover other than that in which it is published and without a similar condition, including this condition, being imposed on the subsequent purchaser.

Printed and bound by CPI Group (UK) Ltd, Croydon, CR0 4YY

www.wardriverpress.com

Praise for Kingdom of Scars

"Quite brilliant, a coming of age story that never flags".
Sue Leonard, *Irish Examiner*

"Evocative, stand out, Macken has a natural flair for the descriptive"
Michael Doherty, *RTÉ Guide*

"Macken imbues his first book with a cinematic quality."
Deirdre Reynolds, *Irish Independent*

"A gritty story about growing up, friendship and betrayal that perfectly captures the confusion and longings of the teenage years, this crossover novel will appeal to adults as well as teen readers . . ."
Sarah Webb, *Irish Independent*

"Eoin Macken's writing bristles and prickles with authentic purpose. *Kingdom of Stars* feels both epic and intimate simultaneously."
Eoghan McDermott, 2FM

"I don't know if I like Eoin Macken. His fabulous face. His Calvin Klein male model contracts. His shimmering six pack. His aquiline jawline. His superb cinematography. His all embracing bravery. His staggeringly successful film and television career. The only respite for the rest of us mere mortals was that at least he couldn't write novels. Turns out he can. Turns out his punch-drunk love-prose will knock you on your ass. Turns out I hate him."
Terry McMahon, Writer/Director

"A wonderful first novel from a new talent: rich, absorbing and gritty. One to watch for the future."

Jim Fitzpatrick, Artist

"Raw and honest, a compelling account of growing up as a teenager – an eloquent and descriptive depiction of a young man reflecting on his experiences as he tumbles through his teenage years. Genuinely written from the heart."

Jack Reynor, Actor

"Gripping, sensitive and utterly captivating, *Kingdom of Scars* is a work of deep insight. A riveting read."

Caroline Grace-Cassidy, Writer

"Author Eoin Macken perfectly captures the voice – both inner and outer – of a certain generation of Irish youth with his debut novel *Kingdom of Scars*. Anyone who has ever had a best friend, a first crush, a moment of awareness that they may never fully understand the world they're a part of – which should be just about everybody – will be able to find themselves in this book."

Rory Cashin, Film Critic

"Sam is immersed in the intoxicating cloud that is adolescence and its insecurities. This is a relatable story that everyone, on some level, can connect with. Macken paints a realistic picture through descriptive and engaging narrative, which pulls the reader into Sam's journey of self-discovery. Each page brings with it a sense of nostalgia, encouraging the reader to remember with fondness and fear their own childhood. It is reflective and colourful."

Laura Butler, *Irish Independent*

Dedication

This book is dedicated to my uncle, the late John Macken, affectionately known as Don.

It's also dedicated to all the lads that I grew up with, for both their friendships and difficult relations, to the girls who taught me many lessons about life, and to both Gerry Haugh my English teacher and Jim Culliton who shaped and guided my experiences in school. This book is fiction, but much fiction has some basis in reality; it's just a question of deciding how much of it you would like to be truth.

The street that I grew up on was called Evora Park, and the band titled "Evora", comprised of lads from this same street, perfectly encapsulates the feelings that I felt as a youth and still feel through their music more than anything else.

The book is finally dedicated to my parents, Maeve and James Macken, who always encouraged my tender forays into trying to be creative. I love them both dearly for that.

YOUTH

There's an energy to them.
A nervous
Swagger that feeds each one, and
Makes everybody around
Shrink into their seats
Like innocuous versions of themselves.

Each boy wears clothes too big
That don't fit.
The track-suit bottoms down
Below the waist, jackets
Hanging like pouches of
Fattened cotton.

Each highlights his own motif,
Separating his
Individuality from the conformity
Of being separate
Which he wears with
Showy hopeful pride.

For some it's hair,
Clipped tight to the scalp,
Or a gaudy piercing
Through the lip or brow.
For others no more
Than a ring on a finger.

But it's the pack mentality
That most concerns the plebs,
This quick instinct
To follow the most virile
That has taken control
In that unquestioning moment,

Where nothing else comes into
Their thoughts but
Adherence to the group,
Dismissing circumstances like
Madmen
Unhindered by consequence.

Yet underneath this bravado.
Below the thin veneer
That hides their character,
Lies a yearning for affection:
A yearning truth
Of humility and loyalty.

Brazen though this appears
It's all a game.
A social ladder
They clamber back and forth
On a daily basis
Searching for themselves.

As we all do.

Prologue

They were definitely following him. He didn't need to look over his shoulder to confirm that they were but Sam did so anyway. He immediately wished he hadn't.

"What ya looking at?"

The voice rang out harshly and followed him down the platform, the rasping syllables bouncing off the railings on either side. They had seen him cross the road to enter the DART station before he had seen them and they had changed their trajectory to match his.

He stared at the arrivals board as he walked, willing for a train to arrive.

"Here, we're talking to ya – do ya have a smoke?" they shouted in his general direction.

He wanted to ignore them and pretend that he hadn't heard but he had to face them. He took a deep breath and swallowed, but there was no saliva.

He turned and shouted back. "No, I don't, sorry."

There were three of them, and more with a straggling

group of girls further up the platform. Ticket inspectors didn't really bother on a Sunday so they were taking their time clambering over the railings.

"Well, go get us one then."

It was a statement buried in ridicule, but it was the sort of threat that was always made to precipitate the start of an aggressive confrontation. Sam heard the screech of the train's horn signalling it was on its way, but they were barely 30 yards back from him.

The train would arrive too late.

"Will you kiss Mary – I think she likes ya?"

He wanted to ask who Mary was but thought better of it. The closest boy, maybe two years older than the others, had his hands in his pockets in a friendly manner, but there was a sharp swagger to his movements. People liked that edgy feeling when there was the possibility of violence, especially when they had little else to do.

"Sorry, I don't want to kiss her."

The boy's face suddenly contorted into a violent mask. "You saying my bird isn't good enough fer ya, is that it? She's not pretty enough for you, but she's ugly enough fer me, is that it?"

Sam didn't know if there was any point in responding to that. He looked over his shoulder to where the train was making its approach in a haze of treacle. They would be more likely to leave him alone with lots of people watching.

The boys pressed on with their inexorable entrapment – ten yards now.

"That's not what I meant – I'm sure she's gorgeous."

The boy's eyebrows rose mockingly. "So now ya do wanna kiss my bird. Why would ya wanna kiss somebody else's woman?"

The train achingly slowly pulled up alongside and then they were on top of him. The nearest smacked him on the side of his head hard and a second punch clipped his ear. Hands grabbed at his bag while the third boy hopped around like an idiot.

Sam ignored the surprised faces that were watching this macabre dance with detached fascination. He frantically pressed the button to the door while trying to keep hold of his bag, and ducked his head in and around to avoid some of the punches thrown at it. The door opened just as the lads further away saw what was happening and began to run down to join in.

Sam struggled halfway onto the train, so that the doors couldn't close, but he couldn't get in without leaving behind his bag which he refused to give up. He had spun to try and twist it out of their eager hands when one punch hit him square in the eyes, and for a moment he lost his balance and it seemed that he might fall back onto the platform.

The train driver leaned his head out from his cab and screamed down at them.

"Get off my fucking train so we can leave, ye little gurriers!"

With one almighty pull Sam ripped the bag from the boy and kicked out, catching the other in the groin. In that split second he was free and he fell backwards into the car. Mercifully the doors closed at precisely that moment and he was safe.

The lads thumped on the door, trying to reopen it and when the train started to rumble forward they ran alongside it for a few yards, brandishing their middle fingers like weapons.

Sam sat back against the opposite doors, on the floor, panting. Nobody offered to help him and after a while he got up and took a seat opposite a guy with his girlfriend. The man refused to look him in the eye. Sam's legs began shaking, and he had to hold them to stop his knees clacking together. He wanted to get sick.

Sam had turned fifteen a few months previously. He didn't particularly like being fifteen.

An old lane ran directly up from Howth train station to Sam's estate, bordered on one side by dense woods with a golf course behind, and on the other by a sloping bank leading up into a lighter wooded area that ran alongside the laneway for half its length. These woods gave the laneway a tunnel-like effect from the trees clasping above, both sides heavy with secret ways into clearings and hacked-open spaces. Eventually the lane gave way to the streets above, leading into the various estates with the woods only on one side. The lane then continued snaking up the hill through more estates, before breaking in two a few times with the woods and golf course still on the right before reconnecting and opening out at the summit.

He was walking up the lane towards his house, still nursing his bruises, when a whistle split the air to his left. He looked up and saw Jesse waving at him halfway up a slope leading into the undergrowth ahead. He nodded and followed him up through the dense forestation to where they joined three other lads – Jayo, Mouse and Washing Machine. Sam wasn't part of the group by any means but they accepted him at times. This was one of those times, and he would always eagerly take it.

"Ya want a drag?"

Jayo spoke to him in an almost fatherly tone. At times like this Sam felt like he almost liked Jayo.

"Yeah, yeah, that'd be deadly."

Sam's voice changed when he was with the lads. He spoke more like them with the odd inflections, the dropping of consonants at the end of words and the screwed-up grammar.

He found himself relaxing. He didn't smoke, but just being in the relative comfort of the lads' company made the earlier events seem distant. It wasn't usually like this.

"We need some more smokes."

Mouse didn't actually direct the question at Washing Machine – it was just a simple statement – but Washing Machine didn't allow it to hang in the air for too long. As they all knew he wouldn't, for he was the grunt of the group.

"Yeah, we do. I'll leg it down and get some."

He paused for a moment, half in hope that somebody might offer him some money to get them. Nothing. Finishing the drag off his cigarette in one long inhalation, he blew the smoke out in Sam's face in a thinly veiled attempt to reassert himself, then hopped onto the high wall behind them and dropped into the undergrowth below. They could hear him scrambling through the bushes to get onto the street beyond, leading to the shops.

They always stood by that wall where it formed a right angle – protected on two sides from the wind and rain, opening out over a sharp ravine where a tired rope hung desperately off a single territorial oak tree. It was hidden from unwanted visitors by the thick growth of trees and bushes all around it. Remnants of fires and broken branches, rubbish and various other bits and pieces – burst footballs and bent golf clubs – surrounded their feet. It was their haven. It was dirty and overgrown, but it was theirs. And that was the most important thing.

Chapter 1

Schooling with Don

He had always enjoyed the walk from the DART up to school. It didn't really make any sense because half of the time it was cold and dreary and his feet hurt. But there was something that excited him about walking past the council flats from Connolly Station up through Summerhill to Mountjoy Square – the sense of danger. He had a physical routine that he used to slip into when he approached. He'd knit his eyebrows together like he'd seen on the television – it made people look very intense and dangerous, he thought. He would bob his head and his hips from side to side, adopting the 'walk' of inner-city Dublin, a little like the lads who had approached him at the station. Safety in replication. Lastly, and most importantly, he'd stare at everybody who passed with malice, as if he wanted nothing more than for them to attempt to start a fight with him. He always felt empowered when he did this, so much so that on odd occasions he actually resented having company to walk to and from school with, as it meant he couldn't do his act.

The school was right in front of him. The big black gates confronted him, with all that separated him from the dark castle being a tidy moat of a tarmac road with cars streaming across it. He crossed the road and slipped in past the gates just as they began to close behind him.

Lessons dragged that morning and at the allotted time he eagerly skipped class and made for his appointment with Don.

Don's room always stank of heavy smoke which hung in the air like a blanket, warm and suffocating. It permeated every pore in Sam's exposed skin and coated them in a thin layer of dark yellow nicotine. Yet it was strangely comforting.

Don sat across from Sam behind that massive oak desk of his that was covered in stacks of papers, folders, files, books, photographs. Sam was convinced half of them had never been moved since he first came to the office but it was hard to tell through the haze of smoke.

"How's class?"

"Fine."

"Home?"

"Yeah, good."

"Anything new?"

"Not really, no."

Don took a long drag from his cigar, but it didn't respond satisfactorily so he relit it.

Sam was fascinated by the flame as it flickered for a moment, testing the foreign air around it, then growing in confidence wrapped itself around the cigar with gusto, burning it quite brutally before abruptly disappearing.

Don's fingers were long. The digits of an artist. He would most likely have been involved in the arts if he hadn't been a priest. But the scholarly profession suited him, as did the less rigorous demands of being mentor to the young men in the school.

Blowing a perfect smoke ring, Don finally turned and looked Sam straight in the eye.

God, for a priest he was damn cool, thought Sam. He realized that he was staring and as covertly as possible shifted his gaze to the window above Don's head, searching for a pigeon. They liked sitting on the windowsill and crapping down onto the courtyard below where they would regularly catch an unfortunate student.

"Are you with us today?"

Sam snapped back to reality, fixing his gaze back on Don's piercing eyes that gleamed through the smoke.

"Sorry, yeah, just drifted there a little bit."

Don watched him for a moment, nodding his head gently. Then he inhaled another deep long drag and allowed his eyes to wander around the room, feigning interest in the heavy books lining the shelves all around.

"You've been doing that a bit in class lately, haven't you? From what I hear."

"Who said that?"

"I have my sources, but I can never reveal them." Don smiled as he spoke.

With Don there was never recrimination, only warm comradeship and a search for understanding. That was his secret: you liked Don so much that you never wanted to disappoint him. It was a Jesuit trait. They were clever, these old Jays, wily like magpies. You were always wary when you saw more than one – it usually meant trouble – but when they weren't around you found yourself yearning for them and wondering why you weren't worthy of their attentions.

"I've just been a bit distracted lately, that's all."

"Why?"

There was a long pause. That was the beauty of talking with Don: he would let you take your time. If you were really lucky you might get to spend two classes in a row in that homely office of his, just talking about whatever came to your mind. Don fancied himself as some sort of amateur psychologist and to him every detail was important. Including the fact you'd made the choice to skip maths. Nothing was irrelevant.

"I guess I'm finding it all a bit boring lately, finding it difficult to concentrate."

"What have you been thinking about instead?"

"Nothing."

"That was a bare-faced lie."

"No, it wasn't."

"You looked away."

"That's beneath you, Don – too cheap."

"It's in all the books."

Sam laughed out much too loudly, but he couldn't help it.

"What have you been thinking about?"

Sam stared Don in the eye. Don stared right back.

Sam knew that this was the point where Don would decide if he was telling the truth or not, and if he thought that he was jerking him around then he'd be heading back to class within minutes. Equally, if Sam had nothing of note to say he would be sent back anyway. He really wanted to miss another class.

What was the truth though other than somebody else's lies?

"I went to a concert at the weekend."

"How nice – who did you see?"

"The Chemical Brothers."

"Who?"

"Hardcore dance and raver band, you wouldn't know them."

"Ravers?"

"Yeah, it was pretty mental – got home late."

Don's interest was piqued. He tried to hide it, but he failed.

Now that Sam had started he wasn't going to stop, but he mightn't give out too many details – just enough to keep Don hooked. He wanted to tell him everything that was really going on – there was something very comforting in knowing that he could say anything and most likely not be judged but actually offered advice. What did priests know about life though? This story was better.

"Any drugs in those kinds of places?"

Sam hadn't expected him to say it straight out, but he had. He might as well have nailed the point to the wall, written on a white flag with heavy red paint. Sam felt a tiny bit less respect for Don than he had moments before.

"Of course – it's that kind of place."

Sam let that hang in air, teasing, just out of Don's reach, unless he really wanted it.

"Sure."

Don looked at him and inhaled from that impressive cigar again without commenting further. Fuck, he wasn't playing the game the way Sam had expected – he probably knew exactly what he was doing and wasn't going to be led in.

Sam wriggled in his seat to make himself more comfortable. There was silence and he felt the need to fill it.

"It was a good night."

Don nodded. But that was it. He didn't pursue it any further. If Sam wanted to tell him more then he'd have to volunteer.

"Your marks are slipping. All of your teachers are reporting that."

Don came straight out with it. So that was why he had no further interest in the concert.

"And the Chemical Brothers aren't playing until November."

Sam stared at Don. How the fuck did he know that? He could feel the blood swarming up through his capillaries and flooding his cheeks, propelling hot air around him like a visible force field. This was trouble. Don was not to be lied to.

"Is that all?" Don continued, a bored tone in his voice.

"Yes."

"Okay."

Don spun away in his chair, swivelling to face the window. At his movement two pigeons on the sill were startled and they jumped off the ledge in a bustle of feathers and cat-like purring.

It was all so seductively relaxing in this office. But right now Sam wished he could leap off the ledge with the pigeons and fly somewhere. Being caught lying hurt because of the pride involved.

"How did you get the swollen nose?"

Shit. Was it that noticeable? Sam had figured it looked fine. Fuck. He had wanted to tell him but he hadn't.

"Football. Ball hit me in the nose."

"Your answer was too quick. Come on?"

"You can't judge that."

"Am I wrong?"

"Yes."

"Okay."

Once you start lying it becomes habit very quickly. Sam had heard that once before, probably from Don during one of their more productive conversations.

Don stiffly kept his back to him, indicating that the conversation was finished, so Sam reluctantly pushed out his chair which scraped across the floor with a petulant squeal. Don's shoulders shook a little from the grating noise. Sam immediately wanted to explain that it hadn't been a childish gesture on purpose but the damage was already done so he didn't bother.

Making sure to close the door behind him as respectfully as possible, he walked back to class with leaden feet, replaying the conversation with Don in his mind over and over as if adding guilt to the past might somehow reveal a reprieve hidden in their words. There wasn't one.

Chapter 2

Bacardi Breezers

The smoke filled Sam's nostrils, rushing up his nasal cavity with all the indiscretion of a thief. He wrinkled the base of his nose and scrunched his eyes close together tightly to try and force away the impatient need to sneeze. He spluttered and heaved three times in a row, then leaned back to catch his breath, proud that he had kept the impulse at bay but momentarily exhausted from the effort. Then the sneeze came, louder because he had initially stifled it.

There was a justified silence as everybody looked at him in disgust.

It was the start of the weekend and the lads had dragged him into the woods before he could argue, his schoolbag left up beside the old oak tree. It was late when he came home and already getting dark so they had crept slowly in single file through the thick bushes and increasing gloom, mirroring the confident steps of their de facto leader Jayo.

Jayo had stopped at the edge of a clearing on the far side

of the woods, holding his hand up like a soldier in the movies. Then creeping forward on their bellies to an overhang above the clearing, they had each taken turns to look down to where a bunch of old tramps was gathered around a smoking fire, drinking cans in the same clothes that they always wore. They were no more than a few feet away and the smell of stale sweat, grimy clothes and thick smoke clogged the air around them, making it hard to breathe, or in Sam's case not to sneeze. His spluttering had echoed through the woods as it if was the only noise in the world.

Jayo shook his head with a show of disappointment but also a gleam in his eye – he was always excited by the prospect of impending violence and now if they were caught by these old tramps they would get a serious beating.

The world seemed to hold its breath before one of the tramps began shouting angrily and Jayo immediately leapt to his feet smoothly and disappeared into the wet undergrowth. The rest of the group followed him in a mess of limbs and crunching foliage and then there were wet branches smashing into Sam's face, threatening to take out his eyes in the increasing blackness as he blindly followed the bodies in front. The mud was alive beneath his feet, feinting this way and that way, daring him to slip. He ducked under a huge bough that erupted in front of his face, grasping an errant sapling that sprung from the ground to keep his balance on the slippery surface. Hard breathing, thick with the heavy scent of stale alcohol, bore down and threatened to overrun him through pure sound. Fear. The adrenaline pumped through his body as he ran, listening in vain for the sounds of any of the lads. They were probably crouched down in the undergrowth, tiny hidden figures lost in the wild night. Fuck. He felt a scrabbling at his back, a hand grasping vainly at his collar. He put his hand on the zip of his jacket, ready to abandon it if necessary, like a lizard reluctantly shedding its tail. It was a nice jacket that his mother had given to him for Christmas to keep him warm on nights like this.

He knew he was about to be caught and his body had begun to tense up when there was a loud thud behind him, the fingers disappeared and a roar of pain and supreme irritation bellowed out behind him.

"That you, Spud? Did ya catch one of de little fucks?"

"No, I fuckin' hurt me leg on a fuckin' tree or somethin'!" Spud screamed back.

Sam kept running, soft leaves slapping the skin of his face like a gentle warning of what could have happened. The woods were on his side tonight.

"I'll fuckin' murder ye, I swear – I know who ye are!"

Spud's voice belted into the gentle air but Sam kept running as the fear receded behind him victoriously.

The voices of the tramps had faded into the distance and his pace was slowing when a body slammed into him and knocked the wind out of him with a loud whoosh. He fell on his hip, hitting decaying branches and rolling over once, but he was up in a flash defiantly looking for his attacker.

Jesse stared back up at him from his haunches as he caught his breath. His eyes gleamed in the darkness like a cat's.

"You were lucky," he said.

"I know."

"They'd have knocked the head off ya. They battered Carney a few weeks ago."

Sam nodded and wiped some of the mud off his face.

"Where did the rest of them go?"

"Dunno. Probably out to the course."

"Yeah – we'd better go find them?"

Jesse nodded and the two of them walked towards the golf course a few hundred yards away.

The rest of the lads were sitting calmly in a small compact group, bathed in moonlight as if nothing had happened. They turned as one to look at the two stragglers emerging from the trees.

Mouse lifted a Bacardi Breezer to his lips and winked patronizingly at Sam.

"I didn't think we'd ever see ya again so I started drinking yours – figured ya wouldn't mind."

"Yeah, sure."

Sam had forgotten that he had given Washing Machine money earlier in the week to buy him some bottles. Washing Machine begrudgingly passed him one from his ugly yellow backpack.

They sat down and Jayo reached out and ruffled Jesse's hair, while staring balefully at Sam.

"You're a fuckin' eejit – why the fuck did you have to sneeze?" he sneered.

Washing Machine spat on the ground. "Yeah, fuckin' dope, we should have left ya!"

"I was gonna trip ya up and leave ya for them – fuckin' deserved it," Mouse said.

Sam nodded, accepting the rap, although he still wasn't clear on what they had actually planned to do. The lads probably didn't know either but were caught up in the allure of having a grand master plan.

"I didn't mean to sneeze but the smoke was killing me. Sorry, lads."

Jayo threw an empty bottle at Sam who ducked and watched it roll out onto the smooth grass. Turning back, Sam found himself face to face with a demon. Jayo's face was contorted into a black hole of venom, his features twisted into an ugly snarl. Sam reeled back only to be pulled into Jayo's body by the grip on his collar. Stale breath reeking of cheap sweetened alcohol raped his throat as Jayo exercised his full control and humiliated him. When he had finished burping in his face, he pushed him casually to the grass.

Peals of laughter broke out.

"Yer lucky I don't beat de shit outta ya – if we'd got caught by those knackers it woulda been your fault."

"Yeah, sorry."

"Whatever."

The banter began to simmer between the lads, but Sam found himself isolated on the outskirts of the group, a pariah of sorts. Now and again insults were thrown in his direction and he shrugged them off with a rueful smile, but his insides burned. He wanted to lash out, catch Jayo right on the nose, maybe break it, but definitely draw blood. Payback for all the injustices he had suffered this week. He imagined the red liquid oozing proudly down Jayo's chin, as the lads offered their overdue respects to him, Sam. He wasn't even sure how they would – he just imagined he would feel it, and that alone would be enough.

Once or twice when Mouse directed a barbed comment his way, or Washing Machine threw his empty bottle at his head, he felt on the verge of jumping to his feet and throwing his clenched fists on one of them.

Washing Machine would be the easiest to overpower, he reckoned, but he'd also be the most dangerous. If he did beat him up he'd have to look continuously over his shoulder in the future, for Washing Machine was sure to retaliate in a much more violent fashion. Washing Machine had a dangerous cornered-dog element constantly brooding inside his under-educated skull and he was wily like an injured hyena.

Mouse would in all likelihood kick the living daylights out of him, and the only hope he'd hold out in that situation would be that Jayo's completely irrational sense of power, fuelled by a desire to keep control of the interactions of his supposed lessers, would eventually bring it to an end.

As for Jayo himself, Sam believed that he would put up a fair fight, and stop before he did too much damage. But he couldn't really predict anything that Jayo would do. Jayo's legend was secure among his peers pretty much for all time, so much so that even if he became old and sick he would be unlikely to be challenged for the fear of what he could do if the mood took him. He had a ferocity within him that could only be described as primal.

A little over a year before, when he was still fourteen, Jayo had been walking home from school, unaccompanied by his older brother for once (another lively force in himself), when he was jumped by three of the bigger lads from the local school. There was a territorial feud between these groups of teenagers from sections of the roads leading up to the council houses, which only faded once the offenders were either in jail, had moved out, or had grown old enough to be tired of it. Jayo was in theory completely overpowered and the three lads were particularly aggressive, with a well-deserved reputation of extended and vicious assault. Jayo walked home however with just a broken nose and some scratches. The other three lads didn't come to school for at least a week, and when the first to do so, Billy Ryan, 'Choco' to his mates, finally did, his right eye was bandaged to his head, his ear ripped by what appeared to be tooth-marks, and his ankle fractured. The other lads didn't reappear until their wounds were much further advanced in healing so nobody fully knew the extent of their injuries. After that incident, nobody questioned Jayo's ability to be much more vicious than the next person, and he commanded due respect. The legend of that story grew to such an extent that kids and gangs from outside the area, some even as far afield as Ballymun and the outskirts of town, knew and respected him. Jayo himself refused to speak of it, always dismissing it with a flick of his head and irritated sucking in of his lips, but he did allow others such as Washing Machine to regale them all with tales of it when the mood took him and they had little else to do except smoke under the drenched forest canopy of rain and darkness. He had never gone overboard in a fight before or since, however, and showed a remarkable sense of fairness that Sam considered went some way to levelling out the constant petty violence he used to assert himself. Most of the time.

"*Ow!*"

The bottle had landed in Sam's lap, bouncing off his skull, and he'd cried out reflexively.

Washing Machine fell over himself, doubled in two with laughter – even Jesse joined in from his quiet position on the edge of the group where he sat watchfully.

Sam threw the offending bottle off himself aggressively into the encroaching darkness as if the dusk itself was to blame.

"Temper, temper, Sammy boy! What did that bottle ever do to you?" Mouse smiled broadly.

Sam ignored him.

"Never seen Sam that aggressive before," Mouse said. "Better watch out, lads. Sam has thrown an unarmed bottle – who knows what he could do next?"

"Fuck off, Mouse!"

Sam's voice was quiet and Mouse blew him a kiss. The lads burst into rounds of laughter and Washing Machine jumped to his feet, never missing an opportunity for exhibitionism, and gave a dramatic reenactment of Sam fighting the bottle, then the bottle suddenly attacking him back and Sam retreating in fear.

Mouse leapt to his feet and poured half the contents of his Breezer all over Washing Machine's pants.

The mood suddenly soured and, while Jayo laughed heartily, Washing Machine scowled and pushed Mouse roughly in the chest. Mouse hesitated a moment, like any bully, unsure quite what response to engage in when challenged physically. Then he caught a glance from Jayo, recognized that he was being challenged and had to respond, and swung out viciously. His fists were a blur as they caught the smaller teenager on both sides of his head. Washing Machine fell to the ground, his legs buckling, and Mouse walked back to his spot with a swagger, having demonstrated his authority. Mouse didn't like having people stand up to him. He didn't have any legend like Jayo's to fall back on – had only his continual efforts at weak intimidation to sustain him. All the same he had shown commendable speed in his punching.

Meanwhile Jesse simply watched with that thoughtful look of his, as if the world was happening around him and he was immune to its foibles.

Sam gave himself an internal pat on the back. There was

no point in a broken body for a little bit of pride. He was a part of the group and that was all that mattered – a little abuse every now and again wasn't that much to accept for the privilege. Besides, as it was, this loose membership of Jayo's inner circle had protected him on quite a few occasions already. And this time Washing Machine was the one that had got punched. Not him. That felt good in a macabre way.

Soon there was nothing much left to drink and, with the mood sufficiently dampened and not looking like it was going to be lifted, Jesse decided that he was going to go home. Sam stood up to do the same, remembering his bag and suddenly acutely aware that he was hungry. If Jayo wanted to stay, the other two would do likewise, but he nodded and they all picked themselves up and, lost in their own thoughts, quietly filed into the thick blackness and back into the chaos of the woods.

Sam always felt some trepidation entering the woods at night when he could hardly see in front of him and instead had to rely on his memory of the paths, or more likely rely on the lads in front of him. It wasn't marauding groups of lads from the roads above, or even the drunken homeless that scared him, but a supernatural fear of ghosts and, after watching the film *Aliens*, improbably . . . aliens. He always had to steel himself at every little twig that broke, or wind that whistled through the creaking boughs, and clutch at the urge to run for the gap of light signalling the road lamps when he saw them, even when he was nominally with a group to support him.

They gradually emerged from the natural depths of the woods into the artificial street light, Sam side by side with Jesse leading the way. Washing Machine was agitated, still edgy after his earlier put-down and he threw some snide comments Sam's way while kicking out at the pavement as if it was to blame. Mouse seemed too distracted to back him up this time, though, and they all reluctantly parted ways and went home with a certain sense of anti-climax.

Chapter 3

Mr Cusack Bares His Teeth

The blinds were stretched their full length, almost to the bottom of the sill, to block out any reflections on the whiteboard. Mr Cusack, the geography teacher, hated sun glare, complaining that his eyes were very sensitive to light – but then Mr Cusack complained about something every class. His opening salvo was generally in the form of a complaint, be it something personal or about the world at large, and his static pupils offered a guaranteed and surprisingly willing audience to air his concerns to.

Mr Cusack seemed to be droning on much longer than usual, and for once Sam really wished that he'd stop and do some actual geography or else there was a very real possibility that he would fall asleep. A shadow appeared on the desk in front of him: a butterfly. It bounced along the bottom of the window underneath the blinds for a moment. Sam watched it flutter gracefully against the pane, the light behind it giving it a soft halo effect. He found himself captivated by its lazy motion and he was quickly being lulled to sleep by its gentle movements.

"*Psst . . . psst . . . Sam . . . Sam!*" Daniel whispered behind him as loudly as he dared. For all of Mr Cusack's protracted disinterest in teaching, when it came to discipline he was as tough as an old boot, so Daniel's whisperings were almost too quiet to be heard.

Sam casually leaned back in his chair, feigning a deep stretch, then dropped his open hands behind his back. Like a shifty criminal passing stolen bounty, Daniel slipped a scrunched-up piece of paper into Sam's eager palm. Sam continued his stretching routine for another few seconds to make it seem natural, then swept forward onto his elbows and peeled open the paper.

"*Heading to Bray, meet those girls, you coming?????*"

Daniel's writing was bordering on illegible but Sam got the gist of it. Daniel was his best friend in school and had met a girl in an arcade a few weeks ago. He was going to meet her again and they had both agreed to bring a friend to make it less awkward and less of a date. Sam wasn't entirely sure that he wanted to go along as a 'plus one' on a date, watching Daniel try and get off with some random girl, so he reread the message a few times, pretending that he didn't understand it. He scratched his face, then his head, picked at his nose, all just stalling for time.

Daniel kicked his chair from behind, and Sam gave him a thumbs-up sign.

"Samuel Leahy, have you taken up sign language recently?"

Mr Cusack's sudden change of tone dragged Sam's attention to the front of the classroom. A pair of beady, green eyes languished on him with that bored, hopeful look that teachers have when they are searching for an excuse to enforce their power and assert themselves.

Sam bit his lip and raised his eyebrows as if the question made no sense to him whatsoever.

Mr Cusack wasn't going to be deterred so easily.

"Your hand signals to Mr Rowan behind you – is it a problem that may best be solved by sharing with the rest of us? The old saying: a problem shared is a problem halved. Or in your case, probably eliminated completely."

"I wasn't making any signals, sir."

"Of course not – it was a trick of my eyes."

"It is sunny today, sir, and you do have problems with the sun glare."

To emphasize his point Sam lifted and shook the bottom of the blind beside him, sending dazzling rays of sun across the room and directly into the teacher's eyes. Mr Cusack brought his hands to his face dramatically, and some of the class stifled their giggles. The butterfly had almost got caught under the blinds and Sam held them up a moment longer to make sure it wasn't going to get crushed. This caused the light to remain blazed across Mr Cusack's face and he almost cursed, but stopped himself midway through the second syllable, and marched pompously towards Sam.

Sam spared the butterfly from a certain crushing and looked up just as Mr Cusack's smirking figure cast a shadow across his desk. The butterfly flew out in front of Cusack and he clapped his hands over it, squashing it instantly.

Sam watched the destroyed little body fall to the ground but, before he could protest the death of the innocent insect, Daniel's note was swept up into Mr Cusack's hands. Distracted by the little loss of life, Sam had left the note resting on his desk in full view.

Daniel wrung his hands in dismay while Mr Cusack

positively beamed with delight at his prize. Clearing his throat, he turned to the rest of the class, momentarily his adoring audience; they always were when the possible destruction of a classmate was on the cards.

"'*Heading to Bray*'. Oooohh, classy. '*Meet those girls*'."

Mr Cusack paused for effect.

"'*Girls . . .*'"

He covered his mouth in mock horror.

"'*You coming?*'"

When he had finished this piece of theatre, Mr Cusack turned back to Sam, flicking his eyes up to Daniel every few seconds as he spoke in a voice loud enough to enable the rest of the class to hear every word fully. Mr Cusack was the star of the show at this moment and he knew it. He would rise or fall in their eyes based on how scathing he was in his put-downs of the young teens in front of him.

"Well, now that *is* interesting. Going to meet some girls in Bray . . . which girls are these now, Samuel? Are they cousins of yours, Daniel?"

This delighted the congregation and, encouraged by the response to his joke, Mr Cusack continued before the boys could launch a witty riposte, which was unlikely to be forthcoming in any case.

"Are they *cute* girls, Samuel? I mean, why would you be interested in meeting *girls*?"

It was a bad follow-up and he was suddenly in danger of losing his audience. Luckily for him he quickly cut out the comedic efforts.

"Be after school, would it now, lads? Well, would it make it difficult to meet them if you were in detention? Probably ruin your plans completely, now wouldn't it? We could send some of the other boys in the class in your place, just so we don't disappoint the girls entirely. Although I'm sure they won't have been too heartbroken in any case."

He had hit a home run, right down the middle of the plate, and he knew it. Neither Sam nor Daniel could think up any response that would swing it back in their favour, apart from lamely saying they would go to Bray after detention anyway, so both played the sullen mute card.

Mr Cusack turned to his captive adoring public and spread his arms.

All the moment needed was some Beethoven, thought Sam.

"Right, who would like to take Sam and Daniel's places to go to Bray and meet these lovely ladies this afternoon while they sit in detention?"

Every hand in the room shot up without hesitation. Except one lad called Mark who wasn't paying any attention and was asleep as usual. Teachers usually left Mark alone because it never seemed to make any difference if they woke him – he would just fall back asleep.

"I think you've made your point, sir – we're sorry for passing notes in class."

Mr Cusack whipped around at Sam's weary voice, his head leaning down towards Sam's, hand cupping his ear.

"Did I hear you apologize to me, Master Leahy?"

"You did, sir. I said I was sorry. So is Daniel."

"Well, he'll have to apologize himself, Samuel – he's well able to talk for himself. Or at least I hope so or entertaining those girls in Bray will be very difficult!"

A slip-up! Mr Cusack had left an opening.

Daniel looked up, eyes glinting. "Depends on how you entertain them, sir."

Mr Cusack reeled back slowly as if stung, then composed

himself – but too late. A chorus of *oooohhhs* reverberated around the room as a mixture of recently broken young voices did their best to create an intimidating atmosphere.

"And how were you planning on entertaining them, Mr Rowan?"

Daniel paused with perfect timing, just long enough to entice everybody in, but quickly enough not to deaden the moment. A real pro, Sam thought admiringly.

"Why, the only real way to entertain girls, sir!"

"Which is, Mr Rowan?"

"Well, if you don't know, sir, I think you're in a bit of trouble at your age? Ask Miss Jones, the career guidance teacher – I'm sure she can tell you if you ask nicely."

There was a stunned silence. The silence was so deafening that it actually caused Mark to sit up and pay attention.

Mr Cusack tightened his jaw and walked back to the top of the class, flicking the note into the paper bin as he did so. To his obvious relief it found its target, after bouncing on the rim.

"Detention today, both of you."

He said it with such casualness that he almost seemed unaffected by the slagging he had received but everybody present knew better.

Daniel put his hand up politely to ask a question.

Mr Cusack indicated wearily for him to speak.

"No problem with detention, sir, but it's not on today. We'll have to go tomorrow instead. Which we will, of course."

"Eagerly," Sam added as a footnote.

"And why is there no detention today, Mr Rowan?"

"It's a Wednesday, sir – we have games after school –

there's never any detention on a Wednesday."

Mr Cusack hid his growing irritation and clenched his hands tightly, his knuckles positively gleaming white like freshly polished ivory. He gave a tight smile and nod of the head to Daniel who graciously accepted this surprising show of good grace with his own tilt of the head. Mr Cusack was usually a very immature and particularly sore loser in anything.

Then a sly smile broke out across the teacher's freshly shaven features. The class suddenly arched back as one in anticipation.

"Very well noted, Mr Rowan, but I have to stay behind after hours today to correct papers, so I shall be happy to oversee your detainment for an hour."

Daniel drew back in shock. "But, sir, we have games – it's Wednesday!"

"Oh, I didn't realize that you do games, Daniel?" Mr Cusack's eyes shone with the scent of victory that was surely within his grasp.

Daniel stuttered, his composure lost. "Well, I, em, no, I don't, sir, but without games I have a half day and I thought . . ."

"Well, you thought wrongly. Now, Mr Leahy does do games usually, I believe, so unless he was planning on skipping them to romp across the city he cannot do detention today – in which case he can do it tomorrow."

Mr Cusack allowed the implications of what he was saying to sink in for a moment. Every boy in the class felt these blows and had to accept that the scrawny individual overseeing their education on glaciation had stepped up to the mark this morning.

Sam reacted quickly, trying to avoid their having to do

two days of separate detention. "It's okay, sir, I'll do detention today with Daniel after school and miss games."

"And miss your games on account of me? Heavens, no, Sam!"

"Oh, I wasn't going to go today anyway, sir – I've hurt my ankle."

"That's too bad, Sam – I hope you get better – but you're still doing it tomorrow. You can, of course, wait in detention with him, but you will still be doing yours tomorrow."

Sam lowered his head, trying to hold onto the riposte that just ached to be released at this stupid teacher playing one-upmanship with teenagers. The sense of injustice built up rapidly and he blurted it out loudly to everybody's delight.

"Sir, this really isn't fair. We only passed a note and you weren't even teaching – you were telling us about your fucking crap opinion on politics, which has nothing to do with geography, and it's almost twenty-five minutes into class and we haven't done any work. You're completely out of line, not even doing your job properly, so I don't see how you can justify this punishment – even putting on detention just for us today – it's absolutely pathetic!"

His voice had risen by octaves. All the recent tensions had boiled to the fore.

Mr Cusack smiled grimly. "I'll have your homework journal, Sam, and we'll write a little note for you to take to the principal after class, where you can explain how you think it's alright for you to raise your voice in class like this to me. Maybe you would like to explain the whole situation to him – and perhaps Daniel's remarks to me also. Then we can let Father Kelly decide on your punishment. Does that seem 'fair' to you?"

"But, sir, ah, I don't believe you – ah –"

"Keep going, Sam. When you're finished complaining you can bring me up your homework journal, please."

Sam punched the desk in anger and stood up sharply, journal in hand like a weapon. The sun had gone behind the clouds now, and the room was much darker than earlier, gloomy and cold the way a classroom should be. Begrudgingly he handed his notebook to a gloating Mr Cusack, who took great pleasure in scrawling a lengthy note across the entire page delegated for the day's homework. With an admirably fake smile he offered it back.

"It's not fun losing, is it? Don't try and test me like this again."

Sam turned on his heel without acknowledging the comment.

Just as he turned the handle on the door to exit the classroom, he felt Mr Cusack's trembling voice rush towards him, hot breath almost at his ear.

"Where the –" Mr Cusack struggled to keep himself from cursing. "Sam? Where exactly do you think you are going?'

Sam turned to him innocently. "I'm just going to go and talk with Father Kelly, sir, like you said."

"I didn't tell you to go now."

"Well, I can hardly miss somebody else's class, now can I? And Father Kelly is never there after lunch, so I have to go see him now, otherwise I won't be able to see him today."

Mr Cusack began to visibly tremble, his hands shaking violently. The whole class watched with something approaching glee and a collective holding their breath, waiting for him to explode and attack Sam, or do something obscene that they could all talk about later. It could be one of those sacred moments when a teacher lost the plot and went crazy. Maybe it would get really good and he would beat Sam to a bloody pulp. Just imagine how much mileage they would get from a teacher's breakdown.

But to everybody's disappointment he closed his eyes, seemed to count to three and then turned back towards the rows of glinting eyes, waving them to their books as if nothing had happened.

Daniel gave him Sam a supportive thumbs-up and some of the class burst out laughing, no longer able to contain their mirth.

Mr Cusack spun around to confront Sam again but he was already gone, the door falling closed gently behind him.

Walking away down the corridor Sam could hear Mr Cusack's voice rising as he berated the rest of the class, the sound fading as he drifted down the hallway.

Chapter 4

Antoinette, and Not the Queen of France

The lost hour from Daniel's detention meant that they were definitely going to be late but Daniel had assured Sam that the girls would wait. Catriona was into him too much apparently. Sam was smarting a bit from having to wait in detention for Daniel, and still facing it tomorrow, but Daniel wasn't that bothered.

He was regaling Sam with another of his faintly amusing anecdotes concerning Japanese manga and Bruce Lee. This was an unhealthy obsession that, coupled with a desire for sharing his increasing collection of porno mags and a growing regard for smoking hash, was beginning to subtly strain their relationship. Sam needed to relax and grow up and not be worried about smoking hash, Daniel would needle him – it was the cool thing to do.

Sam smiled appropriately when prompted, having long stopped pretending that he understood the in-jokes and convoluted storylines that Daniel was reciting, until his monologue took on a fluid beat and he began to describe Catriona, the girl they were on a mission to meet.

Sam's attention levels immediately perked up.

"She's a fucking fox, seriously."

"Yeah, so you've been saying."

"Yeah, but I mean, seriously."

"As opposed to – 'unseriously'?"

"Exactly that – amazing tits on her. Seriously."

Sam waited a moment as Daniel drifted off to stare glassy-eyed up at the roof, lost amidst his own illicit teenage thoughts.

Daniel was essentially bringing Sam with him as a wingman so that he could assist him in getting into her knickers. The deal was simple: Daniel needed a friend for moral support and to have someone to brag to afterwards if it went well, and a back-up plan in case it went pear-shaped. In return Sam might get lucky if Catriona did as she had promised and brought a friend who might feel obliged to make out with him, or so Daniel said. Sam guessed Catriona would bring a friend but for very different reasons from Daniel – probably in case Daniel turned out be a weirdo and she needed some assistance, or in case he was just plain boring in which case she had a ready-made escape. Girls their age didn't need moral support the way boys did, he reasoned. Why would they? They were all pretty and clean with breasts and bums and nice smells – they had to be confident. Sam didn't really mind being used like this – he didn't get to meet girls very often so he couldn't complain.

Daniel smiled across at him like an older brother who had just explained the secrets of sex and after a furtive check up and down the carriage he took a cigarette and lighter out of his jacket pocket.

"You can't smoke in here." Sam gestured at a sign.

"Fuck it, who cares?"

Sam shook his head and stared out the window, watching Dalkey Beach roll by gently. A couple strolled arm in arm, ankle deep in the surf while holding their shoes in their hands. Sam hadn't had a girlfriend yet – he had, in fact, yet to kiss a girl properly if you discounted the Spin the Bottle game he had been forced to play when he was still in primary school. Daniel had had plenty of experience, or so he said. He had an easy way with words, always ready to engage with a quip and could talk actively on a variety of subjects, even if he fabricated most of it. Sam both admired and was painfully jealous of him for this ability that he covertly attempted but consistently failed to imitate.

"I'm sure her mate is hot."

Sam raised his eyebrows sceptically. "No, you're not."

"I am, I am – seriously, hot girls always have hot mates – it's part of the law."

Sam's cheeks cracked into a wide smile. "Gimme a break – 'the law'! Hot girls tend to bring ugly mates, everybody knows that – it makes them feel more confident and ensures that they get all the attention."

Daniel's cigarette dropped out of his mouth which was gaping in a gesture of exaggerated surprise.

"Where did all that come from? I'm *shocked*."

"Yeah, I can see that – keep that face for later – I'm sure Catriona would be bowled over by it."

"Seriously, when did you learn about women? That was just *soo* incredibly . . . *deeee*p."

Daniel made a grating laugh and suddenly jerked his head sideways, loosening his jaw, and a sliver of saliva flew out of his mouth and splattered onto the dirty window beside him with an audible slap. He grimaced and wiped his mouth with the back of his hand.

"I read it in a magazine," Sam admitted.

Daniel turned to Sam with a wide smile and picked up his fallen cigarette.

"You're right – her mate's going to be dog ugly, probably fat."

"So you agree with me?"

"Surprisingly, for the first time when it comes to girls, I will give you some credit for insight."

"Well, if I'm correct, then it raises the question: why did you bring me with you?"

"To educate you. I'm doing you a favour, young Jedi. I am your Obi Wan and you are my star, and only, pupil."

Sam punched him. "You actually need me with you, to make it seem as if you have friends."

"That's regrettably true."

Sam began picking at a scab on his arm. This usually helped him think.

"If her mate happens to be hotter, you're not allowed to switch," he said then.

"Course."

"Shake on it. We stay on track, no sloppy seconds."

Daniel took his hand and pouted. "It doesn't matter anyway – you haven't a clue what to do with girls. So even if I left you and her alone in her bedroom in the middle of the night drunk and her in a thong you'd still come out a virgin."

"You wanna test that?"

"Sure."

"Then leave Catriona alone with me later and then we'll see who comes out a virgin!"

Daniel leapt to his feet and grabbed at Sam, who ducked under his loose hands and reached for his midriff. They grappled for a few moments, but Daniel was out of breath quickly and he begged for a halt to the proceedings. Sam released him and fell back onto his seat, his features calm.

Daniel fumbled in his pockets for his lighter, searching for the calming influence that would come from nicotine. Then he relit the cigarette.

He had no sooner inhaled gratefully when the train ground to a halt at the next stop and without warning a ticket inspector strode on, all business.

Sam saw him moments before he clocked them.

"Shit, put that out quick."

"What, no, why?"

Without explaining, Sam grabbed the butt from Daniel's mouth, threw it on the floor and pressed his shoe down firmly on top of it.

"What the fuck, Sam, they're expensive . . ."

Daniel trailed off as the ticket inspector loomed over them.

"Tickets, lads."

"Yep, sure thing, sir."

Nobody ever called anybody 'sir' unless they were in trouble or unfortunately subservient. The older man looked at them more closely.

"Just finished school then, lads?"

Daniel handed him both of their tickets. Sam ground his foot harder on top of the cigarette – it was only a matter of time before the smoke would begin to filter up. There was a definite smell rising.

The inspector handed back the tickets slowly and sniffed the air. "Not smoking here, are you, lads?"

"No, sir. Some other lads were a few stops before though. Not mates of ours – they seemed pretty rough. We were too afraid to tell them to stop."

"Because you would have told them to put them out, would you, lads?"

"Course yeah, can't be having smoking on a DART."

The inspector nodded, thought about pushing it further, then decided that he really couldn't be arsed and carried on up the carriage to the other passengers.

Neither of the boys moved until he had crossed into the next carriage.

Sam punched Daniel. "I fucking told you!"

"Ah, we got away with it – relax."

"Because I saw him and I stood on it."

"Because I told a great story, that's why."

Sam shook his head. Daniel invariably had a way out – that's why he admired him so much. Bray pier was coming into view in the distance.

"This is it, the end of the line."

Daniel nodded as he fished out his lighter, took another cigarette from the deep crevices of his jacket pocket and stuck it firmly into his fleshy mouth like a poor man's Clint Eastwood.

Sam smiled this time. "You just don't learn, do you?"

"Nope. Not gonna learn until I'm dead."

"What?"

"It's a quote. Sort of."

"From what?"

"Can't actually remember."

The doors of the DART slid open with an easygoing *whoosh* and the two alighted on the platform of Bray station, ready victims to fate.

The footbridge brought them over the tracks and onto the opposite side where Daniel halted suddenly, his breathing heavy again.

Sam looked at him quizzically as he stood there staring at his feet on the gum-flecked platform.

"What are you doing?"

"I'm nervous."

"You're kidding me? *You* – you're nervous?"

Daniel's head bobbed up and down slowly, the tension in his shoulder muscles giving the movement a surreal halting effect.

"But you've already kissed her a few times, I thought?"

"No, I never said that."

"Yes, you did, you said it loads of times."

"No, no, you must have misheard me."

"Oh, right then." Sam paused. "That's a problem, isn't it?"

He sighed and kicked out at an imaginary football in front of him, then mid-kick a thought hit him and he almost collapsed with laughter, dropping to his knees. He couldn't breathe and his body shook.

Daniel lifted his sullen gaze up. "What the fuck's so funny?"

Sam needed a moment to catch his breath, then he stood up again, hands gripping his hips for stability.

"We got into so much trouble today – I walked out of Mr Cusack's class, got sent to Father Kelly's office, got double detention, missed games, sat for an hour on a train to Bray, and now we finally get here and you tell me that you're shy and haven't actually kissed this girl that you've been fucking rambling on about for the last two weeks! It is kinda funny."

"No . . . it makes me feel like a knob."

"Yeah, you are a bit of a knob alright."

Daniel looked at his feet. "What if she hates me?"

"I don't really care. Honestly. Look, if you're struggling, just send her over to me and she'll see how much wittier you are and you'll be grand – I'm your sounding board to bounce off and make you look good."

Daniel visibly brightened and stood up straight, taking a deep inhalation of the cigarette.

"You're right. Cheers."

"You weren't meant to agree with me."

"Sorry, but I kinda do."

"Bastard."

"Yep."

Sam pushed gently at Daniel and they strolled through the exit gates as nonchalantly as was physically possible in dull grey school uniforms, shirts unbuttoned, ties discarded. Once outside they didn't have to wait very long to find who they were looking for – it was painfully obvious from their fixated looks that the two tall slim blondes in short skirts and identical ponytails sitting on the bench across the road were their destination.

The taller, slimmer and blonder of the two stood up, flicked her cigarette out onto the pavement where it smouldered fitfully and approached them. For the first time it occurred to Sam that perhaps they shouldn't have worn their school uniforms.

"Howrya. What's yer name?"

Her harsh accent shook him for a moment, so far removed from the delicate beauty of her features, and he had to swallow the nausea that threatened to crawl out of his belly. His voice broke as his spoke, his balls leaping in and out of his belly.

"I'm Sam."

She nodded and stared at him.

Then nothing.

They appraised each other slowly as Sam came to terms with the shopping-centre beauty in front of him. He waited for Daniel to pipe up and take control – this was obviously the girl he had been talking about, the 'hot' one – but he was silent. Sam turned to encourage him but he wasn't there. He looked around, confused. Wasn't he meant to be hanging out with the ugly friend? This angel in front of him surely couldn't be her? But she was.

A few yards behind him stood Daniel, mouth latched onto the smaller blonde's lips. Fuck.

"I'm Antoinette," the angel said, still staring at him.

Sam had realistically been expecting a nice relaxing afternoon entertaining Catriona's boring friend with no expectations or possibility of falling in love until Daniel had made all his plays and either succeeded or failed trying miserably. Instead Daniel hadn't even had to lift a finger and he had already achieved his goal of getting off with Catriona while Sam was facing the most gorgeous and confidently cool girl he had ever seen in his life. That included the late-night movies on telly. In the moments that it took him to register precisely what was going on, it occurred to him that Antoinette was waiting for him to say something. His palms suddenly felt very heavy and sweaty, just like when he was in an exam and struggling badly, when the wet pencil would slip from its position between his loose fingers. Those same fingers she now enclosed in hers and led him away with from their clearly occupied friends. Her skin felt soft and delicate, but confidently firm and maturely sexual. He wished and prayed that she wouldn't be able to feel the sticky sweat that oozed from the pores of his skin.

He found his voice again, as much a defensive reaction to give her something else to think about as anything else.

"Didn't take them long, did it?"

He smiled hopefully at her and, to his pleasant surprise, she smiled back at him without a hint of condescension. Her smile was radiant and easy, and made the smile warping his own mouth feel distinctly awkward.

"We should leave 'em alone fer a few minutes – let 'em get to know each otha'. I told Cat that we'd meet her down at de pier and get an ice cream – that alrigh' wit ya?"

"Yeah, sure – I have no idea about Bray anyway."

"First time, is it? Where ya from?"

"Howth, the other side of the city."

Antoinette looked at him, her lip curling upwards in that bemused grin that only beautiful women can properly do, and Sam felt his self-esteem drop down through his chest and fix itself solidly inside his left foot, giving him an instant limp.

"Howth? Yer a bit posh, are ya then?"

"No, why would that make me posh?"

"Gimme a break! Goin' to a nice private school paid fer by Daddy and livin' in the poshest part of Dublin!"

"Where I'm from it isn't that posh."

"Yeah, why's dat?"

"Ah, well, ah, just it's not all big houses and all that – there are lots of, well, you know?"

He struggled to give a proper definition of the lads on the roads around him who would beat you up for a fiver, without sounding really posh and describing them as having accents like hers. That would be much worse than just accepting that he was posh in her eyes. He shrugged his shoulders.

"Righ', yeah – what does yer dad do den?"

"So what school do you go to?" Sam changed the subject quickly, the conversation heading in a direction that he really didn't want it to.

"Loretto."

Sam reeled back in mock amusement, the movement breaking the connection between their bodies, and his hand came away from hers. He immediately regretted it but didn't know how to grab her hand again without appearing desperate for her affection or being too obvious about his desire for her. How could he do it like she did, so casually as if it was the most natural thing in the world?

"Wha's wrong wit going te Loretto den?"

"It's just as posh as my school, probably even more so."

"'Even more so'? Who de hell speaks like dat?"

Sam could feel this opportunity slipping away from him, washing over him like a frothing tidal wave, proving that he was way out of his depth. He imagined what some of the other lads in his class would do in this situation . . . well, they wouldn't have let go of her hand, that's for sure – most likely they'd have pushed her up against the wall and kissed her eager lips with the suave detached air of James Dean. He didn't know how to do that so he just stared blankly back at her.

And then she laughed good-naturedly. She must have thought his blank look was a deadpan joke. Still giggling to herself, she pushed her hips out towards him so that they bumped into him gently, the impact sending a frisson of excited energy leaping around his groin. He made a decision which he immediately regretted and grabbed her hand firmly with his. Too firm, he thought, and was about to loosen the crushing grip on her slender fingers when he caught a blush wash over her smooth cheeks and her eyes flicked at him shyly on their way down to her feet. A wave of elation swept over him, followed swiftly by a crushing insecurity. She had blushed for him so, by all the average laws of attraction, she must like him at least a little bit . . . but what if she didn't and he made an ill-advised pass at her only to be rejected out of hand? Or even worse was the thought that, if she did actually like him, she would now have expectations of some sort of confidently subtle gesture to sweep her off her feet. How would he compare with all the previous guys that she had kissed – how had they acted with her? Would he be looked down upon, would she laugh and tell Catriona who would in turn tell an amused Daniel in secret? He couldn't bear the thought of it.

Then she suddenly tripped on the pavement, stubbing her toe between two slabs of concrete. He instinctively grabbed at her flailing body as she fell, catching her by the waist and twisting her around into him. Her stomach pressed hard against his, her thin hips grating against his pelvis. She looked at him, a flicker of amusement dancing around her painfully perfect eyes. Her full lips regained their balance only centimetres away from his, their breath mingling for the tiniest of heartbeats. Thank you, Fate.

He gasped audibly and she giggled, pushing herself away gently.

"I only tripped."

"I was just making sure you didn't hurt yourself . . ."

He suddenly found the perfect gap in conversation to flick a compliment in her direction, and in the split second that it took to cross his mind he knew that it was almost too late – it had to be spontaneous so he just said the first thing that entered his mind.

"You're much too pretty to allow any damage to you."

Damage? What the fuck was that? Who used that in a compliment? And *pretty?* He might as well have been talking about the blue finch in the back garden being chased by a rogue cat. If he could have done it without her noticing he would have punched himself in the gut.

But she was staring at him with a funny look in her eyes.

"Yer dead sweet, ya know dat?"

He swallowed reflexively from the intensity of her look. Unable to hold her eyes for too long, he scuffed his feet on the pavement, being careful not to trip himself up.

"Yeah, do you want to go and get that ice cream?" he asked.

"Not really – ya wanna just come back to my gaff?"

There was that feeling in the pit of his stomach again, the deep heavy dread that weighed him down, physically forcing his body inwards upon itself. It took all his strength to hold it at bay. He looked at her. Her eyeliner was perfectly drawn across her eyes, embellishing her best feature. She really was arrestingly beautiful. Her mouth was soft and shapely, skin smooth as amber, and she had a nose that was small and cute on her face, the type of nose that when she was a child would have received an abnormal amount of playful tugs and rubs from proud family members.

He found himself nodding without even being aware that he had thought to do so. A voice screamed at him inside his head to turn back, go find Daniel – he'd know what to do. He had managed to get her to like him so he should back away, take time out, gather his thoughts and figure out what to do next time, like wear normal clothes, gel his hair, fucking anything. But he didn't, instead allowing himself be dragged along behind her like an eager puppy bounding headfirst towards the wolves' lair, innocently unaware of the danger it was placing itself in.

Her apartment was nice, normal, and probably relatively small for her and her parents together. But they weren't there – at work she said. It felt so exotic being in an apartment instead of a house which always felt like it belonged to somebody's parents. This place could just have easily belonged to her, he imagined. He felt a thrill at being alone with her but he half hoped that her parents would come home and they would be forced to watch television with them, or leave and get an ice cream – then he could act annoyed but be admirably relaxed about the imposition so she would like him even more for being so understanding about it. Her parents would probably like him too.

She asked him if he wanted a glass of water and he found himself shaking his head and then opening his mouth to accommodate hers as she pushed him back against the fridge and slipped her velvety tongue inside and slid it against his teeth. He barely reacted in time then flipped his own tongue into action, bouncing against hers roughly. Something odd hit his molar and he struggled to figure out what it was, managing to push it against his cheek while maintaining his battle for supremacy with her increasingly violent tongue. It was chewing gum, but he wasn't chewing any. The sudden realization that it was hers struck him at the same time as she pulled away from him.

"I just gotta go to de toilet."

"Sure, I'll wait here."

"Well, yer not coming wit me!"

There was a pause for a moment as she examined him.

"Ya don't wanna come wit me to de toilet, do ya?"

"No, of course not."

"Good, I was jus' checkin' – some weirdos out dere, yeh know."

He nodded with an assurance that he hoped gave out the impression that he knew exactly what she was talking about while also dispelling any possible suspicion she might have that he could possibly be one of those weird people. He nodded for probably far too long because she gave him a long hard look, and this time it wasn't a soft quizzical gaze, but had a certain condescension wrapped around it. He had expected this earlier but not now. Shit. He didn't exhale until she went into the bathroom, only half closing the door behind her so he could hear her peeing.

He realized that he was actually chewing her gum and he spat it out reactively, then quickly retrieved it from across the kitchen floor and had opened the bin lid to flick it in when a thought occurred to him . . .

Did he find it sexy that she had 'given' him her gum? No, he definitely did not, but that wasn't important . . . did she find it sexy that she had given it to him? Had she done so in some sort of sexual bonding gesture? Now he could chew her gum and they had bonded, a precursor to the exchange of sexual fluids, so if he got rid of it would it indicate that he didn't like her taste? He heard the toilet flush and he made an immediate decision, the type that has the minimum of thought running through it. Instinct.

"Are yeh chewin' me gum?"

She had applied an extra coating to her make-up quite masterfully, giving it a glowing sheen that screamed out healthy sexy female at him in big bright neon letters. She stared at him disdainfully.

"Eh, yeah, I think so."

"Uh, dat's gross! Just spit it out into de bin or sumtin' – I'm not kissin' yeh again if yer still chewin' it."

He lifted the bin lid again, cursing himself.

She welcomed him over to the couch and he followed her dutifully. If he had a tail it would have been wagging. Sitting down on the couch she flicked on the television, turning over the channels a few times before settling for some cartoons in Irish for some unexplained reason – he began to wonder why then internally chided himself to focus. He noticed that his hands were beginning to sweat again and he closed his eyes, begging them to stop, reasoning with them that it wasn't warm enough inside the room to justify releasing excess water from his body so therefore they should just stop. Science. His hands didn't listen. He was sitting beside her awkwardly now, unsure of how to position his body in a comfortable position that was both accessible to her and cool-looking at the same time. How did James Dean sit on couches? She looked so elegant, her legs crossed one over the other with such disdain that it had to have been practised over time. Her neck arched upwards like a royal swan, eyes beckoning him into her expectantly and all fluid suddenly flew from his mouth, leaving it as dry as timber. He couldn't move, nothing worked.

She gave him a rueful smile and leaned towards him, her left hand drifting downwards onto his crotch. It took all of his energy not to jerk away but his body stiffened with tension and she must have felt it because when she pressed her lips against his she paused and stared searchingly into his eyes. He felt like he could melt into her at that moment if he wasn't so nervous about trying to do the right thing. He desired nothing more than to curl into her and have her wrapped around him like a soft consuming blanket, her skin caressing his body, her lips against his, her eyes allowing him to drift deeply into their pools of green magic. It occurred to him that he could fall in love with this girl if she allowed him to. The kiss was much softer this time. This second time was more patient, less exploratory and much more enjoyable. Sam felt as if honey was being poured into his mouth and his tongue was swimming through a crystalline pool of sugar. Her lips sucked him towards her, pulling him onto her, her hands lifting up his jumper and slipping inside his shirt to slide along his skin. She dragged her own top up towards her chest and then pushed against him. Shock waves raced through his entire frame as the skin on their stomachs humbly touched. For the first time in his life he felt like he was being sucked downwards into a well of individual, suffocatingly beautiful moments. Everything that he touched seemed to be sculpted from a bed of pure perfection, a surprising exploration of harmony.

The front door rang, giving them both a jolt, and she pushed him off quickly, a look of fear twisting her features.

"Fuck, that's me ma!"

Sam fell off the couch, guilty despite having achieved nothing more than a brief drift of his fingers across the flesh of her neck and belly. He was immediately rueful, and then elated at having got onto the couch with her in the first place. He knew that Daniel would be jealous as Antoinette was far prettier than Catriona, not that he would admit as much.

He realized that he hadn't thought about anything much

else apart from this girl for the last hour, which was very unlike him.

The sound of teenage laughter breezed into the room. He knew that voice.

Daniel bounded into the room and gave him a massive slap across the back, then cupped his hand over Sam's ear for secrecy.

"My god, she gave me a blowjob!"

Delight was etched across his face like on a wood carving, never be removed for eternity unless you took out an axe and chopped it to bits. Sam kept his composure, wanting for all the world to leap into the air and scream out smugly about the joys of kissing Antoinette while simultaneously desiring nothing more than to thump Daniel for interrupting them. But all he could do was smile and proudly angle his body a little away from the others to hide his ardour.

Chapter 5

Violence Is a Virtue in Some Cultures

His chest rallied against the pressure that forced the breath from his lungs as his arms pumped ferociously, and pummelled through the late spring air. His body arched around the corner of the street, momentarily leaning sideways like a slumping rubber band, as he inexorably ground down the distance to the quays. The traffic lights kept turning red for pedestrians but he ignored them and leapt across the road like a gazelle despite the crushing weight of the bag on his back. The 31, that Holy Grail of buses that flew directly by his house without taking a tired long detour like the following buses, was just a few hundred metres ahead. He could see it, tantalizingly close. Catching this bus gave him at least an extra forty-five minutes of freedom at home to do what he wanted with before it got dark, and when you were a slave to the schooling system any free time was treasured. He doubled his efforts, willing his tired legs to move faster.

The indicator flashed on the side of the bus, a timid flickering of faded orange neon. His whole body screamed in defiance and he thought that his lungs would burst like overinflated balloons. The heavy vehicle lumbered away from the footpath, trembling under its own weight like an old rhino at a watering hole.

"Don't bloody leave yet . . . wait, wait, wait, wait, wait!" Sam begged under his breath as he skipped and rolled past the static bodies of other bus-waiting civilians.

The bus edged its nose out into the stampede of pre-rush-hour drivers desperate to avoid the traffic and unwilling to accede any ground. Irritation gripped the driver and he took a trained gamble, swinging the rusted metal beast abruptly out into the maddening rush of traffic, then conceding defeat in a cacophony of bleating horns.

Sam finally reached the bus and stretched out his fingers in desperation, nails scraping some more paint off the beast's dying skin. Another few giant steps and he was pressed up against the window, face pleading. His left fist thumped the door to get the driver's attention. Minutes seemed to pass by as the bus trundled forever forward, a few feet at a time. Sam kept pace with his prize, ignoring the bored looks from those already settled into their temporary seats. Finally the driver's head turned and he stared directly at Sam who indicated for him to open the door. The driver took one look at him and smiled like the devil, then slowly turned away and finally guided his aging friend out into a gap in the traffic.

Sam stood deflated, his bag dropping off his shoulders onto the grimy street, and watched the bus drift away into a warm haze of what might have been. That extra forty-five minutes was never more priceless than on a clear evening like this. The sun caressed the roof of the double-decker, haloing it like an alluring thing of beauty.

He had to cough suddenly. Bent double, he spat out the remnants of his exertions, watching the spittle drip pathetically onto the road, as useless now as the time he just lost. He stood back up and waited for the arrival of some of the other lads from school. They'd be here in a few minutes, just in time for the next bus no doubt. They would be fresh and clean, having endured nothing like the pain that he had just punished himself with. He trudged back to the bus stop, distracting himself with some thoughts of Antoinette from the day before.

They came late. So late that they almost missed the bus. Sam was already sitting upstairs, halfway down the gangway, against the window. Sitting downstairs was out of the question, an unwritten rule reserved it for grandmothers. Upstairs, the front of the bus was frequented by the younger kids, either doing their homework, pressing up against the window for leverage, or tossing spit-filled lumps of tissue paper across at each other's heads. They generally calmed down once the bus filled up with all sorts but the first ten minutes belonged to them and their sugar highs. The middle section was usually where girls from other schools, older college guys and working adults sat. The back was where the cool kids always were. Sam used to sit at the back when he was younger but now that the ribbing was intolerable he didn't.

The boys all clambered up the stairs together, giving each other space to move and then swiftly closing in on the back seats like a fly-trap squeezing away the vacant air. They were five boys from his year. Not from his class, but the same year.

The first to saunter by tousled his hair as he passed, in a roughly humiliating way that only your peers can really execute properly. This was Greg.

"Sammy, good afternoon."

The next few all smirked at him – they were in playfully dangerous moods.

"How was school, Sam – you learn much?" Greg continued.

"I heard that you gave cheek back to Mr Cusack the other day?" Darren chided.

"No way, what did you say?"

Greg and Darren were leading this together.

Sam ignored the sarcasm, and kept his gaze focused out the window.

They took the empty seats at the back of the bus and proceeded to unload their possessions on to the seats in front, taking as much unnecessary space as possible. Darren, too cool to need to be conventionally good-looking, lit a cigarette and stood up against the window to breathe his smoke out into the air flying past. Greg slouched back, feet up on the next seat and stared hard at Sam. Greg was smaller than Sam, but the wittiest of the group. He wore his good looks around him like a cloak of invincibility, his prowess with girls from the surrounding schools emblazoning him with a loud confidence. He took a particular enjoyment in Sam's discomfort.

The other three were almost irrelevant when Greg and Darren weren't around, but in their presence they became virulent servant imps whose sole purpose was to serve and entertain their superiors. They took a specific interest in jokes at Sam's expense – nothing more physical than some objects thrown in his direction, yogurts maybe, and some head-ruffling; any physical abuse was generally infrequent. What they did was much worse, however, trading on the qualities of slow psychological destruction in which young girls were supposed to excel: the consistent unravelling of another's self-esteem through words.

One of the underlings, Barry, jumped onto the seat behind Sam's and spoke directly into his ear, but loud enough for the others to participate in the conversation.

"So what did you say to Mr Cusack that got you *double* detention?" he said, gurning.

Another, John, overweight but stereotypically funny, whistled in mock admiration. "Wow, Sammy, you're in danger of becoming hardcore!"

"Quick, Barry, get away from there – Sam might talk back to you!" Greg called out.

Barry scrambled away from Sam's head, cowering behind him. "Please, Sam, don't – don't do to me what you did to Mr Cusack – I couldn't handle it, I'm sorry, I'm sorry!"

Greg flicked open a packet of Maltesers, casually popped one into his mouth and flicked the other in Sam's direction. It missed and bounced off the window beside his head. The entire bus was eerily quiet, sadistically listening to the exchange going on at the back. Sam felt completely alone and wished for the millionth time that he had managed to get the earlier bus.

Barry resumed his duties at Sam's ear, smelling around his collar like an inquisitive dog. "Sam, you smell, in fact you stink – doing a bit of exercise, were we?"

Greg kicked his foot against the seat to get somebody's attention. "So what did you say to 'Cusko'? I wanna hear it word for word from the lion's mouth."

Sam shrugged his shoulders and muttered to himself. The strange aspect of it all was that he actually longed to be a part of their company, to feel their acceptance, and be involved in the group, even if it would have meant taunting somebody else in the manner the guys taunted him. At least, he already knew that he would happily sit in the shadows and watch, a part of it by association. He longed for it, and it was this desire that always broke him. He finally turned to them, almost apologetic.

"I didn't really say anything."

He wanted to regale them with his story, but knew that it would be twisted into some form of hurtful slagging. He knew it was safer to lose himself in observing the activity that bustled on outside the confines of the bus, unaware of the war that was silently being waged inside its unforgiving windows.

Darren chipped in. "Ah, come on, man, fucking tell us – everybody's been talking about it in school!"

Darren was outwardly the nicest of the group, so probably the most dangerous. Sometimes himself and Sam walked to the bus together, Sam tagging along, never sure whether he should walk alongside or say his greeting and then walk either faster or slower. He usually gauged from Darren's reaction to him what to do. Sometimes they talked and got on relatively well – not quite bordering on camaraderie but nothing hostile. At times like that he quite liked Darren and hoped he would get invited to the parties he heard that he held in his house, featuring girls, music and alcohol.

He turned around to face them, directing his story at Darren who smoked casually, the cigarette balanced between his fingers like a real pro.

"Ah, he just found out that me and Daniel were going to Bray to meet some girls."

"You were going to meet some girls?" Darren replied in a friendly manner.

"Yeah."

"Cool. Good man."

"And so he threatened us with detention."

"Shit, not cool – so what did you do?"

"Well, he began telling us that we wouldn't be able to entertain them if we couldn't talk for ourselves and Daniel said it depended on how we planned to entertain them."

"Oh yeah – like you wouldn't be entertaining them by talking!"

"Exactly."

"Very smart. I'd say Cusko didn't like that."

"No, no, he didn't."

Sam began to grow in confidence as he engaged all of their attention. He knew his storytelling was very weak, that he had no sense of timing or delivery, but right now they were apparently listening to him. Eager to impress, he continued.

"So he told us that we were getting detention and I got really angry, fed up with being treated that way by that eejit, so I told him that he was a brutal teacher and wasn't able to give us detention and he had wasted the whole class talking shite."

"You didn't actually say 'shite', did you?" Darren was skeptical.

"Well, I can't remember – I think I did."

Darren nodded to him and threw the butt of his cigarette out the window where it got caught in the slipstream of the air rushing by and flipped around in nauseating circles like an acrobat on its journey to the grass verge below.

Greg stared at Sam with his eyebrows raised in disbelief, moving over as Darren sat back down beside him and took a few Maltesers. Greg took one himself and rolled it around his fingers, then offered it to Sam.

"You want one?"

"No, I'm fine, thanks."

"Why not?"

"I just don't want it."

"Can I tell you something, Sam?"

Sam leaned in expectantly. "Sure – what?"

Greg hurled the piece of chocolate into Sam's eye at the exact same time as he spoke, causing Sam to reel back and bang his head off the window.

"That was the gayest story I've ever heard – you're such a little faggot. I bet you and Mr Cusack went off to a quiet room and you sucked his dick like a little queer after class, or did you do it at detention instead, you little pansy?"

Sam blushed bright red and turned away but Barry grabbed his hair and pulled him backwards, laughing as his stretched his neck against the cold metal seating.

Greg smirked and continued, his voice getting louder. "Why do you even tell a story like that when it's obviously bent?"

"You all asked me!"

"Yeah, but we thought something cool had happened, not your gay little fit. Grow up and get some balls. Your whole class just thinks you're a twat and I heard Cusko was telling that story in the staff room while they all shat themselves at how thick you are."

Barry pulled Sam's head harder and the hairs on his head strained to stay in contact with his skull. He squirmed which made it hurt more.

"Stop, stop, let go!"

"Why, what are you going to do, faggy? You want to suck my dick like Cusko's, yeah?"

Sam could have lashed out. He could have done something to protect himself but it seemed better not to provoke them any more and just hope it would end soon.

The girls from Manor House, the nearest girls' school, started piling onto the bus, their eager chatter preceding their march upstairs. Barry's enthusiasm increased when he heard them and Sam suddenly felt a huge wave of embarrassment descending. The first two girls immediately saw what was going on and smirked. Girls that age always seemed to side with the bullies. Barry began tapping Sam on the forehead with his free hand like he was playing a bongo and the girls laughed in appreciation. It was finally too much for Sam. He lashed out with his fists, whipping his body around and catching Barry on the side of the ear.

Barry immediately let go in fright. He pulled back for a second, and time seemed to freeze as the girls all turned and stared as one.

Greg and Darren stared in shock but that passed as quickly as it had occurred and the five lads were on top of Sam in a heartbeat, a combination of their fists thumping every available body part and evil hands scrabbling at his clothes. Within a few violent seconds they had managed to get the jumper and shirt off his body and pushed him down onto the floor between the seats using their feet to keep him there.

Greg took ownership of his garments with a dramatic flourish and held them in front of Sam's face. "You going to apologise?"

Sam didn't respond, the cold of the dirty floor at his

naked back and the shoe on his face provoking a numbing shame.

Greg sneered, then opened the window and stuffed the clothes out casually. The whole bus looked on in astonishment as the wind swept them up and opened them out like giant flags of shame.

They flew into the air like grey and white butterflies, floating along the currents gently, seemingly content at their freedom. Gasps broke out amongst the occupants, followed by giggles and loud bursts of female laughter. Barry and the other two minions released their hold on Sam, removing their offending feet from his back and face, and high-fived as they sat back in their original seats.

Sam looked at his clothes drifting away in horror, wanting nothing more than to remain where he was, hidden from the scathing eyes of everybody else on the bus. But his mother would kill him if he came home without his uniform – it was far too expensive to replace for no reason. He'd have to walk up the lane topless past the lads playing football on the street too. The huge ramifications that this would have for the respect that Jayo and the lads might have for him – for all they knew he was popular in school – smacked him in the jaw harder than any of the blows he had just taken and so he jumped to his feet, ignoring the sparkling eyes riveted on him. Grabbing his bag, he bounded down the stairs, doing his best to ignore the taunts that cascaded after him. Pressing the stop button desperately every few steps he prayed that the driver would let him off before the next stop, but no. He was forced to stand, clutching his bag to his naked chest, at the front of the bus until it stopped again by default.

The grannies peered forward at him, as if wondering if

they needed new glasses after all, while everybody else did their best to stifle their sniggers. Even the driver had to work hard to contain himself. The bus slowed agonizingly to a halt and Sam raced off, hitting full stride for the second time that day as he ran back the way he had come to try and retrieve his possessions. The lads stuck their heads out the window, their jeers spurring him on away from them faster and faster. Something smacked his head hard but he kept going, until he felt something cool and watery dribble down his shoulders. Reaching back, he felt soft lumps of a creamy substance come away in his fingers. Yoghurt. He kept running though, resolving only to stop once he had got his clothes back, and restored some lost pride. All he kept thinking as he ran was thank God Antoinette didn't get this bus.

Chapter 6

Fishing, and Other Things

The events on the bus had deeply shamed Sam and he woke up on Saturday morning with a sense of lethargy that he had never felt before. His body was heavy and sloppy as if it was filled with water and moving only swilled the liquid inside uncomfortably. It was best to not move in such circumstances, he reasoned. He closed his eyes and pulled the covers back over his head. His bed vaguely stank of stale sweat and old farts but he didn't care – when it's your own smell it's almost enjoyable.

He must have slept until after four because when he finally arose to relieve the pressure on his bladder the sun was no longer finding gaps in the curtains – it had moved around to the other side of the house as evening approached. He was thirsty and his breath felt aggressively dirty so he went downstairs for some water, refusing to brush his teeth in support of his self-loathing.

His mother was happily pottering around the back

garden and she waved to him, her hat shielding her eyes from the evening sun, oblivious to his suffering. For a moment he was angry at her for not waking him up as he had missed a beautiful day, then he felt ashamed for being annoyed at her.

The lads were outside, just beginning their daily kickabout. His body still felt clogged and ached in the same dull way that it would after a hard day's football practice. He watched the lads play for a few minutes, wanting nothing more in the world than to join them and feel the release of tension that it would bring. But he sullenly stuck to his guns and trudged back upstairs. The lads would knock for him and then he could reconsider if he wanted to play. He would only join them if they begged, he decided.

The lads never knocked and the evening approached with its delightful inevitability. Sam didn't manage to pass back into sleep and when there finally was a knock on the door he sprang out of bed and was down the stairs and opening the door before the second knock.

"Your mum there?"

It was the milkman, one sinewy arm outstretched with the bill for the week's delivery. Sam looked past him to the empty field. They had never knocked for him. He sagged further into himself.

"Son? Your mum?"

The milkman was staring at him impatiently. Sam nodded and went back inside, closing the door behind him on the unfortunate man.

"Mum? Door."

He heard her muffled voice in the kitchen but he ignored it and went back upstairs. He began dressing. His mother's sparkling voice drifted up to his room as she bantered playfully with the milkman, which soured his mood even further. Nobody else should be enjoying anything about the day if he wasn't. He hadn't showered so he took dirty clothes from the wash basket: he was going to smell as he felt.

"I'm going out, Mum. Back soon."

"I'll keep dinner for you."

"Okay."

Weekend sunshine always puts his mother in such a good mood that she would never question what he was doing.

As he walked down the laneway he dragged his feet as if he could somehow transmit his mood into the ground. It was an unbearably fine evening that made everything worse – the world around should be forced to share in his melancholy. The lads weren't at the swing. He thought of all the possible places that they could be on a day like this then continued down towards the pier. Mouse liked fishing for dogfish when the mood took him and Sam knew the spot even if he'd never been there by official invitation.

As he walked he thought of Antoinette and wondered what she was doing. Probably with another lad back at her apartment, he figured. A girl like that could never spend a day alone – she was just too beautiful. The euphoria of kissing her had flatlined. It had been a few days ago now so she'd had ample time to regret it. He had wanted to ask Daniel for her number but he hadn't been in school since. He should just ring him and ask him to get it off Catriona but he felt stupid doing that. What if Daniel asked Catriona, and then had to tell him that Antoinette didn't want to see him again? No, he would just wait and let her get his number off Daniel.

The place where the lads would occasionally fish was on the far side of the harbour, just beyond where the trawlers were repaired. They would sit on a stone platform that ran around the outside of the pier a few feet above the surface of the water.

Washing Machine announced Sam's arrival with a surprisingly good impression of a booing crowd. Sam nodded, trying to be cocky for show, but his hands felt unnecessary to his body so he shoved them into his pockets. This always looked cool in the movies but pulled his pants tightly around his arse and made walking more of a chore. It also served to emphasize how awkward he was.

Mouse and Jayo were sitting on the lower level of the pier wall looking down to the sea below on the exposed side of the harbour. There was a gentle swell and almost no breeze which made the evening perfect for some light fishing. It was just the three of them.

Washing Machine saw him look around for Jesse. "Jesse just left to get some cans off Jacky."

Jacky was Jesse's reliable older brother. He was a relatively consistent source of alcohol because he didn't care for the vagaries of underage drinking laws, instead appearing to see himself as a sort of warden guiding the lads through life by allowing them do whatever they wanted.

"He won't have got enough for you." Washing Machine made sure that Sam knew this before he sat down.

Sam wasn't in the mood to drink but he still wanted to have the option.

Jayo nodded to him and Mouse gave him the finger, neither looking away from the spot where their floats bobbed gently.

"Caught anything yet, Mouse?" Sam inquired.

"No."

"Dogfish, yeah?"

"Yeah."

"Where did you get bait?"

"From a bait fairy."

Mouse never looked at him but the other lads smiled. It was funny.

"Yeah, I heard about those – was she hot?"

"Shut up, Sam."

He fell silent and watched the little floats having a great time in the water. Minutes passed by and nobody said anything. It was a very peaceful form of camaraderie and gradually Sam felt himself relax. The evening sun was warm and he took his jumper off – it didn't smell as bad as he had thought, maybe the smell of the sea was overpowering it. As he rearranged his seating position he saw Jesse approach around the corner.

"Here comes Jesse, lads," he announced before anybody else saw him.

They all turned and raised their hands in greeting. They never did that for Sam. Sam had nothing better to do so he watched Jesse approach slowly, picking his way across the rocks along the waterline. It would have been much easier to approach along the pier and climb over the pier wall but it wasn't a good idea to be seen carrying bags of cans in the open. Except that he wasn't carrying anything. Sam thought about saying something but the messenger always got shot in his experience.

Jesse finally clambered alongside them.

Jayo stuck his hand over his shoulder for a can. "Good lad, Jesse."

Jesse grimaced and didn't respond. Jayo craned his head

back as if it were the most difficult action possible.

Jesse sat down and shrugged his shoulders. "Jacky wasn't around," he muttered.

That was it. The lads nodded and carried on with what they were doing. Nothing. Jesse began watching the floats. That was the way it was with Jesse, there was never any drama. He never created any and nobody else brought him into any. If he couldn't get any cans then he had obviously tried and failed and that was that. If Sam or Washing Machine or even Mouse had failed to get something that they had promised there would have been a minor riot, but with Jesse there was simply acceptance. He was just too cool and calm to ever have an argument with. He sat there, face as impassive as always. He was either the smartest or the dumbest guy in the world, Sam had always reasoned.

"Catch anything yet, lads?" Jesse always spoke languidly and sparingly, so that everybody always listened.

"Few bits, nothing really, hardly trying," Jayo replied brightly.

Jesse nodded. Quite how Jayo could determine any varying levels of effort in casting a piece of whitebait attached to a hook attached to a weight attached to a line to the sea bed and waiting until something happened wasn't disputed. Apparently they weren't trying because of how they were sitting with their feet up, as if sitting straight-backed with their arms cocked for the battle of a bite would have made a difference. Posture made all the difference in fishing apparently.

"Why didn't ya play ball with us earlier?" Jesse asked Sam.

"You never knocked for me."

"That's cos Mouse saw you looking at us through the window."

"I wasn't watching you."

Mouse chimed in. "Yeah, ya were – you were wearing a gay red T-shirt."

"How is a red T-shirt gay?"

Nobody responded. It just was apparently.

"So ya watched us and didn't come out – why?" Jesse persisted.

Sam bit his lip and looked out to sea. He wondered if he could tell them. They were his mates after all. Sort of. Maybe they would accept ownership of his travails and would meet him after school to seek retribution on Greg, Darren and the rest. Unlikely.

"I wasn't feeling great."

"Time of the month?"

"Fuck off, Mouse!"

"There you go – definitely the 'time', lads," said Mouse. "It's okay, Samantha, it happens to all young women. You can have a chat with my mum about it if you want?"

Jayo hooted with laughter and high-fived him.

"Your mum wants to chat about other things with me, Mouse," Sam mocked.

It was a relatively solid comeback – although it didn't really make sense the lads got the idea.

Washing Machine did the standard 'ooooing' noise – anything to increase the tension.

"You makin' a joke about havin' sex with my ma?"

"Eh, yeah."

"Why? That's a bit gross."

"No, it's not. Your ma's hot."

Mouse looked at the lads and shrugged. "Samantha likes older women."

This had really backfired on him. He tried to come up

with a quick response. "No, I don't, just your ma."

Mouse arched his eyebrow. "Suit yourself, man – you stick it in where I came out. Maybe you're a bit gay for me?"

Jayo guffawed. "Are you, Sam – are you a little bit gay for Mouse?"

"No, Jayo, I'm not, are you?"

That was the wrong thing to say. Nobody ever slagged Jayo even when he weighed in on a conversation.

He looked at Sam with that evil grin that just begged you to test how genuine it was. "Careful, Sammy."

Sam nodded, his apology implicit in his silence. Nobody said anything again, the fun gone from the joshing, and they all resumed doing nothing. The swell was getting stronger with the incoming tide and it slapped against the bottom of the wall hypnotically.

Chapter 7

Stealing Never Hurt Anybody

The last vestiges of the day were leaving them and the floats had barely moved. On one occasion it seemed like something might be happening when Jayo's float was briefly pulled beneath the surface and Washing Machine had leapt up in such excitement that he slipped and almost fell into the water. The float bobbed back up like it was all a big tease and when Jayo reeled her in he found the bait was totally gone and a small crab was hanging to the last bits of flesh. Washing Machine grabbed the little creature before it dropped back into the sea and took great pleasure in smashing it against the wall.

Jayo decided that he'd had enough. "Come on, lads."

They all stood up promptly as if they had only ever been there to wait for orders from their general. Sam was the last to his feet. The sea had encroached upon much of their path back along the rocks so Jayo climbed up the wall and onto the pier itself. They all followed in his slipstream.

The pier was emptying slowly, some stragglers still enjoying the end of the sunlight. The lads fanned out abreast of each other, feeling intimidating in their little gang of five.

Jayo swept ahead with seemingly no real purpose except that he was heading the group and so had to lead them somewhere. A small dog barked behind them and then a tiny white ball of fun raced forward, skimming in and out of their legs like a fish would in coral. Washing Machine tried to kick out at it but it dodged gracefully then raced back to him happily. After a moment he bent down and patted it gently on the head.

"Sprinkles – here, girl – come here!" a nervous voice rang out behind them.

Sprinkles left her audience and rushed back to the small fat man who bent down to sweep her into his arms protectively. He had seen Washing Machine try to kick her and he caught his eye accusingly.

"Nice dog, mister." Mouse nodded in greeting, all sarcasm.

"That could protect you from all sorts of birds and frogs. Ferocious!" Jayo added.

The lads laughed, even Sam. The man stood up on creaking legs, clutching Sprinkles tightly to his chest. Without a word he walked brusquely past them.

"Take care of her now," Mouse warned.

"Yeah, don't let any squirrels eat her!" Washing Machine added.

Mouse looked at Washing Machine. "Why the fuck would a squirrel eat a dog?"

"I dunno, whatever, fuck off."

Mouse flicked Washing Machine's ear and he flicked him

back, then Jayo slapped them both like he wanted to play too. Banter always ended whenever Jayo joined in though – they were all too afraid of his schizophrenic switches.

The game was obviously over so Jayo walked on. Sam strode alongside him. The light was almost gone by now as they reached the train station near the laneway leading back to their hideaway and their respective streets.

"Who's got smokes?" Jayo asked the group.

Jayo smoked more than anybody else but he never actually bought any: this was Washing Machine or Jesse's job. Mouse would buy his own and reluctantly share if he was in a good mood. Jayo hadn't said it to anybody in particular but somebody would answer.

"I'll get some, Jayo."

"Good man, Washo."

Washing Machine glided over the ground towards the shop in an excitable fashion similar to the little dog's. Sam watched him go, and put his hands in his pockets again. He was feeling a little better, the thought of school quite distant now. They leaned against the wall, each in his own fashion, and waited.

Mouse began carving into the concrete of the wall with a pocketknife.

"Gimme a quote, Jayo?" he grunted.

"Like what?"

"Something, anything, I dunno."

"'Ride me'."

"That's shite."

Mouse began carving into the stone with difficulty.

Sam leaned in closer. "Whatcha sayin'?"

"Sammy's a fag."

"No, you're not!"

"I am."

He was. He had begun on the 'S'.

Mouse looked at Jayo and they shared a smile. Jesse was drifting off, eyes vacantly gazing at the train station.

"There's that dog again, lads," he mumbled.

Sam looked up. Jesse was indicating the little white dog tied against the railings of the pub beside the DART station. The fat man was nowhere to be seen.

Jayo's eyes narrowed and he stepped forward, suddenly alert. "Let's take her, lads."

"What?" Mouse replied.

"Let's take the fucking dog."

"Why?"

"Why not?"

This was where Jayo's nasty streak came into play and when he was in this mood there was nothing that was going to stop him.

"Who's going to do it?" Jayo challenged the three of them but nobody answered.

"Pussies." Mouse glowered at the other two.

"You want me to do it?" Jayo asked.

Mouse continued staring at Sam and Jesse, trying to avoid having to say no to Jayo himself.

Again nobody answered which was the same as agreeing. They all knew that Jayo wanted to be the one to do it but by including them he made them accomplices for not arguing against it, or it at least felt like they were.

"I'll do it then."

Jayo was in cahoots with himself. Without waiting for a response he strode forward on the balls of his feet, scanning for any sign of the small fat man. He must have gone inside the pub, for a piss maybe. Sam hoped for the small fat man's sake that he didn't come out before Jayo had robbed the dog because Jayo didn't react well to being confronted and in this kind of mood he was liable to do anything. Jayo was across the street in a few brisk strides. Sam watched transfixed as the little dog yapped and flirted brazenly with Jayo – it really didn't know any better. He grabbed at her lead, pushing her away from him with his other hand. Then once she was free he grabbed her roughly under his arm, lead trailing. Sprinkles yelped with pain at his heavy touch but he ignored her and began marching back across the street at the same time as Washing Machine came back with their cigarettes.

One of the barmen from the pub was standing outside having a cigarette. He was a few years older then they were, perhaps nineteen. He watched the whole event and seemed aware of what was happening but Jayo shot him a look and he averted his eyes. Jayo had that effect.

"I'll trade ya a shite dog for those smokes, Washo?"

"Sure the box of smokes is bigger than that thing!" Washing Machine whooped to Jayo.

Jayo winked at Mouse as he strode past them and into the lane. He was playing it cool but you could see his nervous excitement. They all quickly followed. Sam was the last in line and he chanced a look back but the small fat man was still absent. He would regret leaving his dog alone later but who ever thought that their dog would get stolen? Sam felt sympathetic towards him, knowing the upset that he would surely feel. There was nothing that he was going to do, though. He'd had enough of being a social pariah lately so he wasn't going to do anything.

Once inside the safety of the laneway, the trees and the wall shielding them from view, the lads broke into whoops and cheers. Jayo held the dog aloft as a prize. Sprinkles seemed to enjoy the attention.

"Fuck you, fat man, we got 'Sprinkles'!"

They passed the little dog around triumphantly and she licked them each in turn, proud to be the centre of attention. Then Jesse carefully put her down on the ground. She was oblivious to what was going on and she barked cheerfully at them, demanding more attention.

Mouse sneered at her. "Little slut, she doesn't care who she's with."

"Bet she loves peanut butter!" Washing Machine laughed.

"Yeah, dirty bitch," said Mouse.

Sam didn't understand and he looked at Jesse who wasn't really paying attention. Mouse caught him glancing at Jesse for support.

"The fat man makes her lick peanut butter off his balls, Samantha – don't pretend that ya haven't wanted to try it?"

"Now he can use her. Here, try it out!" Washing Machine picked Sprinkles up by the scruff of her neck and shoved her into Sam's crotch.

Sam tried to push away but didn't want to hurt the little dog. She didn't like this game and turned her head, squealing a little.

"Shut up, ya stupid dog," Washing Machine growled as he jostled her through the air.

Jayo had lost interest already and started walking up the laneway. Mouse quickly followed and Washing Machine looked lost with the dog in his hands.

"What d'ya wanna do with the dog?" he asked, needing direction.

Jayo shrugged. "Leave her – she can find her own way home, that's what dogs do."

Kingdom of Scars

Jesse finally piped up. "We can't, lads – she might run across the road and get knocked down."

Jayo indicated that it wasn't his problem with a dismissive wave of his hand and Washing Machine handed Jesse the lead.

"You take her then."

The dog was thrilled to be back on the ground again. Washing Machine followed the other two boys up the laneway leaving Sam and Jesse with the dog. She sat on her haunches and looked at them expectantly.

Suddenly a voice broke out shrilly. "Sprinkles! Sprinkles! What are you doing with my dog?"

The small fat man had found them and he was waddling towards them as fast as his stubby legs could carry him. The dog turned towards his voice, but seemed nonplussed about his arrival to save her. As he got closer it was clear that he'd been crying. Sam felt guilty, as if it had been all his fault.

"Oh, Sprinkles! You're okay! Why would you take my dog – why? Did you hurt her?"

Neither Sam nor Jesse had anything to say so they just stepped back and let the man take the dog. He didn't appear angry – he was hurt and confused that somebody would do something like this to him.

"She's fine, we didn't touch her," Sam reassured him.

The man swept the dog into his arms, clutching her as if it were their last moments on this earth together. It was a little dramatic. The dog even looked a bit embarrassed. Sam nodded to Jesse that it was probably time to leave and they turned away.

Now that he had the dog back in his grasp, the man's eyes blazed and he almost spat after them: "Who do you think you are, taking somebody else's dog? Little pricks!"

Jesse raised his eyebrows but shrugged – fair enough.

Then the man pushed Jesse. It was a relatively feeble gesture but Jesse had to take a step back, more out of surprise than anything else.

Unfortunately this was the moment that Jayo and Mouse chose to turn back and call for Jesse. Jayo had an almost brotherly affection for Jesse. He never picked on him, and seemed attuned to his sensitive nature. They had a quiet bond which the others never understood and declined to comment on for they couldn't quite explain it. If the man had pushed any of the others Jayo would possibly have ignored it, but he would always jump to Jesse's aid. He immediately broke into a run, racing towards them.

The fat man saw Jayo approaching at a sprint and for a moment seemed to consider standing his ground, then thought better of it. He had probably not run as quickly as he did then since he'd been a teenager himself, if ever.

Jayo caught up to him easily with the athletic nonchalance of youth and then stopped short inches from his back, letting the man scurry in fear at how close he was, his breath literally on his neck.

"Keep running, fat man."

Jayo was generally a purveyor of few words, but what little he did say usually was enough. He waited until the fat man was out of sight before he relaxed his body and turned back to the lads. They all waited until he had reached them before following him up the laneway.

For some reason the fat man made Sam think of Antoinette and, fuelled by illicit thoughts, he left the lads at their spot by the swing to carry on home.

Chapter 8

Learn To Smoke Before You Try It First

The first lunch break of the school week on a Monday morning was always lethargic. The weekend was gone and its slipstream left behind the looming clouds of another dire five days of schooling.

Sam was slowly recounting to Daniel the details of his weekend, the highlight being the story of the dog and the fat man. Daniel seemed interested. His sharp eyes were fixated upon him like a hawk, enjoying the wary waiting game before the inevitable kill. He didn't blink until Sam had nothing left to say.

"Sounds like it was a great weekend, but what about next weekend?" he asked coyly.

"Next weekend? I don't know."

Sam began to eat a peanut-butter sandwich, examining it with far too much enthusiasm. Two of Daniel's better qualities were his patience and absolute tunnel vision.

"Sam." He spoke quietly. "Sam. Come on. Yes?"

Sam began chewing and gave a noncommittal shrug.

"That doesn't mean anything – stop being a prat and just say yes."

Daniel was unrelenting and they both knew that he would eventually get his own way.

"Okay, fine, fine – Jesus!" Sam said through the side of a mouth filled with sticky peanut butter, which always tasted better when eaten with an open mouth.

Daniel wasn't satisfied. "What does that mean – 'fine, fine'? Is that a *yes*?"

Sam indicated that his mouth was full and implied that if he didn't swallow he would choke but he nodded his head.

Daniel wasn't convinced and he shook Sam's shoulders with the brio of a young bullock. "Come on, come on, come on, come on!"

"Okay – that's a yes – relax – fucking hell!"

Daniel spun on his heel dramatically, bashing into two younger boys beside him who up until this point had been distractedly minding their own business.

"Watch where you're going," Daniel growled at them.

"But we didn't move – we were standing here," the taller boy replied confidently.

Daniel smiled goofily. "Who cares – guess what?"

"What?" The boy was wary about where this was leading.

"Sam's parents are away."

"Oh. Cool?"

"Oh yeah, very, very, very cool."

They smiled, and one of them gave Sam a thumbs-up.

Daniel shook his head. "Don't do that."

The young boy nodded and dropped his thumb. There

was a moment when it seemed as if he was waiting on further instructions but Daniel had already moved on. He stuck out his tongue at Sam in the universal symbol of giving a woman oral sex, or "fucking her with my tongue" as he might have succinctly put it were he trying to impress his peers. Sam pushed him away but Daniel persisted in trying to lick Sam's face.

The second young lad laughed at that and Daniel turned back on him.

"What's so funny?"

"Oh, nothing, sorry."

"Damn right."

The poor lad looked like he might shit himself and he began the process of grovelling, his eyes downcast, subservient, but peals of Daniel's laughter split his mumbling.

"Ah, fucking hell, how could I be angry when *I may get laid*!"

Sam watched this meaningless expression of Daniel's masculinity with disinterest.

"*May* . . ." he said. "Fundamentally the most important word in that sentence – 'may'."

"Oh, lighten up! This means that Antoinette will be here too, doesn't it?"

Daniel's enthusiasm had this ability to burrow under your skin and tickle you with its joy. Suitably ignited, Sam's excitement began to worm its way out of his gut and fill his belly like a hungry swarm of bees. His arms tingled and electricity swept through his sinews, jolting them into action, and the two friends danced around like merry leprechauns, each lost in his own illicit thoughts.

The two younger lads just watched, unsure what to

make of it but afraid to comment either way – so they just stood there meekly.

Daniel seemed to have it all worked out already, and he spent the rest of the working week eagerly fine-tuning the operation. It was possible that he had planned the entire operation over the weekend in advance of Sam giving his consent to have a small, with emphasis on the 'small', party while his parents were away for the weekend. Friday was the obvious choice of day. In Sam's eyes it gave ample chance to rectify anything that might go wrong before his parents' return on Sunday evening – in Daniel's it gave them an extra day for whatever might happen to continue happening.

On the Friday they got the bus together after school to Sam's. Daniel was amply prepared, his gym bag filled to bursting with extra clothes, enough for at least a week – an outfit for all and every possible occasion plus accompanying deodorant and aftershave. Sam wasn't shaving yet and, while Daniel only did occasionally, it was the smell and sense of increasing maturity that made the scent a necessity. Condoms of course had been acquired. Daniel had at least two packets of every type, "just in case".

They didn't get Sam's usual bus, which was a blessing as they would have been sure to get questioned by Greg, Daniel and the rest, although Daniel's gregarious presence and surprising camaraderie with everybody in school would have lessened the grief. Instead they went to the renowned off-licence down the road from the school. This shop was infamous for proudly holding the most lax underage alcohol laws in the country.

Sam was going to let Daniel do it himself but Daniel was

insistent: "A Jedi warrior can't have sex without first having proven himself."

"By buying alcohol?"

"Obviously."

The off license was down a small staircase off a side street. Inside it was dank and dark, smelling of sweat and sharp vodka. An old man behind the bar hardly lifted his eyes off the counter where he was reading Page 3 of the *Sun* newspaper with admirable patience.

"Yeah?" he said without looking at them.

Daniel took control. "Two bottles of vodka, six Smirnoff Ices and six Buds."

"And a bottle of Coke," Sam added.

"Yeah, Coke too."

The old man dragged himself away from the half-naked Page 3 model and set about getting their order.

Plonking it on the table, he grimaced.

"You lads old enough?" He still didn't look at them.

"Yeah."

"Yep."

"How old are ye?"

"Eighteen!" Sam said just as Daniel said, "Nineteen."

"Yeah, nineteen!" Sam blurted out. "Since yesterday."

"You want our ID's?" Daniel asked.

"Not really."

They paid up and Daniel cheerily looked at the naked model.

"She's got great tits, hasn't she?"

The old man finally looked at him.

"Don't make me want to ask for your ID's."

Daniel nodded, swept their loot up into his arms and they left the shop gratefully.

When they had emerged into the clean clear air that had

never tasted so nice after being suffocated down below, Daniel looked into Sam's eyes.

"Stage three complete."

"What were stages one and two?"

"Stage one: convincing you to have a party. Stage two: convincing the girls to come – well, Catriona agreed and she's going to pass on the invite to Antoinette."

Sam nodded as they began to walk to the bus stop. "Oh good, I was going to ask you about that."

"I've got it all under control."

"Good."

Once they got home Daniel set about arranging drinks and glasses and making sure that he had pizza numbers – "setting the house in order" as he liked to say. There wasn't really that much to do so it was finished pretty quickly and Daniel called Catriona to check when she'd be arriving.

Sam had nothing else to do so he sat on the couch to think about what was about to happen. A large framed family picture of him and his parents sat on the fireplace. It felt like they were staring at him so he turned it around. He couldn't flirt with Antoinette with his mother watching.

"Sam?" Daniel called him from the hallway.

Sam went out to him. Daniel looked at him solemnly, his hand covering the receiver.

"Why are you looking at me like that?" Sam asked.

Sam was used to Daniel's incessant play-acting but this seemed serious.

"Did you ring Antoinette?"

"Well, no – why?"

"Have you rung her at all yet?"

"It's only been a few days. Or maybe a week. Maybe a week and a half."

Daniel slapped his hand to his face and waved him back inside so that he could finish the phone call in peace.

When he came back into the living room he stood opposite Sam with his hands folded like Father Kelly giving the school's weekly compulsory Friday morning Mass.

"Samuel, Samuel, Samuel," he intoned softly as if to an errant child. "Have you not learnt anything from your Jedi master?"

"Don't do this *Star Trek* crap."

"*Star Wars*, my young Skywalker!"

"Okay, whatever!"

"I'll forgive you that slip of the tongue because you are obviously under extreme emotional duress, but what do we know about girls?"

"Seriously?"

"Very seriously. What do we know?"

"Fuck off!"

"This is a serious issue."

Sam didn't enjoy being scolded in this mocking fashion. Daniel was enjoying himself however.

"Obviously you don't know nearly enough, which is what tonight is for, to change all that. But there are ground rules that any young warrior must know before he is to take his sword into battle."

"You watch far too many films."

"True. But I have forgotten more from these films than you have learned from your limited life experience. Anyway, when a boy likes a girl, and this boy kisses said girl, then to follow up on the desire for courtship is a prerequisite to getting the girl into a pattern fit for mating."

"Seriously, I can't take this any more."

Daniel threw up his hands in exasperation. "Why the fuck didn't you call her?"

"And say what? I haven't got a clue what to say to her in person so how in hell could I hold a conversation with her over the phone?" Sam was serious.

"Good point."

"Besides, I don't have her number."

"*What?*"

"Eh, I was just so thrilled to have kissed her that I completely forgot."

"So why didn't you ask me?"

"I figured . . . well, I dunno."

The truth was more complicated. Getting Antoinette's number would have meant he would have been under pressure to ring her, and then he was setting himself up for a fall. As it had stood he'd emerged unscathed and with a story of sufficient merit to boast about, nonchalantly of course. If he met her again and it went badly it would destroy the previous memory and embarrass him no end. He couldn't take the rejection that he figured was inevitable, his reasoning being that once she spent more time with him and was aware of how inexperienced and uninteresting he was then her interest would fade rapidly. Then, of course, he had got pushed into this 'party'.

Daniel helpfully explained that what he had done might have inadvertently been a good thing because he had played hard to get, played it cool, so she now would want him more, but that was a fine line apparently and if he had gone past this weekend he would have stepped over it for good.

Daniel went back outside and called Catriona again, who helpfully was with Antoinette at the time. Antoinette, it turned out, had been a little put out that she hadn't been invited by Sam personally and had been waiting, if not hoping, for him to contact her. According to Catriona anyway. In any case she had persuaded Antoinette to come over to Sam's for the soirée on the promise that it was to involve just the four of them.

Sam's gut almost dropped through his knees and smashed into the floor when he heard that. Just the four of them meant that Daniel would be off with Catriona within minutes, leaving Sam for the entire night with Antoinette, and she would be expecting him to be cool. He wasn't sure why he was expecting more people because he certainly hadn't invited anybody else but he had just assumed that Daniel would have had something up his sleeve. He seemed to have it all planned out in such detail that it would have been rude to interrupt his meticulous preparations. But, as it turned out, Daniel hadn't invited any more people anyway.

Daniel waved away his complaints and began explaining some of the things that he should do – in between recalling his own conquests, of which there suddenly seemed to be a surprisingly large amount. Daniel had lost his virginity when he was thirteen supposedly. Sam hadn't yet touched a girl's breast, yet alone seen one naked.

But, as Daniel proudly proclaimed, while handing him some of the condoms, one of each type, size, flavour and colour, that was all about to change.

By the time they had gone over everything dusk had been and gone. They were inside the kitchen just finishing a first calming drink together when the doorbell rang and Sam froze. Suddenly nothing seemed to work, his muscles were set in rigor mortis, and even the saliva in his mouth was immobile.

The world began to move in slow motion as Daniel left the room and returned with Catriona and the most beautiful girl in the world. Sam seemed to float up to the ceiling and he watched in morbid fascination as his body worked on autopilot, a smile smearing his face, his arms hugging the delicate creature in front of him. Then she kissed him on the cheek like old relatives greeting each other before Sunday lunch and Sam was sucked violently back into his body. He found himself staring dumbly at her. Thoughts ran through his head so fast that he had to close his eyes momentarily to gain a semblance of control over them. She hadn't kissed him – she had kissed his cheek which didn't count – his grandmother kissed his cheek. Should he kiss her properly – fuck, what should he do – should he ignore it because he was going to kiss her later, or should he kiss her now, a statement of intent – or play it cool? Fuck, he couldn't even ask Daniel because he already had his tongue down Catriona's throat.

And then, just like that, the other two had left the room and gone outside, and he was alone with Antoinette. This had happened much quicker than he had anticipated even in his worst imaginings. He hadn't even been granted a grace period to ease into her company. For the first time that evening he wished that he was watching television alone. He poured them both some vodka and Coke to pass some time and they sat awkwardly on the couch.

Daniel and Catriona came back from outside within a few minutes, a giddy look on each of their faces. Evidently Catriona had decided that she couldn't just leave her friend alone so soon after arriving. Daniel, on the other hand, clearly had no such qualms. Sam and Antoinette were in the middle of a conversation that was devoid of any finishing point, discussing the most mundane things about their respective days that they could drag out of their consciousness: what time school had finished and how difficult the maths course was this year. Relief swept through Sam when Daniel walked back in to join them.

Daniel immediately set about creating an atmosphere by putting Bob Marley on the CD player, which Sam to his quiet shame hadn't even thought of doing.

Fifteen minutes later Daniel was dealing cards amidst a raucous drinking game. Sam felt the weight melt away from his shoulders – maybe it was the alcohol, or maybe the smiles that Antoinette kept slipping his way, but he began to feel relaxed and finally his humour crept out and into the group. They were a willing audience.

Three full glasses of vodka later and Sam found his lips pressed against Antoinette's. The taste of wet salt on his upper lip mingled with her scent was intoxicating. The vodka began making him dizzy and he had to concentrate on what he was doing to keep his tongue moving in tandem with hers while simultaneously not losing his balance on the couch. He had his head bent awkwardly to allow hers to stay straight and a crick formed in the back of his neck. Hot pain soon began to move down his spine, but he didn't dare break the spell of the kiss – he had to let her do that, he resolved. Moments later she pulled away and he wished that he had been the one to do it.

"Okay, I got something to really get this party started, kids!" said Daniel.

Sam looked at him in surprise as he produced a small clear plastic packet containing what looked like a clump of dirty soil-flecked grasses he had plucked from the back garden.

"The best grass in Dublin, I promise!" he announced triumphantly.

Daniel held his arms aloft and waited for the adulation to roll in.

Antoinette clapped her hands and giggled while Catriona grabbed his hands as he lowered them and kissed the backs of them like he was Caesar himself.

This moment later explained to Sam why Daniel was popular with girls and his peers: he was the person to get you the best weed, and he knew how to roll a joint better than any drug dealer.

Daniel wetted his lips and began his latest masterpiece. Sam blanched internally. He had never smoked before, but judging from the girls' active participation in Daniel's 'process', they were not amateurs.

When it was passed around Sam was third in the little circle they had made on the floor, but he gave it to Antoinette, a gentlemanly gesture that backfired as she sucked on it like a pro, attempting a cigarette circle with her exhalation before passing it back to him. Daniel smiled hazily at him as he tried to copy the others' mannerisms, taking a deep drag on the lumpy joint. He closed his eyes with a wide fake smile, keeping his mouth closed. There was silence and Sam could feel them all staring at him. His throat began to burn and suddenly it was aflame with hot stones clawing at his insides. His eyes whipped open and he doubled over, coughing hoarsely.

Catriona clapped her hands in glee and tears ran down Daniel's face in his struggle to speak.

"You're not meant to swallow the fucking stuff, you dope! You hold it in! You hold it, and then exhale. If you swallow it, well, that's what happens – Jesus! Ladies and gentlemen, Sam has just lost his hash virginity!"

Sam held his throat gingerly. It felt as if a tiny soldier was grating coarse sandpaper along its soft inner lining. His eyes welled up with unavoidable tears of pain as he managed a smile, but regretted Daniel's reference to 'virginity'. Antoinette gave him a knowing smile, or at least he thought that's what it was – it could have been pity but his vision was blurred and he felt lightheaded so he couldn't be sure. He wished that Daniel had warned him, or even given him some basic tips, until a thought drifted into his aching head – that maybe it was part of the way Daniel operated. He did always need to be the leader, the better one, especially with girls present. Sam batted the thought away like an irritating gnat and finished his vodka. It made his throat sting even more but drinking water would be too degrading.

Antoinette leaned over and stroked his cheek gently. "Ya should have a glass of water – first time I smoked it almost raped de throat outta me."

"Yeah, you're probably right. You want some water too?"

She arched her eyebrows in that achingly sexy manner she had, exuding dominant sexuality. "Nah, honey, I'm not de one chokin'."

He nodded and went inside where he drank half the local water supply in famished gulps until he could swallow without pain again.

When he came back to them Daniel was on his feet with his conquest, and a glint in his eye that positively lit up the room.

"We're gonna go upstairs – that cool, use your room?"

Sam nodded. They had already discussed this – he would use his parents' room tonight to sleep in. He hadn't really believed that Antoinette would stay over but he definitely didn't want Daniel having sex in his parents' room.

Antoinette was looking at him with a gentle provocative grin. "I missed the last DART a little while ago – it's alrigh' to stay over, isn't it?"

That layered question drifting huskily out of the delicate throat of the most beautiful creature that he had ever seen, let alone had the privilege of actually touching, should have sent Sam's self-esteem spiralling into ecstasy. Instead it numbed him and his chest constricted involuntarily. He was in uncharted territory. She was sitting on the couch in her mini-skirt, supple legs crossed one over the other, kitten heels pointed at him. Her back was arched slightly, thrusting her rounded breasts out from her tiny ribcage while her eyes looked up at him demurely, lips parted in that submissive manner made famous by budding pop stars. He found himself staring at the smooth skin over her cheekbones, the rouge of her make-up projecting a healthy glow around her sculpted features. If it were possible she was, in Sam's eyes, too beautiful. Then she stood up gracefully, like a swan, and danced over to where he stood transfixed by her. She seemed to move over the floor like an angel without touching the ground. He was in love, or it could have been the grass mixing with vodka. Either way he felt her breath pushing against his teeth, her breasts heaving gently like tiny animals, her unblinking eyes smiling coyly at him.

"Ya didn't say yes – would ya prefer if I got a taxi an' went home?"

She didn't mean it – she was only speaking to allow her husky voice, seductively enhanced by cigarettes, to affect him.

"No, I think you should definitely stay." His voice spluttered out of him, the pitch harking back to his pre-pubescent halcyon days and he cursed himself silently.

Her eager lips against his neck broke his thoughts and he let out a gasp. Her hand grabbed his, pushed it against her breast and pulled the other around her waist, holding her tight. He was in a trance and he let her dictate his movements, much the same way as she was manipulating his thoughts.

She brushed her lips across his cheeks and whispered into his ear which vibrated with desire. "We should go upstairs."

He nodded.

His parents' room was large, with ensuite bathroom, the whole decor done in simple chestnut wood and porcelain fittings, with soft lighting that could be manipulated to different settings. Most importantly the bed was big and wide.

It was strange that she led him to the bed and not the other way around – usually the girl had to be coaxed, he would have thought, but Antoinette was positively eager. Her obvious desire and domineering manner made him uncomfortable but that vanished when she pulled him on top of her. They kissed hard, teeth banging roughly against each other then biting each other's skin, neck, shoulder, cheek, anything in reach. When she lifted up his shirt and did the same with her top, he gasped into her open mouth at the touch of her hot skin against his. Their bellies pressed and rubbed against each other with a seething animalistic desire. She slipped her hand underneath the tight buckle of his belt after a few more moments and he immediately hesitated. His hands suddenly felt clumsy, his touch heavy, his teeth in the way. Sweat dripped from his brow onto her forehead and he hoped feverishly that she didn't notice. His hands became clammy and he fumbled childishly for her bra. As he did so he felt her stiffen slightly – only for a brief moment but it was enough to register and he felt all his desire leave him, afraid of embarrassing himself further.

She reached for him, her hand having forced its way beyond his belt and she stopped kissing for a few seconds as she concentrated on searching for him. He pulled back, aware of what had happened, wiping the sweat from his brow. She stared at him in incomprehension.

"I've gotta go to the toilet real quick. Drank too much water."

She smiled and stroked his arm. "Don't be too long."

He smiled back, hoping that it masked his inner turmoil and, flipping over onto his back, in what he hoped was an athletic movement, he slid off the bed and went into the bathroom. He could hear her every move through the thin frame of the door, and listened as she took off her clothes, the sound of tights peeling off her legs both exciting and disturbing him. He knew that once he went outside she would be next to naked – there was no going back now. He couldn't go to the toilet, not with her listening, and if he took any longer she might think that there was something wrong so he bounced on his heels, willing for something to happen. He flushed the toilet even though it was clean, splashed his face with water and stared at his own reflection. 'Pussy,' it seemed to grimace at him and for the first time he found himself hating his own features.

He found himself imagining being on the bus, with Greg and Darren laughing at him, Antoinette sitting between them, her hands on each of their legs, caressing them gently.

Greg's face contorted in an evil expression. "Couldn't get it up with a naked girl, huh? Fucking faggot!"

He felt his cheeks flushing with imagined shame and he walked out the door, indicating to Antoinette that he had to go downstairs without giving her a chance to react.

From the downstairs loo he could hear little pants from Catriona mingled with Daniel's heavy grunts. Antoinette couldn't hear the trickle of his urine into the bowl down here and he gratefully relieved himself and tried to pull it together. He grasped at his penis and attempted to make it harden, willing it to do its job. It gave him no reaction.

He made his way back up the stairs with dead weights in his feet and wished with all his might that something would happen – a Garda raid, anything. Yet he couldn't think of anything that could plausibly occur to rescue him from oblivion.

Opening the door, he saw her before she knew he was there and he stood still, breathing her in. She lay on her back, her head turned slightly away from him, wearing only knickers. Her soft nipples caught the shadows and drew in his drunken gaze. Blonde hair cascaded down the near side of her face, hiding her eyes from his view, but her lips protruded gently. He ached for her and found himself waking up below, stirring from a terrible slumber. He was quickly on the bed beside her, hard and ready. She turned into him, noticing his ardour and they kissed, then she gave him a gentle caring smile and reached for him, clasping him through his pants in her hand.

"We'll take it slowly."

For some reason that simple and giving gesture knocked the wind out of his chest like a sack of bricks. He felt his masculinity being questioned – the girl was going to dictate to him how it went and be kind enough to help him gently through what should be the greatest event in his young life.

He nodded but already knew how it would go.

She squeezed him delicately and he felt himself begin to deflate in her grasp.

She let go of him and pressed play on the stereo remote. Despite himself he laughed as Paul Brady filtered into the room. She looked at him, indignant, the impudence on her face making her seem young and childlike.

"It was de best dat I could find!"

"It's a good choice."

"I know."

She undressed him and they lay side by side in their underwear, bodies lightly touching. Sweat filled his armpits in puddles like burst water balloons and he hoped it didn't smell. She kissed his nose and traced her lips down his neck, chest and along his hips, easing off his boxers. Pleasure swept through him as her gentle wet mouth opened and closed. She eventually eased up off him when she felt he was ready and sat astride his hips, her pelvis grinding into him. Then she arched back, lifted her legs up into the air and removed her knickers in front of his disbelieving eyes. Leaning forward again she kissed him and lowered her body on top of his, her warm nipples scraping his skin. A condom appeared in her hands and, smiling, she reached down and tried to slip the rubber skin onto his hard flesh. She struggled for a moment and he felt her hands scrabbling – it was uncomfortable but he said nothing, too afraid to move. She sat up, trying to position herself. He realized that he could feel nothing and he panicked, the blessed calm of the last few sacred minutes lost in the swell of his fears. He didn't know what to do, how he should move inside her, how he should touch her – should he move at all or just stay still . . . he had no idea. She pressed down on top of him to no avail and she grimaced, trying to guide him inside but he was shrinking fast and she wasn't able to stop it. He closed his eyes and wished for the bed to swallow him up and suddenly the erotic beauty of her naked body was washed away and she was just a skinny naked figure sitting astride his hips, the spell broken. She became aware of it at the same time, and embarrassment overtook her, which she expressed with an irritated sigh to mask her own inexperience.

Apologizing with a scarcely audible mutter, he yanked the covers over both of them and they lay there for a few minutes.

Paul Brady stopped in the middle of a track and the disc skipped over itself, with a gentle clacking. Then it was silent and the only sound was of their own breath.

Then she spoke. "It could be de johnny – take it off and we'll try again, yeah?"

He wanted to say no, that he couldn't handle going through that ordeal again so soon, all desire having long since emigrated from the husk he now inhabited. But she seemed hurt and he knew that he had to try at the very least.

He pulled the condom off and they lay there under the covers looking at the ceiling as he began to stroke her body insecurely. She replied in kind and her fingers traced the contours of his skin down his ribs and thighs. She was so subtle and wonderful in how she touched him and he wished that he were the same. His fingers pushed into her roughly, and despite the yielding from her body he knew that he didn't possess the same degree of skill that she did.

The fear of not being able to please her covered him like a leather skin, a dungeon enclosing him and sapping him of any power that he might have had. There was no response from between his legs when she reached for him and this time she got visibly annoyed but, to her credit and his chagrin she made another excuse for him, which was actually worse than the reality.

"Could be da drugs, heard it happen before. I'm getting' tired – gotta get home early tomorrow. Ya wanna go to sleep?"

"Yeah, you're right, it's getting late. Gotta stay sharp for those maths exams."

She didn't laugh and his lame joke hung in the air between them, a final nail in the coffin.

He got out of bed, very aware of his own nudity, turned off the lights and leapt back into bed. In the darkness she curled into him but eventually she moved onto her side, facing away – maybe because he was so slippery from sweat.

He hardly slept all night, trying intermittently to awaken himself and, when he did manage to, then wishing that he had the courage to waken her, but fearful that if he did then the pressure would overwhelm him again. It was exhausting.

The morning sun awoke him to the sight of her naked body half hidden by the duvet, the sheet lying across her waist. Her make-up was smeared and she wasn't quite the divine angel she had been before, but his head hurt and nothing else mattered apart from getting some time to himself to pretend that the shameful event had never happened. His inabilities last night had ruined the marvellous experience of seeing and touching his first naked female.

Catriona and Antoinette left for the DART with cute and cunningly placed kisses, and Sam thought that maybe she didn't mind at all. She seemed positively nourished by the night with him, and made such a show of it to the others that he began to think it had gone much better than he had remembered.

But Daniel looked at him with a grimace the moment they had left.

"Uh oh, bit of trouble in Paradise?"

"Fuck off!"

Daniel hugged him though and smiled, his own joy evident in his energy. "Don't worry – she likes ya a lot – trust me, *a lot*. Now wait 'til you hear what we did – I didn't sleep all night!"

He could be an awful bastard sometimes, but Sam listened to him anyway.

Chapter 9

Manufactured Indecision

She was all that he could think about. The image of her lying naked on the bed, eyes turned away, breasts heaving, filled his mind and clouded his senses. But it was tainted. Whenever he tried to re-imagine it, he couldn't get past those same harrowing moments – every time that he imagined approaching her, what had happened would happen again and his hands would get clammy. He found that he couldn't alter what had happened even in his own imagination. He could still feel the embarrassment.

The pen slipped out of his hand, slippery with wetness. He looked down and saw that the palm of his hand was stuck to his copybook, pasted as if with glue. Even the memory of it was overpowering. He lifted his palm gingerly off the paper but the ink was stained and illegible. The page was ruined – he would have to rewrite his work for this class.

He always met with Don on Mondays. He liked to think of

it as their 'thing'. Don would arrange meetings with all the other kids but Sam was one of the few who were regulars each week – and more often if he had a pressing need to discuss something important. The Jesuits, and Don in particular, were encouraging of this practice. Part of it was born less out of concern for their students' well-being than to maintain their own narcissistic reputation as being strong social influences, but they were genuinely inclusive and didn't want their boys to feel isolated at such an important stage of their development. It was a huge part of the ethos of their order. Naturally Sam had figured this out and took advantage. Some boys would avoid these meetings like the plague. Daniel was one such and steadfastly refused to change his mind no matter how convincing an argument Sam gave about their benefit for skipping class. Secretly Sam adored these interactions and needed Don's validation, even if he would never openly admit it.

Standing patiently outside Don's office he wondered if he would be allowed in. He had knocked but there was no reply. Sometimes Don would take a while to open his door, so it was never clear if he was actually in his office or not. He knew that he had the appointment with Sam so if he wasn't in then he would surely arrive at some point.

Unless he was deliberately staying away.

Sam had been ashamed after being caught lying about the drugs and the concert at their last meeting so had deliberately missed their appointment last week without explanation. Don had twice since passed him by in the corridor and not even acknowledged him. Sam had been surrounded by other kids on both occasions but he still expected to be noticed.

If Don didn't want to see him it was because he was angry and was making a point – he hardly ever missed an appointment with anybody, always rescheduling in the extreme circumstance that he did. If he didn't want to see Sam it was because he was extremely unhappy about being lied to and it was going to require an awful lot of grovelling to make amends. There was now the very real possibility that Don wouldn't ever fully trust him again because his word was tainted. Fuck. He shouldn't have bothered making up something to talk about last time – had class really been that boring?

The door never opened after twenty minutes of standing outside and knocking. He checked his watch – only thirty-five minutes until school ended – either Don was deliberately missing the appointment or was in his office and wasn't going to open the door to punish him.

Again the image of Antoinette flashed into his mind, making his belly tumble inside of him. She really had been incredible-looking naked. He wondered if he would ever see somebody that naked again. But wasn't he going to be meeting her again? Of course he was. So if he had got her naked once then surely it was a dead cert to happen again? Yet he couldn't escape that nagging feeling that he had missed his chance, that that was it. He hadn't really got her naked – she had got herself naked. Besides, when was he going to be able to have a party in his house again? Daniel possibly might because his parents were very liberal and might very well leave him the house so that he could specifically have sex, but he'd probably then just have Catriona over – he was selfish like that.

The bell for the end of school rang and he realized that he had been standing against the door lost in his thoughts for the entire period. He remained there for at least ten minutes longer as the corridor filled up and pretended that he was waiting for an appointment after school so that he wouldn't look quite so pathetic.

The lads were already at the swing, staring out over the ravine reverentially in a line when he pulled himself up the slope leading up from the laneway. He had tried to do it as quietly as possible but at the last moment had lost his footing and would have tumbled back down if he hadn't clutched at a fresh sapling to stabilize himself. There were times when he felt like a cat, lithe and graceful, and occasions when he felt as ungainly and stiff as a mechanical doll. He felt like that today – his limbs were heavy.

He knew that he should ring Antoinette later tonight as a follow-up from Saturday. Daniel had instructed him to, and the responsibility was weighing him down. He could simply forget about her, never contact her again and spare himself the agonizing insecurity and constant self-recrimination. He half wanted to do that but knew that Daniel wouldn't stop berating him if he did, and that would be more painful in the long run. He also fancied the knickers off her and just seeing her naked again would raise his self-esteem immeasurably.

The lads were all looking at him, still standing in a line like lemmings about to leap.

"Yer some space cadet, ya know dat?"

He found himself staring at a contemptuous Mouse. They were all looking at him as if he had something important to say. Jesse, Jayo, Mouse and Washing Machine, the four lads from his gang. His gang. Sometimes it was his gang.

"You're always staring off into the distance like that retard Gar from up the street," Jayo mocked.

Sam stood up straight and let his schoolbag fall to the ground at his feet.

"Well, what are you all doing just standing there?" he countered.

Jayo broke the line to reveal a huge pile of recently cut sally branches against the tree where the swing was.

"We're preparing." Jayo said.

Mouse picked up one of the biggest sallies and slashed it through the air like a samurai sword, ending with a high-pitched scream and the sally only inches from Sam's face. Washing Machine clapped his hands like a child. Some people couldn't clap very well, Sam thought.

"We're going to have a war."

Jayo's voice was calm but unnerving at the same time, maybe because he was so still, almost Zen-like, and for all that Sam could see, with no apparent reason. At times like this Sam was pretty certain that Jayo was at least a little bit insane.

"De lads up de road, Skinsers an' de rest of dem, dey challenged Jesse today," Jayo's steady voice continued. "So we had to say yeah."

"Meaning what exactly?"

"We have pride of de road at stake – we're meetin' dem out on de course in front of the woods in ten minutes – we've been waitin' fer ya."

"Yeah, I missed the bus."

"Grand, yer here now. Grab as many sallies as ya can carry an' let's go."

Sallies were essentially like bigger, longer, harder, more flexible sticks of rhubarb, the stalks of newly grown bushes of some sort which were perfect to harvest for this purpose at certain times of year. When ones with the optimum size and weight connected with exposed flesh they left marks on the skin that mightn't leave for a week. You used them in a whipping motion, in the style that Bruce Lee would use numb-chucks in the movies, and the best for this were the long and skinny ones. The older thicker ones were similar to hitting somebody with a heavy stick but the elasticity of the sally made it slightly gentler and almost impossible to snap or break – you had to cut them from their bush with a sharp knife in a sawing motion. The main thing about sallies was that they hurt. A lot. Sam had got one to the eye last year from Jayo, and his eye had refused to close properly for three days, the soft tissue underneath the eyelid swelling up like a ripe tomato.

He wasn't sure he was in the mood for this – this kind of woodland combat could last a while – but, if he left, the lads would make sure he regretted it – but then, if he was late in, he mightn't have time to ring Antoinette.

Mouse abruptly shovelled a huge pile of the stalks into Sam's arms and spun him around. Choice made. They all saluted each other grimly and then slipped into their familiar single-file column behind Jayo, sliding back down the slope to the lane and cutting across into the woods proper.

It was probable that Jayo didn't actually like any of them individually, Sam thought. He was definitely hard enough to hang out with the older kids in the other groups, but it was obvious that he enjoyed being an unquestioned leader. A teenage dictator, sometimes he would lead them in a complete circle around a clearing when they crossed through the woods and nobody would say anything.

Having Jayo gave the others some much-needed street cred, generally enough to avoid being picked on by other gangs, so allowing him to have his moments of absolute control was a small price to pay.

They were deep in the forest now, moving surprisingly swiftly along one of the many half-paths that would continuously appear and disappear, nature usually reclaiming it before it could be acknowledged as an actual 'route'. The forest bordered the golf course on every side, maybe a quarter to half a mile thick in places, with certain areas even deeper, sometimes so dense that you could get turned around and not know which way was which. Then you never knew who you were going to stumble into – the woods were thick with other groups of more violent kids, random men drinking from stale beer bottles and crazy guys with golf clubs who weren't even playing golf but just wandered around collecting lost golf balls with one-eyed dogs and a crazed stuttering walk.

Near the edge of the forest bordering the 9th green, Jayo put his finger to his lips and began to creep forward with his chest low to the ground.

"If we're meeting them in the open why are we creeping?"

Sam's voice projected louder than he had meant, and it seemed to echo in the silence of the forest surrounding them which was quiet and still, as if it knew there was a war about to begin. Nature was holding her breath, reluctant to disturb the concentration of these youths.

Washing Machine clipped him around the ear like he was a petulant child and violence blazed in Jayo's eyes as he hissed like an angry snake: "Shut de fuck up, ya muppet!"

It all happened so fast that everything was just a

misshapen blur, like something from a Salvador Dalí nightmare. Shapes darted in and out of Sam's eye-line like crazed nymphs, their body parts blending into the forest and merging, melding, gliding like thick green and brown shadows. Jayo bellowed a war cry and his hand flashed up and down, using a sally like a scythe, spinning in and out, ducking and weaving. A teenage Warrior God. An almighty swishing sound broke the stillness as innumerable sallies sliced through the air and the painful wet smack of them meeting with the bare flesh on arms and faces sent tremors through them all. Sam dropped his own bundle and grabbed the closest sally to his hand as they fell through the air. It was small and thin, perfect for delivering a killer slice to the face. Some kind of alien feeling flooded his senses, primal and earthen. His muscles felt larger and his movements quicker. Lithe and cat-like, a panther. One of the boys from the streets above came charging at him, wielding an enormous sally like an axe but it was a jerky unsure movement and Sam ducked under his insecure slash and whipped his own arm out, feeling his sally connecting with the boy's face with a surge of satisfaction. There was nothing that could be made out clearly without staying still for a second and that was far too dangerous – keep moving, he thought, as he spun and slashed, a dancer of death, his feet moving across the forest floor like a ballerina in tandem with the upper body thrusting and delivering ferocious blows at the air.

Slap! The sudden stinging across his face was incredible and he stopped moving for a moment to register the shock. He yelped in pain as a second was dealt, then a third. He dropped his own tattered sally to the ground and lifted his arms up to his face for protection but the pounding was unrelenting, the back of his head and hands on fire. One of the two boys beating him punched him in the ribs violently and he collapsed onto his knees, the wind punched out of him.

All around him there were individual scuffles that were threatening to become much more dangerous than they should have been. Washing Machine had already been disposed of and was in a crumpled heap by a tree. Jesse was faring well in one-to-one combat with a taller lad, Sticks – they were on the same football team and there was a respect and even a smirk in their fighting that was almost playful. Mouse was filled with aggression, knocking one lad to the ground and then hitting another with his fist, though taking as much as he gave.

But Jayo was the devil incarnate. He held two sallies, one in each hand and his fists moved in a circular action as he alternately whipped three boys in front of him. One was Skinsers, a wiry little boy, older by a few years but perhaps because of his small size compelled to relive his younger years on a loop. He was not usually to be messed with because in a fight he was a pit bull and wouldn't give up – he wore you down so you either had to really beat him or he got you when your nerve failed. And he was fast, and vicious. But here Jayo was easily knocking him for six. The stories about Jayo flickered in Sam's mind and he was glad that he was on his side.

The attack suddenly subsided and Skinsers held up his hands in defeat but Jayo ignored him and slammed his fist into his unprotected face like a sledgehammer. There was a loud crack and Skinsers dropped to the ground unmoving. Blood slowly trickled out of his left nostril, then with increasing speed like a dam slowly breaking until it was a flood. Everybody stopped moving and Sam took the opportunity to kick out at his distracted savager, tripping him off balance and onto his knees in the muck. But he ignored Sam, his attention on Skinsers who was still not moving.

Jayo stood back. A triumphant smile curled at the edge of his lips, not betraying a trace of concern.

The sally fight was a tradition with the lads around here, although nobody quite knew where it originated from, and it usually took place a few times a year when the bushes' growth was at its peak, and lasted as long as the appetite was there for it. But there were unwritten rules, and 'no extreme violence' was one writ loud and bold. It was as much about speed, taking each other by surprise in the forest as had happened, as it was about the actual fighting. It was a fun fight – there was never a huge amount of malice in it, the bruises and physical humiliation notwithstanding.

But Jayo had crossed the boundary, hitting a surrendering man, and he knew it. There was a very fine line bordering an act of brutality and participation in what accounted for fun.

With this one act Sam could feel the mood of the two groups change.

The boys from the other road hardened and the tension was palpable as they waited for Skinsers to get back to his feet. Once he was standing and the fear of having to bring him back to his parents injured had subsided, Carney, the larger of the group who had been fighting Mouse and winning, squared up to Jayo, pressing his head against his forehead aggressively.

"Wat de fuck was dat about, Jayo? Fuckin' not on!"

"Fuck off, Carney!"

"You fuck off! I'll fuckin' deck ya!"

"Try it – come on!"

Jayo's cheeks went blood red and the heat in the forest seemed to sear, crackling like a frying pan. All it needed was a spark and the tinder was going to ignite.

Carney and Jayo began to push each other back and forth with their foreheads like two young bullocks, each waiting for the other to make the first move. Then Jayo had had enough and suddenly flipped his head up, the movement pushing Carney back and suddenly sparks erupted. Carney let his fists fly at Jayo who immediately responded and the two biggest in the groups fell into the undergrowth scuffling, knuckles bruising and beating on each other, far beyond the scope of the mock 'war'.

Skinsers watched with interest, wiping his bloody nose on his sleeve.

The groups stood apart, a few feet from each other, waiting for the titanic tussle to come to a close. They didn't make eye contact.

Carney had Jayo by the throat and neck now, pushing his face into the mulch, forcing him to eat the dirt. "Come on, ya fuck, swallow it up!"

Mouse and Washing Machine watched in morbid fascination but nobody helped. Perhaps they were all too scared. Carney was big and violent and, like some of them up the road, had brothers who dealt drugs, with rumours circulating that he did a bit of running. He drank with them and most likely carried a knife, which they were all painfully aware of.

Carney let Jayo go, taking his knees off his back. Dirt lining his lips, Jayo scrambled to his feet, and tried to regain his wounded pride while cleaning the smelly mass from his face.

The other group disappeared into the forest as quickly as they had come, Skinsers and Carney the first to leave. Surprisingly none of them said anything – they just left as if they were strangers who had just passed the others on the street.

The shock of what had been barely two minutes of intense violence seemingly stretched into an hour for Sam and the others.

The birds were tentatively making sweet birdsong again, and the forest had come alive with teeming life as if a switch had been pushed. This forest had been privy to far more dangerous events than that of scuffles between fifteen-year-old boys. A nose bleed and some muck in the teeth wasn't going to be remembered for that long. For the lads, however, there was nothing more important than what had just happened.

They stood in silence, not knowing what to say. Suddenly Jayo turned and without any warning violently pushed Washing Machine to the ground with his left forearm so that he tumbled over and cracked his head on a protruding tree trunk. A barley inaudible whimper escaped his lips but to his credit he didn't scream out in pain. The other lads immediately diverted their eyes and followed in the slipstream of the tense figure of Jayo as he thundered past them. He didn't exude an anger to them so much as a tangible fear – pure fear that reached out and gripped them individually by the throat and sent shivers rippling down their spines. They weren't respectful of his anger or shame but afraid of what it might mean for them. Their fear was protective – nobody wanted to be the one who bore the brunt of Jayo's humbling because it always threatened to be brutal. In a sense Washing Machine was lucky that he hadn't suffered worse, and he was aware of it.

The lads melted into the bushes silently. Jesse tripped on a submerged root and scuffed his knee but didn't break stride and kept following Jayo dutifully.

A strange thing happened that evening. For the first time Sam felt accepted. There was no truly solid line of friendship in this group that couldn't be sliced up with a relatively sharp incident but on the surface they would stay true to one another in a fight. That was what Sam thought anyway. Maybe they allowed him to feel he was part of the group to mock him and behind his back maybe they were laughing or waiting for the right time to humiliate him, but for the moment he was a part of their little gang and that was enough for now.

They stayed by the swing until late, trading their war stories and building them up considerably until it was even decided that Jayo had actually got the better of Carney. Even Sam was suitably honoured, most especially with the regaling of how he had tripped up his adversary when the fighting had stopped. "That took balls," they had said and Washing Machine had re-enacted his sweeping action until the laughter had died away and they all parted, going their separate ways.

When Sam got home it was very late and he forgot to ring Antoinette.

Chapter 10

Strength of Nerve

After school the next day Sam made his way directly to their place above the ravine but found himself alone there.

Daniel hadn't been in school again so he had been spared the lecture about not calling Antoinette. It was strange – he had awoken dreaming about her, but he was dismissive of it now. Finally he was part of the group here and she had no hold upon that. For the first time since he had met her he no longer felt the constant tightness in his chest and he could think of her without feeling his body sweat. He was free and he had the light bruising on his face to prove it. He didn't need the stress of a girl when he had a group of lads who looked after each in a fight – nothing was more important than that.

He lifted the solid lump of wood that served as their swing out of its nook in the lower branches. The night before they had all had one very definite celebratory swing to confirm their sally-fight victory and he had almost enjoyed it.

He held the swing in his hands. It was heavy and rough, the wood like an ancient ornament that would decorate a museum, the weight indicating how valuable it could be. The rope was tied tightly around the middle and hammered in with a few nails to make certain that it wouldn't slip off. This particular rope – there had been many different swings and ropes over the years – was stolen from one of the fishing boats down at the harbour. Mouse had said that his dad, who worked on the trawlers that went out into the Irish Sea and down to the Atlantic for weeks on end, would help them out but had been proved very wrong and for weeks afterwards had the marks to prove it. So an expedition had been formed and a suitable rope was acquired. It was this rope that Sam now held in his hands. How many hands had it passed through on its journey here, how much grief had it saved and crises averted in a storm on board its previous home, he wondered? Now it was being used as a plaything.

He stood on the edge of the ravine and looked down. It was a steep drop to the bottom which was filled with old concrete slabs, disused metal and a shallow muddy pond. A forgotten dump right in the middle of the forest. He had clambered down only once before with the others as part of a joint dare but the climb back up had been arduous so he wasn't inclined to do it again, especially not alone. Over the tops of the trees that flanked the ravine he could just about make out the sea and part of the harbour. If you got some good height when you swung sometimes you could see the entire bay but you had to get dangerously high for that.

He fingered the rope absentmindedly, toying with the idea of leaping out across the ravine without anybody to impress, just for the sheer joy of it and to reaffirm his newly acquired sense of manhood. The feeling that only being in a gang gave to a boy. Antoinette might have emasculated him but she couldn't take that away. He had only ever previously got on the swing when the lads were there – the fear of falling off took away any pleasure for him. The swing was more of a symbol of masculinity. He looked around him. There was no sound of anybody approaching. He was alone. The swing loomed large in front of him. Should he do it? Wouldn't every other lad in a gang do this if they had the chance, because it was manly to do it alone? He came to the conclusion that he simply had to do it, for himself, to reassert the fabric of his self-esteem that Antoinette had ripped at.

He pulled the wooden 'seat' down level with his waist and readied himself to leap into manhood. The swing was deliberately a little high to give it some tension and a better arc and so the only way to get on it was to grab the rope high above your head and jump up in the air as you pushed out off the edge. This only gave a split second to get your ass on the wood before you were hanging out in the empty air with space all around you. That was what made it so much more difficult – if you missed getting on the lump of wood you could be in trouble. You could lift yourself on it first before jumping but then without somebody pushing you wouldn't get enough power. If it was weak then you didn't get the down swing to take you back over the edge and you would would just hang out above the ravine. The only way back in then was if somebody reached out a branch to pull you back in.

Taking a deep breath, Sam leapt into oblivion.

The air swept past him along with the trees, branches and leaves necessarily out of focus. He had managed to get on the seat but struggled to get comfortable on the wood, a little jutting lump on the top digging into his ass. The swing moved back towards the hill and he hauled himself up a moment and back down, lodging his hips down around the rope. The hill came into view under his shoes and then was gone again as quickly as it had appeared and he was back into the nothingness. He had got a good swing. Elation pumped through him, and a broad smile tore open his face. For the first time he felt the ecstasy that thrill-seekers regularly search for, that addiction from the drug of facing your fears and passing control over to nature's whim. The swing did three more full lengths and then began to slow drastically. Sam turned his head as he felt his momentum recede, the soft breeze now gentle upon his skin again and not like sliced air rushing past. The bank was a few feet behind him and he was moving towards it but not quickly enough. He should have jumped off earlier but his speed had been too much – now he wasn't going to reach the edge. He drifted almost close enough but before he dared leap off the swing it gently drifted back out again. Panic set in and he began to swing his body against the rope, trying to give it some extra momentum. It began to work and painstakingly slowly on each turn he crept closer to the bank, at one point stretching his foot out and managing to dislodge some loose earth right on the edge.

But that was it. The swing slowed again and came to complete standstill and so did he. Hanging down from the tree branch, ten feet from the safety of the bank. He hollered out hopefully but still none of the lads had arrived.

"Jesse? Jayo? Washo?" he shouted out. He refused to call for Mouse.

Maybe they could hear him if they were walking up the

lane. He shouted out again and listened but heard nothing.

"Hey, lads! Anybody!"

Their clearing was so hidden from the laneway that nobody would ever come here, and would not even hear him. That's why they liked it, the hidden seclusion. He was alone.

Sweat began to moisten his fingers and his grip loosened on the rope. His hips hurt and the wood was digging uncomfortably into his crotch. The swing moved gently in the wind but apart from that it was static, and so was he. He had no way of getting back to the bank and the twenty-foot fall below was simply not an option. He tried using his body to swing back towards the edge again but the tension on the rope kept pulling it back and he just couldn't get his foot onto the edge no matter how hard he tried. He almost got his toe onto it, but without traction and with the pull from the rope like a spring he was gently brought back to the middle where he swung around, the rope turning itself in circles until he felt ill. He dared not throw too much of his weight into the swing, for fear of losing his grip and falling off. If he had been but six feet above the ground no doubt he would have stretched his body backwards like a plank of wood and eventually through violent abuse of the swing, his body and aerodynamics, would have made it, but this high up the fear gave tension to his every movement.

He hung there for almost twenty minutes hoping for somebody to come but still nothing. He eventually faced up to the reality that he had to do something before it got dark and he knew what it was. He brought his gaze upwards and looked at the branch fifteen feet above him. If he made it that high he would be fully thirty-five feet above the concrete and rocks below. It was a long fall down. Washing Machine had climbed the rope once under extreme duress from the lads so if he could do it out of peer pressure then Sam could do it out of necessity. Reaching up, he took a firm grip on the rope a few feet above his head and lifted himself off the swing seat. He hung in the air by his hands, the bottom of the rope and the wood now flapping uselessly without the tension of his body to hold it. He just hung there. Now what? Wrapping his foot in the rope below he tried to give himself some leverage but that didn't work like it did on television. He took a deep breath, removed one hand, took a grip a few inches above and held tight. Then he moved the other hand. Each time he removed a hand his body gave a little shiver of fear until halfway up his arms were aching so much from the effort that the shivers went unnoticed. He now found himself in a complete conundrum. He couldn't change his mind and just go back down onto the wood swing because he feared he wouldn't be able to control his aching arms and sliding down the rope would surely shake him loose – he had no choice but to keep dragging himself upwards and so he gritted his teeth and painstakingly, inch by inch, climbed on.

Eventually, in triumph, he made it to the top.

It was here that he encountered a second major problem. He was hanging for dear life just below the massive branch above but to reach up and wrap his hands around the bough was impossible. His reach wasn't long enough and under the strain he didn't think his one arm could take his weight as he stretched for it. His hands began to slip and burn and tears formed in his eyes. How the fuck had he got himself into this mess? He closed his eyes tightly and went for it.

Reaching up he clawed at the knots in the rope where it jutted out from the tree limb and found a grip, then kicked his legs into air and, with his nails digging into the tearing strands of rope, managed to get his chin up onto the tree branch. Now with one hand below and one above he had to make an act of faith in the rope holding, and his nails not breaking. All he needed was a second to let go of the rope and get his other hand over the branch – and he got it.

Finally he wrapped his arms around the branch, got a leg over it and hauled himself onto it gratefully. The bough wasn't as sturdy as it looked from below, nor as wide, and he was suddenly just as vulnerable, only now with his back to the trunk erupting from the dirt where safety beckoned. He got a solid grip on the bough and eased himself backwards. A few feet closer and enthusiasm overruled his nerves for a moment so he looked behind him. Craning his neck awkwardly back he almost lost his balance, the gulley below teetering into view, and dizziness shook him, but his hands dug into the bark of the tree and he steadied himself.

"Careful. Slowly," he said out loud and then he felt his shoes hit the trunk behind him. Sitting up, he spun around and hugged the trunk gratefully, relief washing over him.

He climbed down the tree as quickly as possible and collapsed to the dirt beside his schoolbag, his head nestling into the hard familiar books comfortably. The swing was still out there, hanging fitfully in the breeze, dangling mournfully out over the now unthreatening drop that he had defeated.

He felt a sense of achievement. He had accomplished more in these last few minutes than he had all day at school, maybe even all week, but there was nobody to tell it to. Nobody present to see his extreme feat of masculinity.

He felt a pang of loneliness. He couldn't tell the lads as they would just mock him and force him to climb back up and collect the swing, which he wasn't going to do. He would leave that to Washing Machine. Daniel had never seen the swing, so even with a detailed description it wouldn't mean much. There was nobody to share it with so he caught his breath, mentally photographed the memory frame by frame, picked up his bags and went home.

It confused him that the lads had never shown up. They always came after school like clockwork, and the fact that not one of them turned up at all meant that they must have made plans without him. Three of them went to the same school while Mouse travelled some distance like Sam, although not half as far. It hurt to think that they would have agreed to do something without him – surely after the epic sally-fight bonding they wouldn't?

There was nothing on television and his mother was in one of those moods where she wanted to chat. Not talk but chat – there was a marked difference. Chat involved gossip. Small irritating lumps of useless information about neighbours and family gleaned from her myriad of sources. If she was a detective for the CIA her skills would have been invaluable, here she was a nuisance. He sat there, trying to watch anything on the television and praying for her nattering to stop or for his father to come home from work to entertain her. He was careful to feign interest – a skill that he acquired from his father after careful observation, and honed to perfection to prevent any offence. His mother was a smart woman and her articles in magazines as diverse as gardening and lifestyle were well received and respected but she had an innate need to project hot air to alleviate any stress she might be feeling. He just wished that he didn't have to bear the brunt of it tonight. She was in the midst of a spiel on a family predicament when he suddenly remembered Antoinette.

With the perfect excuse he left the room and went upstairs to his parents' bedroom where he could make a private phone call, unlike in the hallway where he would be overheard.

The phone loomed large and ominous and looking at the bed brought all the memories flooding back. He hadn't been in this room since that night. The phone was within touching distance of what should have been a seminal moment in his life, but had instead been privy to the event that he would try and erase most intently from his mind. He sat down on the soft mattress, took his shoes off, pulled his socks down over his toes to get them comfortable and adjusted the collar of his shirt. He picked up the phone then immediately put it back down again and cleared his throat loudly. He needed a glass of water. Cursing himself, he put his socks back on properly and bounced down the stairs.

When he was finally settled on the bed with a glass of water in front of him, he swirled the cool liquid around his mouth twice to wet his lips and dialled the number. Taking a deep breath he leaned back to get comfortable but slumped awkwardly into the pillows. Off balance, he had to roll onto his side to drag himself upright again. Just as he got himself straight and was exhaling loudly, there was a sweet voice on the other end. He hadn't even heard it ring.

"Hello?"

He held his breath automatically but his stomach muscles couldn't hold him up and he fell back down into the pillows with a thump and a loud gasp of air.

"Eh, who is dis?"

She sounded impatient. Fuck. He had to say something. The idea of hanging up flashed through his mind but he swatted it aside. She had picked up the phone so quickly maybe she had been waiting for him to call. Yeah, right.

"Eh, hi, Antoinette, it's Sam – sorry, I just lost my breath there – I slipped on the bed."

"Ya slipped on de bed? How de fuck did ya manage dat? Hi, by de way."

"Yeah, no idea. Hi, how are you?"

"Grand, yeah, you?"

"Grand, yeah, grand. It isn't too late to be ringing, is it?"

"What – since last Saturday? Nah, relax, it's only Wednesday."

"I meant late, as in tonight."

"Oh, nah. Sure it's still the evening."

He settled back into the pillows, resigned to being stuck there for the rest of the conversation – at least it was comfortable.

"You answered the phone so fast I didn't even hear it ring."

"Oh yeah, our phone is funny like dat – it rings twice here before it does on anybody else's end – dunno why. I had jus' stopped talkin' te Catriona actually."

"Oh nice, how is she?"

"She's grand. Ya know herself and Daniel mitched off school an' went te Funderland today?"

"Oh right, yeah, of course."

"Why didn't yeh come?"

"Oh, were you there?"

"Yeah, I was. Obviously. I thought you might be der."

He hesitated, completely unsure of what to say. She sounded annoyed, as if he had not shown up for her on purpose. Daniel had actually taken the day off school and gone out with both of the girls and not even told him. Not only that but made him look bad in the process. He felt cheated and angry but couldn't let that on to Antoinette.

"Yeah, sorry, I wasn't feeling well today, didn't actually go in to school."

"Ya alrigh'?"

"Yeah, I'm grand now, didn't tell Daniel actually – I didn't realize it was today that you were going in."

"Yeah, it was a last-minute thing – he only rang last night."

Sam hesitated again, thinking. Did that mean that Daniel had rung Catriona or had he rung Antoinette too? He decided to just let it go, but he couldn't and visions of Daniel kissing Antoinette forced their way into his clouded mind. It didn't make any sense though.

"Catriona had to go early though, so meself and Daniel hung out – he's good craic, yer mate."

Sam had a lump in his throat. "Yeah, he's cool, one of my best friends."

"Sound, yeah. Cat's mine. Dey seem te like each other anyway."

"Yeah, they do – cool when your friends like somebody."

"Yeah, it is."

The conversation was going nowhere fast and he knew it. He had to find a way to rescue it but he couldn't think of anything to say.

Sweat formed on his forehead and he had to wipe it away with the pillow beside him. She heard the fumbling.

"What are yeh doin? Are ya jackin' off while yer talkin' te me?"

"What? No, of course not. I was fixing the pillows."

"Righ', yeah. Pity ya ain't jackin' off – ya need de practice."

He was stung into silence.

"I was only jokin', sorry."

"Yeah, I know, don't worry, it was funny."

He laughed out loud to show that he wasn't offended but it sounded like he was mocking her. She didn't respond. There was an uncomfortable silence between the two of them and he had no idea how to fill it. His mouth felt dry but he didn't dare drink any of the water in case she heard. Maybe it was better just to leave it, forget about her, leave her perfect figure and glossy lips to the imagination where nothing could affect him, go back to the swing where he was able to be a man.

Then she spoke again, her voice having dropped an octave. It was incredibly sexy.

"I gotta go soon – me ma hates it when I'm on de phone fer too long."

"Yeah, mine too."

"Listen, Sam . . ."

"Yeah."

"I really like ya – I think yer very cute."

His heart almost skipped a beat and that lovely warm feeling that flushed his body from limb to limb filled him up and he drifted upwards towards the ceiling. His mouth felt supple.

"And I really like you. I think you're absolutely drop-dead gorgeous."

If he had been floating upwards driven by the seduction of her voice, now he collapsed back to the mattress with a painful thud, cringing. What a fucking stupid thing to say!

"Ah, thanks – dat's really nice of ya."

He felt a little bit better. His ear was stuck to the phone, trying to decipher every little tonal change in her voice for an idea of what she really meant. She seemed genuine. But she was a girl, and he knew they were all natural actresses. He began talking without really knowing what he was saying.

"So listen," he said, "we should hang out, maybe do something?'

"Yeah, dat'd be nice – wat ya thinkin'?'

He actually had no idea – he'd never suggested something like that before in his life. He racked his brain at top speed for ideas, flipping through film stills in his head for any form of reference.

"Well, we could go for an ice cream . . . you could come out to Howth and I'd show you around? You didn't get to see it last time."

She laughed at his joke and the tension in the back of his neck released a little. It did sound nice – they always ate ice cream by the sea in movies.

"Yeah, I'd like dat – okay, how about Friday den?"

"Yeah, Friday would be perfect."

"Okay, grand – em, will I meet yeh at de DART station den?"

"Yeah, I'll wait at the entrance for you. About what time?"

"Well, I'm off school at three. Let's say five – gimme enough time te get over der."

"Okay – five it is."

"I won't be late, I promise."

"Don't worry, I trust you."

"Okay, grand. Well, have a good nigh' – see ya Friday."

"Bye."

"Bye."

The phone clicked down on the other end and he had to concentrate to stop his hand from trembling as he lowered the receiver gently. He stared up at the ceiling in disbelief. There was no way it could have gone that well, not even in his imagination. Had he dreamed of telling her that he thought she was gorgeous? Although that was much too far, he felt stupid for that. Suddenly he was worried. What was he going to do with her out in Howth? Why hadn't he suggested the cinema or something, head into town? Much better, much more things to do. He was still thinking about every little possibility later when he got into bed and then he finally remembered what she had said about Daniel. He would have to ask him tomorrow.

Chapter 11

The Truth about Friends and Girls

Daniel looked at Sam with that sympathetic gaze that parents use on their children when they aren't getting what they want and have to be cajoled into submission. Daniel hadn't been in school again on Wednesday and so it wasn't until Thursday that Sam had been able to confront him.

"It was a last-minute thing."

"Last minute?"

"That's what I said."

"Then why did you organize it the night before?"

"That is last minute!"

Daniel had just finished explaining to Sam what had happened, or the watered-down version that he wanted Sam to hear. According to Daniel he had only had the idea the night before, had rung Catriona and she eagerly agreed. He had no idea that she was going to bring Antoinette. According to Catriona, he said, she had presumed that Sam would be coming and so she had brought her.

"I could hardly call you that late, could I?" Daniel reasoned.

"Yeah, you could."

Daniel clucked at him and arched his eyebrow. They both knew that after 1 a.m. was too late to call his house – his parents would not have been happy. Sam wished that he had a phone in his bedroom like Daniel, and like Catriona had apparently, or else parents who wanted to help their child socially rather than ruin things with rules and curfews.

"You wouldn't have mitched off school anyway," Daniel said.

Sam wasn't going to give him an inch – he was already too close to worming his way out of this. Daniel just had a way with words.

"I would have mitched. You should have waited for me and intercepted me on the way to school."

"Seriously?"

"Yeah."

"You're saying I should have got up early just on the off-chance I could meet you before school and maybe convince you to come to the arcades for the day with me. With Catriona and I."

"'Catriona and *me*'."

"Grammar doesn't matter when you're with a girl. No, I would not get up early to meet you like that. I arranged to meet Catriona late that night and that's it."

Sam didn't believe him. He wasn't sure why, but there was something in the overly confident manner Daniel had when he was explaining, as if he had thought it through and was fulfilling a premeditated dialogue. He didn't bother saying that he felt hurt at Daniel not thinking he would abscond from school but he wanted to ask why he'd then spent all that time afterwards with Antoinette – surely there was some sort of etiquette? If the roles had been reversed he felt certain that he would not have entertained Catriona for a similar length of time because she was Daniel's girlfriend of sorts in his eyes.

Daniel was looking at him expectantly.

Sam had said everything in his head again and now he was too drained from considering all the different possibilities to express it in words. It was easier just to let it go, like most things, especially with friends. Better to just let them lie and keep your thoughts to yourself until it all worked out.

Daniel smiled broadly. "So I heard that you're meeting Antoinette on Friday?"

Sam looked at him sharply. "What? Who told you that?"

"Catriona, who else?"

"Right, yeah, last night?"

"Yeah, I think Antoinette rang her and then she rang me or something."

Sam suddenly felt distinctly uncomfortable with Daniel knowing all his business – he wasn't sure why. It wasn't even the sting of irritation and embarrassment that he had felt in finding two used condoms in the bin of his room after that night, which indirectly highlighted his own failings, but something deeper in how Daniel seemed to be relishing the little courtship that was going on between him and Antoinette, almost voyeuristically enjoying it, watching it the way sadists watch live news on airplane crashes, begging to see the crash and destruction.

"Do you want me and Catriona to come with ya tomorrow?"

"Why would you do that?"

"I dunno – be fun, the four of us."

"The same way it would have been fun for me to come along yesterday?"

Sam didn't know why he let it come out like that after just deciding not to say anything, but if Daniel couldn't see how his offer was degrading then fuck him.

Daniel didn't take it very well. "Oh, okay, it's like that? I do recall helping set you up with Antoinette, you know."

Sam looked at him in disbelief. "Eh, you had nothing to do with it – you left me alone with her immediately and ran off with Catriona – you had no idea what she was even like. You brought me to help *you* out."

"I've known Antoinette for years. I knew she was hot."

"Gimme a break."

"You're an ungrateful prick – you're just pissed off about what happened with her. Not my fault you couldn't hit the back of the net."

Sam stared at him. They were eyeball to eyeball and people in the yard were beginning to pay a distracted interest in their exchange.

Sam was careful to keep his voice down. "What the fuck are you talking about?"

Daniel looked away as if he had said too much and regretted it already. He sighed and put his hands on Sam's shoulders. "Let's just forget it, man."

The bell for the end of break went and so they left it at that but Sam couldn't escape this feeling that Daniel knew more than he should, and his closeness to Catriona, who seemed to know everything about Antoinette and him, was uncomfortable. Something had changed between them now. He didn't trust him any more.

The rest of the day, with the football practice that followed after school, was hard to focus on. His thoughts were broken as if they were one big glass jigsaw sitting in his brain that had been smashed into a hundred pieces. He spent every waking moment trying to piece them together. Antoinette. Daniel. The lads. Antoinette. Antoinette. It was just becoming noise in his brain and nothing was making any sense.

On Friday morning he was so tired from over-thinking and not being able to sleep that he was tempted to skip school and pretend he was sick, but that would backfire because then he wouldn't be allowed go out and meet Antoinette that evening.

Thankfully Daniel wasn't in school again. It was the fourth day that week that he had been absent. Sam didn't like it that on the very day he was supposed to be meeting Antoinette Daniel was off but at least it meant he could just focus his thoughts on Antoinette alone without having to avoid talking to Daniel. He pretended to his French teacher that he had a meeting with Don to enable him to skip the last class, which meant that the moment the bell went he was the first one out the school gates and was actually early for the 31 bus. Naturally the bus was then late and he found himself praying that Greg and Darren wouldn't manage to make it also. Today of all days he needed to get home unmolested and with his confidence intact.

It was only when he was on the bus that he had the idea of getting her a present, something cute. That was what people did on dates, wasn't it? Or did you only do that if a girl was your official girlfriend? Would she be his girlfriend after today? Would he have to ask her or would it just be assumed? They had seen each other naked and were now meeting again – that had to count for something. He was getting excited at the possibility of Antoinette being his girlfriend when he remembered that the last time he had seen her was that fateful day and his balls shrank and wormed their way upwards into his belly. The fear, clammy hands and the tightness of his chest was back. He needed to concentrate.

His parents always ate early on Fridays so that the weekend could begin in earnest, a tradition of his mother's. They both asked him the usual questions – how were things going at school, how was football training etc. He was too distracted to answer, their needling made him edgy, and he was unable to eat properly. It felt like the evening before Christmas Eve when it was always both too far and too close, making everything else much less important. In between their harassment he watched them eat – they had an easy manner, a learned pattern between them in how they ate, shared wine, tidied up the dishes together. There was such an easy loving rapport between them that he felt very blessed to have parents like them, and they were lucky to have each other. He wondered if that was how himself and Antoinette would be in the future.

They were eating ice cream with some freshly baked apple pie when he came out with it, and immediately wished he could take it back.

"I'm going on a date with a girl this evening."

He blushed and felt uncomfortable sitting next to his mother while mentioning going on a date with a girl. But he had wanted to tell somebody who wasn't Daniel.

They fixed their eyes on him with interest.

"Who is this girl?" his father asked.

Sam didn't want to get into it any more than he had to,

so he scooped a particularly large lump of ice cream and pastry into his mouth and nonchalantly shrugged his shoulders in the vague hope that this would satisfy them.

It merely piqued their interest.

"Where did you meet her?" his mother cajoled.

"Is it the first time you're going on a date with her?" his father wanted to know.

He shook his head, hoping that was sufficient but knew it wouldn't be.

They kept staring at him, waiting for an answer.

"No, I've met her before a few times, but she's coming over today – we're going to go for an ice cream and stuff."

His father nodded and swept a big calloused hand out onto Sam's shoulder with a thump. His strong calming fingers dug into his shoulder blades and he shook him gently but firmly.

"Good lad – well, I hope that it goes well."

His mother looked at him in that motherly manner that he found so irritating. It would have been much better if he had just kept his mouth shut.

"Do you want some money to treat her?" his mother asked.

This was unexpected. He looked at her in surprised hope, trying to contain his desire.

"Yeah, well, that would be great."

"Okay, honey, I'll give you some money if you clean up the kitchen after dinner – you need to treat a girl if she's going to come all the way out here. You should take her into town afterwards – go to the cinema – girls love that."

He couldn't believe it. They were actively encouraging and even trying to assist in his date with Antoinette. He wasn't completely sure but it must be a good omen. He tidied the kitchen in record time and swept up the money they had left on the table.

He showered quickly and sat on his bed to decide what to wear. It had only occurred to him moments before while he was lost in the heady warmth of the hot water that he hadn't got a clue what he should wear. That seemed a complaint he had always associated with girls – they were the ones who never knew what to put on that complimented their figures or was appropriate for the situation at hand. He wondered what was appropriate here. They were going out for ice cream, but then they might go into town. He really hadn't worked it out beyond the first few minutes – he'd be quite happy if they just sat on the pier kissing all evening – as long he kissed her nothing else really mattered. So what was he going to wear? He had a nice new pair of tracksuit bottoms his mother had bought him a few weeks ago that he hadn't worn much yet – he was keeping them for special occasions. They were black with a large white stripe down each side and heavy industrial buttons running down the outside of each leg so that you could pull them open like you would with a piece of Velcro all the way up to the hips. He decided to wear them and a new jumper that he had got for Christmas which was very white. He felt a little bit like an ice cream as the jumper enhanced the stripes on his trackies but he did look clean and fresh, like he had made an effort. Once he had spiked his hair and cleaned all the gel off his hands – it was hard to get off and always made his hands sticky for hours afterwards – he was ready to go.

It was five forty-five. He gathered up his wallet and keys and swallowed down a huge glass of water in one go. His heart was pounding in his chest. She was going to be here soon. His mother came in the front door just at the very moment he was leaving, the two almost colliding.

"Oh, hi, are you off on your date then?" She seemed excited for him.

There was nothing wrong with how she said it but she was his mother and it took all the fun out of it, deflating it slowly like when the lads' football hit a bramble and died a lonely but inevitable death.

"Yes, I am – okay, gotta go."

"Good luck – be calm now – give her a nice compliment."

He waved his hand as he half-skipped, half-jogged away from the house towards the laneway leading down to the station. He didn't want to be late.

The lane seemed much longer than he could ever remember. He had to reel himself back from running full pelt down the inviting downhill stretch – he had to keep his calm and not sweat, that was a priority. As he walked tensely down the hill he passed various characters coming home from work, late from school, just wandering, all sorts. He felt proudly dressed, smart but very casual, the way he imagined she would expect him to look.

Then he thought he saw Jayo and Mouse approach. The lads! Shit, what would they say? He would look a bit ridiculous to them probably. He still hadn't seen any of them since the sally fight at the weekend. He had wondered where they'd been all week but then he hadn't been around much himself.

It wasn't the lads but two older boys that he didn't know, so he gave them a cursory nod to be cool, which they ignored.

He would be passing right by the entrance to the slope and the swing though – what if the lads were there? If he clambered up to check they were there they might sabotage him, or he'd get mud on his clothes. What if they saw him down by the harbour with Antoinette? Fuck, he really hadn't thought this out – why did he say Howth where he was certain to run into the lads and get embarrassed? He had almost got to the end of the lane when the tree line broke and the station stood there in all its glory, basking in the approaching evening light. Too late now to do anything – he could only hope they didn't see him.

He slowed his pace – she might see him approach if she was already there and he didn't want to look too eager. Approaching the station he checked his watch, pulling back the tight cuffs of his jumper – it was so new that it was still a little stiff to the touch, like it had been recently starched. The face of the watch flickered and read 5.58. She should be here any moment. He put his hands in his pockets and fingered his wallet absentmindedly in one and picked his nail in the other, just to give his hands something to do and prevent him wringing them anxiously.

The air was sweet, the smell of approaching summer was in the wind and swallows were beginning to fleck the skyline. A huge black-backed seagull bellowed hoarsely over his shoulder from its domineering vantage point on the wall overlooking the street. He nodded to it: two kindred male spirits on the hunt for females. He felt empowered: he had a girl coming all the way over to his part of the city for the sole purpose of seeing him – not with a friend, not for a party, just to see him. For the first time he just knew that he would say the right things. He knew that what had happened before was now irrelevant. He felt a slow but steady surge in confidence.

He sat down on the steps at the station and waited. He needed to do something else to stop fidgeting, so he picked at the paint on the railing he was leaning against. He made sure that his back was straight and his posture exuded strength and purpose. A train arrived and a squirming mass of exhausted bodies pushed and pulled their way off, impatience taking precedence over good manners. Sam had to leap to his feet and get off the steps to avoid being trampled by unforgiving overworked shoes. He looked up at each face that appeared through the doorway, expecting hers to be the next one each time. The mad rush quickly slowed to a trickle and then the train was empty. This was the last stop and so the vehicle sat still, idling on the tracks, catching its breath.

Antoinette was nowhere to be seen.

He walked up the steps carefully, keeping his powerful posture, and casually checked the train-times on the screen. He didn't want to make it too apparent that he was waiting for somebody. The next train was in eleven minutes. She must be on that one. Besides, it was only 6.05 – she was a girl and they were never on time. She was probably doing the exact same thing that he was, trying to be cool. He wondered if she was nervous. He hoped that she was, that she had thought about this as much as he had. He doubted it, but it made him feel better to imagine her being nervous and fearful of saying the right thing and dressing in the best manner.

He strolled over to the newsagent's across the road and bought a packet of chewing gum, thinking that it was a blessing that she was late otherwise he wouldn't have had any. Its tiny proportions belied its importance. Having a fresh packet of chewing gum, both for yourself to chew and to offer as an icebreaker meant that it was not as insignificant as its small size suggested.

The next train arrived and this time he leaned back against a car facing the station opposite the steps so that he could observe everything with a detached air. The faces rushed by and then there she was, radiant, her blonde hair catching the light. But she was rushing off too quickly, her head down. She looked up and it wasn't her. The unknown girl, the Antoinette impersonator, clambered into a waiting car which drove off at breakneck speed. She was about the same age as him, maybe a year or two older, incredibly attractive, and she clearly lived in the area – he wondered how come he had never seen her before. Maybe he would again if he kept his eyes open.

Antoinette. He refocused. Had he missed her by staring after the other pretty blonde girl?

The train had emptied, regurgitated all of its contents. And she was nowhere to be seen. He began to get a little anxious, but it was still only 6.19. He had been early, too expectant. He slunk back up the steps and peered in through the glass, not wanting to be seen by the teller again checking the times. He preferred to be as clandestine as possible. His heart sank into his chest, dropping deeper than usual. The time for the next approaching train read 6.41. That was over twenty minutes away! What was he going to do for another twenty minutes? He'd go nuts! She would be almost forty-five minutes late. He reckoned that at least she would be contrite so maybe it would be a positive thing – she would want to make it up to him and be impressed that he was in such upbeat form despite having had to wait so long. He confined himself to that thought and ignored the creeping suspicion that she wasn't going to come.

Pushing any negative thoughts away he strolled along the road towards the beach, kicking out at a forlorn empty Coke can that lay against the curb. Discarded and forgotten, they were kindred spirits.

He felt thirsty so he went back to the shop, ignoring the assistant's stare. He probably wasn't staring and didn't even remember him, but at times like this it felt like everybody was watching you. He drank the Coke slowly, careful not to rush through it for fear of getting wind and burping constantly when she arrived. He had felt like an ice cream or a bar of chocolate but he would wait until she arrived for that. He wouldn't want to have another Coke when she came but he might have to – he'd just pretend that he hadn't had one recently.

The wait was arduous. People kept driving by and staring at him – in the glare of the evening sun his white jumper reflected the light so he was illuminated. He felt exposed sitting on the steps so he went inside and sat on the bench, deciding that he didn't care what the ticket-teller thought – when he saw Antoinette he would be envious and see that the wait was well worth it. He imagined her naked and wondered how soon he could get her like that again – she really had been incredible.

Finally the train approached. Sam got up hastily and went outside to take up his position against the bonnet of the car. It seemed like the best spot because it was casual enough without being arrogant and gave him the perfect view so that he would see her before she saw him. People began filing off, not as many this time, the after-work rush having dissipated somewhat, but it was still a sizable crowd. Ejected like sardines from a tin can, plopped out into the sunlight, shielding their eyes from nature and getting back inside to the artificial glare. He tried to look down at the ground while keeping his peripheral vision fixed on their faces, being cool. He half wanted her to notice him first, then she'd have to approach him, and he could pretend that he wasn't bothered.

But she didn't notice him first because she wasn't on this train either. She had to be on this train. She couldn't be this late. He rushed up the steps and through the barriers but she wasn't on the platform. He was back inside before the teller could say anything and he just waved at him uncaring, his frustration taking over. He began to list all the possibilities of what could have happened – maybe she had got detention, or got sick, or got off at the wrong station. What if she was at Howth Junction? That station was four stops away – it was an easy mistake to make. Well, it wasn't that easy but it could happen. He wondered if he should get the train there just in case she was waiting and she thought that he was late. Then if she wasn't there he would also be able to check the next train that came and see if she was on that one. He gave it serious thought before dismissing it. The next train was in fourteen minutes, just after seven. She would be on this one.

The train came and went with Antoinette nowhere to be seen. He didn't know what to do. He had thought that everything was organized. He had arranged it firmly with her over the phone, they had talked about it and set a day, place and time, even activities. She just hadn't come. And she hadn't even called. She didn't have his house number, he then realized. But she could have got it off Daniel if she had really wanted to. Maybe she had rung when he was down here and she had spoken to his mother. That would be a disaster. He wanted to wait for the next train but he knew somewhere deep in his stomach that she wasn't coming. He felt like vomiting. He trudged across the road and had begun the long climb home when the worst thing possible happened.

They were coming down towards him. His mother and father were out walking, maybe going for a drink. They didn't notice him at first, engaged in an active discussion about something – politics or something adult. He kept his head down, pretending that he hadn't seen them, but when he was a few yards in front of them his father looked up and spotted him, stopping in surprise.

Sam wasn't in the mood for talking.

"Hey, Sam, are you not on your date?"

It was an excruciatingly painful moment.

Sam stood there, head bowed, trying to keep his shame contained. His parents slowly realized that their son had been stood up and didn't know what to say. So nobody said anything. Even his mother was lost for words.

Sam nodded and walked past.

"Do you have a key?"

He nodded back at his father and put up his hand in the affirmative. They watched him as he moved away from them, his hunched-down figure a shadow of the energetic bundle of enthusiasm that had left the house an hour ago. Now he was broken. Any confidence that he had gained earlier had disappeared with her non-appearance. Last Friday night's non-action now felt like it was going to reverberate forever.

Chapter 12

Immediate Redemption

The morning of the day after being stood up Sam was lying on his back on his bed, eyes open, unblinking, focused on the *Reservoir Dogs* poster above his bed. He didn't really have any huge attachment to the film but a kid in his class, Seán, who knew all the latest hip urban dance and rock music, as well as being the only judge of indie film in the school, had mentioned that it was the best film of all time. He didn't care much for Seán but everybody respected his opinion. It had been venerated in all the reviews though too, and the poster was cool, so it seemed the kind of film you had to like as a teenage boy. He did like the film, particularly the uber-violent Mr Blonde who had scant regard for anybody else apart from himself, but he didn't get the furore over how it was shot and the dialogue etc. Right now he was staring at Mr White who stared morosely back at him. It was plainly apparent who would win this staring match.

He knew that his mother was standing at the bottom of

the stairs because he could hear the stairs creak when she shifted her weight and he knew she was debating with herself whether she should go up and console her only child. He sorely hoped that she wouldn't. His father came out of the kitchen and he could hear them talking softly about him. He strained to listen. Then they both retreated to the conservatory. He was thankful for the lack of intrusion and told Mr White on the poster so. It was going to be bad enough having to face Daniel on Monday, let alone his parents now. He wished he hadn't mentioned anything to them. That would teach him a lesson at least.

His muscles felt sore, tired perhaps from being taut for so long. He was still in the clothes that he had worn yesterday evening, having gone straight to his room, shut the door and lain down in this same prone position. He wasn't actually relaxing on the bed, it was more a static state of rigid shock, similar to rigor mortis where the body cannot and does not want to move. He was surprised that his blood was still running considering his brain felt on the verge of shutting down. Could the mind simply stop the body functions from operating if it was desired enough, or there was no desire left at all? He became aware of his breathing. It was generally at times like this, times of deep and completely meaningless thought that he noticed his lungs breathing air in and out, and how he had to make an effort to stop them doing so. Once he did then breathing seemed a chore, a tiring and difficult thing and he felt as if he had to concentrate to fulfill each complete inhalation and exhalation. It was exhausting. He fell asleep again.

When he awoke his mother was at the door of his room, gingerly putting only half of her head around the frame in a gentle act of submission.

He sat up and rubbed his eyes groggily. His mouth felt stale and there was an acrid taste on his tongue.

She looked sympathetically at him but there was calm hope in her voice when she spoke.

"Some of the boys have just knocked for you – to play football, I think."

He nodded, masking his surprise. They rarely knocked unless there was a big game about to happen, in which case everybody would scatter and knock on every door where there lived somebody within three years of the same age and invite them out for a game. When the weather was warm and bright they had some belters out there. He relished those kinds of games – they would last for hours and became more than just skill and endurance – they became transcendent. The feeling of joy experienced in playing those games was greater than he could possibly describe to somebody who was never involved. It was in those moments that he was truly happy, without a care in the world. He hoped that's what it was. Then he could forget today.

She withdrew her head and left. He rose to his feet, then lost his balance and had to hold himself up against the chest of drawers as the blood returned to his feet and the prickly numbness passed.

Ambling downstairs as if it were an early Sunday morning and not late on a Saturday evening after he had just slept through the entire day, he went to the front door. There was nobody there. Turning around in rising irritation to berate his mother for making him get up unnecessarily, he caught sight of some movement behind the trees at the front fence. There were three figures sitting hidden from view by the branches. His irritation subsided and he padded out across the paving slabs in his socked feet.

The lads were sitting on the fence like three impatient crows waiting to depart on some trip to visit tender carrion. Jesse looked up at him, but Washing Machine was more interested in the wart at the end of his little finger and Mouse never acknowledged him anyway.

Jesse nodded and Sam returned the compliment.

"We're headin' out drinkin' tonight – Jayo's just getting ready – we're meetin' him in ten minutes by the swing – you comin?'

The way it was delivered it was as if Sam should have been aware of exactly what was going on, or at the very least expecting it. He hid his surprise at being invited to join them. He had gone drinking with them on a few rare occasions but they never called in specifically to ask him to join them – it usually happened by chance, after playing football or down by the swing and he happened to join in by default.

"Gimme a few minutes."

Jesse nodded and looked back out towards the forest. Mouse hadn't said a word, and looked a little bit surly, probably annoyed at having called in to Sam's house no doubt. Sam figured it would have been Jesse who had knocked – their parents knew each other to say hello at church – and Jesse was always nice to him – he was always friendly to everybody though.

Sam hadn't bothered inquiring where they were going – it wasn't important really because he was going to go no matter what they said. He padded back to his house quickly just in case they left without him.

Washing Machine had made some smart comments about Sam on the way to the swing which had raised a few laughs but now he was quiet. They were just five youths walking around on a Saturday night and they all felt the comfort of being part of a gang.

The swing was back in its normal place, in its nook on the tree, when they went down and nobody had said anything so Sam could only presume that Washing Machine had been made go out and retrieve it – or they might have used a long stick. He wouldn't know unless they happened to mention it, otherwise he'd be giving his secret away . . . although he was proud of having climbed up the whole length of the rope and did want to tell somebody. Maybe he'd tell Jesse later when he was drunk. Or even Jayo – if he was in a genial mood he might be impressed.

Getting alcohol could be tricky if Jacky wasn't around. The lads would wait near the off-licence and covertly ask people as they passed by if they would get some booze for them. The gardaí patrolled the common areas and off-licences on weekends and if any parents spotted you looking suspicious you were sure to be given a major telling-off back home. It wasn't easy. Now, even when they had got their prize after pooling their money – Sam luckily had money left over from his failed date – they had to hide the bottles by stuffing them into various parts of their clothing. Washing Machine took the brunt of the labour, filling his pants and underwear with cold bottles of sweetened alco-pops and waddling behind them like a constipated duck. Their saviour this evening had been a friend of Jayo's brother. She was almost nineteen, Sam reckoned, and was dressed in a tight-fitting pair of jeans and simple blouse covered with a killer leather jacket. She held a cigarette in her painted nails while she chatted to them, enjoying the eager attention that they gave her and her well-expressed ample cleavage. She seemed so much like a real woman that they were all a little tongue-tied, each hoping that the other would say something witty that would account for the entire group. She got bored after the initial flirting had worn off and she had lost interest in the effect of her pouting at them to fuel their imaginations, so she sashayed off to get their Holy Grail. She was quick, a real pro, and even made them follow her down an alley a few hundred yards away before giving them the gold, as much for her benefit really as theirs as she would be in deeper trouble if she was caught. When she left, Sam could have sworn that she winked at him, but more likely he had hoped that she would and the fading light had played a trick on his overactive mind.

They followed Jayo to their drinking point, which was a twenty-minute trek back past their respective homes. They detoured on the roads above their own, but only where it was safe to – certain areas would invite trouble from other groups of boys, especially after the fiasco of the last sally fight which would have deeper repercussions in time. They eventually found themselves in the middle of the forest at the top of the golf course, beside the old reservoir. From here a person could see out across the whole of Dublin Bay and beyond, all the way up to Skerries. They cracked open a bottle each, using Washing Machine's over-worked teeth. Sam winced every time that he stuck a bottle neck between his enamels but he was not only happy to do it, he absolutely insisted. They drank as they walked, bantering with anybody joining in.

"You never got a blowie!" Jayo taunted Mouse.

"Fuckin' did."

"You maybe but Washo never did."

"Yeah, I did."

"Yer ma doesn't count."
"Fuck you, Mouse, it was your ma."
"Ooooohhh!"
"You can't even spell blow job!"
"B – L –"
"I was jokin', faggot."
"I'll ask yer ma how to spell it next time."
"Burn!"
"Nice bird who got us this though, wasn't she?"
"Yeah, I'd fuck her."
"We'd all fuck her."
"Except for Washo, he prefers ma's."
"Jesse is into dogs sure."
"They have their merits."
"Shut up, Sam."
"I'll go hang out with yer ma then."
"That doesn't work as a joke."
"Oh. Well, fuck you."
"Fuck you back."

The banter carried on much the same, about imaginary sexual escapades, with the inevitable jostling beginning when Mouse pushed Washing Machine down an embankment once they had struggled to the top. Then Jesse and Sam followed suit as a game of gladiators ensued, with Jayo quickly taking residence as the reigning champion. Each time a challenger had made his tired way to the top, Jayo was upon him and had flipped him back down before he could draw breath.

They had left their bottles in plastic bags at the top of the bank while playing and suddenly Jayo, having declared himself champion, grabbed the bag and made a run into the darkening forest.

The other four scrambled up the embankment after him, screaming threats at him.

Jayo was sprinting along the edge of the reservoir, his runners splashing in the lapping water.

"Come back, ya bollix!"

"Yer dead, Jayo!"

"Come 'ere, ya slow bastard!"

Jayo wasn't the fastest and the others gained on him quickly, Jesse and Sam getting there first and simultaneously dive-bombing him into the undergrowth. At first Sam thought that Jayo was going to hit him and he regretted his over-eagerness in the chase but Jayo just laughed and they all lay in the undergrowth, drinking another bottle each.

It went on like that for the next hour or so, trekking deeper into the forest on top of the hill until they could only see by moonlight the well-worn trails they each knew from selling golf balls or crossing during the day.

The night began to cool and they had stopped, intending to light a small fire, when they heard voices in the darkness.

Mouse put a hand to his lips. "Shh, don't say anything!" he muttered.

The voices weren't getting any closer, however – they were emanating from a point in the forest below them.

Careful searching revealed a campfire glowing in the bushes and faint figures around it.

"Sounds like Mick and Paulie and the lads," Jesse whispered.

Mouse nodded in agreement and they all crept forward towards the group. When they were close Jayo stepped in front and hailed them.

"Alrigh', lads?"

"Who's dat?"

"It's Jayo."

"Oh righ' Jayo, sound – who's wit ya?"

"Few of de lads."

"Cool, come on over, sure."

There was a large group around the fire, about twelve or thirteen lads and half that number again in girls. They were all fairly inebriated and Sam recognized only Paulie and Mick from his football team. They barely nodded to him but shook hands with Jesse and Jayo. Jesse was probably the best player on the local team on his day if a little too lightweight – he was a delicate sort of athlete. Everybody seemed protective of Jesse in some shape or form,

The lads sat down and joined the group, taking a position to one side of the fire. It was nearing the end of its ear, but would stay strong until the early hours at least, the large black pile around it testimony to how large it had been to begin with.

The rest of the lads were unknown to Sam, some a bit older, from around the area and maybe further afield. Some must have been doing drugs – pills and E most likely– and the smell of hash drifted through the air. Washing Machine went on a mission to get some and came back successfully with two joints, but none of them wanted any – the lads weren't really the druggy sort.

Sam drank his last bottle while sitting beside Jesse, trying to examine the faces in the firelight. It was a strange sort of atmosphere. Nobody said much, but seemed to just enjoy being in the company of others while they lost control of their senses. Sam wondered how they would all play their usual Sunday match tomorrow then quickly forgot about it.

He didn't know when he had begun to notice but a girl was staring at him through the firelight. She was beautiful, similar to Antoinette, although he could only really make out her reddish hair and slim figure in the dark through his glassy eyes.

Jesse had also spotted her and he whispered into Sam's ear. "I think she likes ya."

Sam shook his head and gave him a gentle dig but didn't take his eyes off her. After the ruinous day that he had just experienced, this could be a welcome reprive. Biting his lip he leaned back over to Jesse and asked him who she was.

"Have no idea – here, Washing Machine, who's that bird?"

Washing Machine shook his head but got to his feet and was over to her and back again in a few moments, having no compunction about chatting her up in his happy state. He sauntered back slowly in a half circle, half by choice, half by lack of control of his muscular functions, then half-fell on top of the two of them, supporting himself by resting his arms on the backs of their necks.

"She likes Sam."

"Really?"

"I told ya." Jesse smiled.

"What's her name?" Sam asked.

"I dunno, but she said for you to follow her."

Sam looked at Washing Machine in surprise but at that moment she got up and her fiery head disappeared into the gloom. Sam scrambled to his feet and stumbled after her, on a mission. He was immediately swallowed up in the gloom and totally lost his bearings but he bumped into her a few feet into the bushes and she grabbed him without any words. He couldn't believe his luck when her soft lips pressed against his. Her mouth was hot and wet. They lowered themselves to the ground and he rolled on top of her, passion overtaking him. He was only ten feet from the fire and the group but the bushes hid them, and in the darkness nobody could see anything so it didn't matter anyway. She was eager and her hands raced all over his body but concentrated on one area. He didn't waste any time either, the alcohol completely alleviating him of any negative past experiences and any fear. He was up for it and so was she. He found the sensitive softness of her nipples and began to knead her breasts like he'd seen in a film while she forced her hands down his jeans and began to slide her hand up and down his penis. She couldn't get her hand all the way past his belt and around him but her fingers created enough of a sensation and he returned the favour, his fingers pushing off the forest floor and down her belly and into her jeans. He scrabbled around her hips for a few moments, unsure if he should undo the buttons on her jeans to get his hand in until she arched her back and opened them for him with her spare hand. She was incredibly wet and his fingers slipped inside her easily, pressing upwards against her pelvis. She gasped and bit his ear so roughly that it hurt but he grimaced and bore it, his focus on his own pelvis where her hand was doing magical things. He wished he had been this hard for Antoinette, then he forgot about her and enjoyed feeling like a god. They gyrated like that for a few minutes, pressing and bumping against each roughly, their hands groping and grasping, their teeth smashing, her mouth biting his neck. Her skin smelled like a girl's skin should smell and he lost his nose in the arch of her neck, his nostrils inhaling the scent of her hair, unkempt and containing the entirety of the forest, but sexy. He climaxed in her hand that was still deep in his jeans but until it was over he didn't even think about the aftermath. He just enjoyed the moment, thankful more than anything else that it had occurred.

Once he had reached orgasm, he suddenly and inexplicably lost interest in touching her. He couldn't explain it but it suddenly felt dirty. Her skin didn't smell quite so sweet, her sweat was overbearing. His hands felt sticky and her groin was annoying in its incessant humping motion. He withdrew his hand to her obvious annoyance and then he hardly knew what happened. She got to her feet, tidied herself up and moved back to the edge of the fire beside her friends, all within a few moments.

He lay there on the forest floor, too tired and satisfied to move, but completely and utterly bemused. Shaking his head he began to laugh a little, not sure whether he should be proud or ashamed of himself. He needed to pee so he did and then joined the rest of the lads.

Jayo wanted to go home when he rejoined them so that meant they all did.

On the way back they were halfway down the hill when Mouse burst into a shriek of laughter, followed by the other three. There had been a strange silence up until that point but Sam had hardly noticed, lost in thought about the girl whose name he didn't even know and with whom he had just shared his first real sexual experience. Sam looked at them sharply when it dawned that the laughter was at his expense.

"What's so funny?" he inquired, words slurring a little.

"Did she suck ya off?" Mouse gloated.

"What?"

"Did ya ride her, yes or no?"

"No, fuck off."

"Ya didn't – are ya sure?"

"Yeah, I think I'd remember if I did."

"So what did you do – we heard ya moanin'!"

"Nothing . . . she just . . . ya know . . . Why do you care anyway?"

Four pairs of eager eyes shone in the faint moonlight, waiting for him to elaborate. He figured it was because they had heard them moving about and were being immature and wanted to know the gory details.

Mouse was in his element, running this inquisition. "She just did wha', Sam?"

"Ya know, she just . . ."

"Did ya frig her?"

"What?"

"*Frig* her! Stick yer fingers in her pussy?"

"Yeah. I guess."

"Oh Jesus!" Mouse held up his hands theatrically to the others who groaned with mock distaste.

"What?" Sam didn't understand.

"Did she wank ya off?'

"Yeah – what the fuck's going on?"

There was silence and then Mouse jumped around in a crazy circle, his mirth taking over. Washing Machine and Jayo couldn't breathe from trying to stifle their laughter and they doubled over and howled with glee.

Jesse had calmed down sufficiently to explain to Sam. "That girl, yeah?" he said slowly.

Sam watched him impatiently, his weight shifting from left to right. He nodded, willing him to come out with it.

"She's got a bit of a reputation."

"For what?"

"For getting around."

"So what?"

Jesse paused dramatically for a few moments, looking at the other lads bent over double on the grass.

"She does it with everybody. For a few beers, a lift, a bit of cheeky cash."

There was a pause.

"Fuck off."

"Seriously. She's been around the block with everybody, that girl."

Sam's face dropped and Jesse dropped back into the hyena-like laughter the others were engaged in.

Fuck. The joy of his victory had been especially short-lived.

Washing Machine goaded him further. "Make sure you wash your hands later!"

Mouse had his say, determined not to be outdone. "I'd get myself checked out if I was you."

Sam gave him the finger but couldn't help feeling dirty. This girl had 'been around the block'. He was just one of many. He didn't feel special any more.

"She's fucked everything that moves around here, all the lads from up the road," said Jesse. "She wanted to fuck Mouse last week but he turned her down point blank."

"And you all knew?"

"Course we did."

"You're all pricks."

"Well, if you enjoyed it then that's all that matters, righ'?"

Sam gave them the finger and walked ahead, but they carried on goading him the entire way back home. He felt dirty. With Antoinette it had felt pure, or would have been, yet he had been traumatized. Then when he seemed to have got lucky and had a special story to tell it had been ruined. Maybe they were lying and just jealous, and maybe she was sweet . . . but maybe not . . . she had been almost too eager.

They hung around together for a bit longer sharing a cigarette but he wasn't in the mood. He bid them goodnight at the edge of the road with a brief wave that became a middle finger as their catcalls followed him.

When he went to bed he had to wash off the mulch and small twigs that had lodged themselves in his clothing and the folds of his skin, his waist being covered in tiny remnants of leaves and muck.

Then he went to bed and stared up accusingly at Mr White on the poster. He slept fitfully.

Chapter 13

Death in the Laneway

The remainder of the weekend had been tiring. Sunday's football match was a disaster as he had suffered a terrible hangover that tormented him. His body was heavy, every movement of his muscles making him nauseated. Surprisingly neither Mick nor Paulie seemed to be suffering any visible side effects. Sam found his head ached and his vision was out of touch with reality, his depth perception completely failing him. At one stage he stretched to control an innocuous pass from his goalkeeper and succeeded in knocking it off his shin directly to one of the opposition players, who almost scored but hesitated in surprise at the gift just long enough for Mick to nick the ball back. Only Mick didn't berate him for that, he simply gave him a thumbs-up and grabbed his balls with his other hand.

His manager Bobby didn't even wait until half time to remove him, like he usually did when Mick was obviously hungover – incensed, he dragged Sam off after barely fifteen minutes into the game. "I didn't expect that from you, Sam," he had scolded.

Sam spent the rest of the day in front of the television, feigning tiredness after a hard match. His mother didn't suspect anything, or at least she let on that she was oblivious, maybe because she was still embarrassed for him after Friday and believed that he needed something to hold onto, to re-assert himself. She was right.

He was late into school on Monday. He slept in and had to run for the train. He cursed every step of the way, his shoes skidding in the light rain that licked the surface of the pavement like a greasy chip-brush. He missed his early train so he had to run from the station towards school to be on time but gave up halfway, resigned to his fate of detention on Wednesday.

He'd had very sexual dreams last night with the unnamed girl from the campfire – he refused to label her negatively despite the claims of the lads – they were probably just winding him up. From what he had remembered, or wanted to anyway, she was gorgeous, and it had been extremely pleasurable. He just wished the same thing could have happened with Antoinette. Why had he not been nervous with the girl at the fire?

He was still mulling it over in his head when he walked into class and it was almost a shock to find himself there. He had to stop drifting off into his own thoughts.

The entire class was staring at him. Then the teacher turned around. It was Mr Cusack.

Sam tensed up, waiting for a reaction, but Mr Cusack shook his head silently and waited patiently as Sam took his place down near the back of the class. As usual he sat in front of Daniel who gave him a knowing smile. Class trickled by painfully slowly and Sam kept his mouth shut.

"I heard about Friday."

"I'm sure you did – you probably knew about it before I did."

"Bit harsh."

"Sorry if you're sensitive."

Sam didn't look up from his sandwich as he spoke. He had no concrete reason to be angry with Daniel as such but he was the only person apart from his parents who knew about that whole event and he was ashamed.

"Yeah. Catriona rang me to tell me."

"That's great."

"Don't you want to know what happened?"

"Not really. I think I've suffered enough embarrassment."

Daniel looked at him quizzically and then realization flickered across his face. "Oh yeah, heard about that too."

Sam threw his sandwich against the wall suddenly, frustration overloading him, and he squared up to Daniel.

"What did you hear about exactly?"

The rest of the class stopped their conversations and all eyes turned to the duo in the corner.

The rain was pouring down heavily so lunch was allowed in the classrooms and the room was full with the sickly suffocating smell of sweat, jam, peanut-butter, Bovril, cheesy crisps and body odours. A standard classroom of young, male teenagers.

Daniel grimaced at Sam, holding his hands up to placate him. "Maybe we should talk about this later."

"Fuck off, Daniel."

Sam stormed out of the classroom like a petulant child.

His success with the unnamed girl, the greatest sexual experience of his life, should have at the very least, if not erased, then diluted the pain of being stood up, but it seemed to only amplify everything, reinforcing the aggrieved feeling that he carried with him at present like a shadow. He had been able to forget everything about Antoinette over the weekend when out drinking with the lads, but now back in school and seeing Daniel it was all re-awakened. And it hurt deeply.

When school ended he found he just didn't have the energy to run for the bus. He felt jaded and, although the rain had stopped, the atmosphere in the city felt tense and uncomfortable. So he took his time, allowing Greg and Darren to forge their way ahead. He decided to take the next bus thirty minutes later, unable to face any potential suffering at their hands today – it would be just too much to bear.

Scuffing the toes of his shoes into the ground as he walked, he pondered what he would do if he ever saw Antoinette again, how he would react, what he would say. He would long to kiss her – that was certain – he craved her touch, but more importantly her acceptance of him. He kicked out at the surface of a puddle in the cracks on the pavement and sent a spray of filthy water into the air, wetting a young woman passing him by. She scowled at him but he ignored her – it was just easier than apologizing. He still had twenty minutes left before he got the bus so he looked around for something to do.

He found himself standing outside the Easons shop on O'Connell Street – Easons were the biggest book and stationary chain in the country. Slipping inside the glass doors he made a beeline for the magazine section. It almost took up half the floor, six rows deep on two sides, containing almost every magazine that was available in Ireland, England and the majority of America and Canada. He picked up a generic football magazine that held interviews with all the top football stars for United, Liverpool and all of the other English teams, but nothing Irish. He scanned through it and looked at the price – he really didn't want to buy it. He held onto it though, then walked to another section where he picked up a porno magazine and slipped it inside the covers of the football one. He would have to be eighteen to buy the porno. He did have a fake ID card – they pretty much all had them in school – but it actually said that he was seventeen. It was a long-term plan. Last year a group of them went to get their bus passes renewed. The form had to be stamped by the school and then processed by Ianróid Éireann. The simplest way of forging it was to change the date on the form with Tipp-Ex after it had already been stamped. There was no point in changing it to say that you were eighteen – they'd get suspicious about that and would ring up the school to check. So the solution was to get it early in the school year and then change it to say that you were seventeen, so that within a few months or by the next year anyway it would state that you were eighteen. They never suspected that anybody would try and get a fake ID to say that they were seventeen. You just had to wait a little longer to get the benefit. Even if a bus pass card was out of date it was still accepted for age ID so it was perfect.

He stopped at the counter and, when the cashier was busy, plucked one of the Easons colour-coded paper bags off the shelf. Whenever you bought a magazine or book in this shop, it was put into one of these green, white and blue striped bags and that was just as good a proof of purchase as a receipt so the security guards never checked. Sam strolled around the shop, casually picking off the bar-coded price tag on each magazine so it wouldn't set off the door scanner, then he put both magazines inside his Easons bag. Even if he were stopped now he would say that he couldn't find the receipt, and when it was this busy they were unlikely to open the tills to check. Besides which, the porn magazines were never registered under their title and so they all went under the same generic price tag – this meant that the shop couldn't tell who had bought them or if any porn magazine had even been purchased that day.

He casually walked out of the shop as if nothing had happened and nobody paid him any attention. Once out of sight of the shop he opened his schoolbag and tucked the magazines in alongside his school books. He usually felt nervous robbing mags and didn't do it that often but such was his mood today that he almost didn't care if he was caught – part of him wanted to be chased down the road, to get that adrenaline rush.

He read most of the football magazine on the bus home – it was a waste of money to buy them when they were read in such a short period. He couldn't remember clearly the first time he had ever stolen one but it hadn't been well planned and he was incredibly lucky to have got away without getting caught. It wasn't sleight of hand but brazen luck that carried it off. He seemed to remember just walking out of the shop with the magazine openly in his hand, but it was such a chaotic memory that he couldn't be sure. He just knew that he had somehow managed to pick up a magazine and walk out without anybody noticing.

Beginner's luck. After that he had paid more attention to how it should be done, but he still indulged himself only rarely and only then if he had a good feeling about it and was in a bleak mood where he didn't care about consequence.

There was a strange commotion when he stepped off the train. People were walking with their hands over their mouths as if that helped contain their shock. Maybe they thought something might fall out of their throats if they didn't clutch their mouths tight. He was in the kind of mood for such inane observations. There was a garda halfway up the laneway and he held out his hand to stop him walking further.

"Sorry, son, you can't go up this way," he grunted, palpably unhappy at being there.

"I live this way – I'm just around the bend," Sam replied politely.

"I'm sorry but you'll have to go another way."

"Are you serious?"

"Yes."

"This is ridiculous."

"I'm not going to tell you again."

"I'm almost there – you can't stop me."

"Yes, I can. Go back the way that you came. Now."

He was going to continue arguing, or maybe just run past, but the garda shot him a look. There was no messing around here. He turned and trudged back down the lane but once he was out of sight he dove into the woods, finding a hidden trail that he knew led him directly past the site where the garda was. Keeping his hands in front of his face to ward off the branches that dug into his skin from all angles, he struggled through the overgrown pathway, brambles tearing and ripping the outer layer of his jacket and tugging at the material on his bag. Once the thorns clutched at his bag so decisively that he was almost pulled back onto his arse by the pressure and he had to pluck the invading plants out individually, but despite the effort he wasn't turning back without finding out what was going on.

Eventually he reached a spot where he heard sombre voices and the low crackle of walkie-talkies. But the brambles had grown into a wall so thick that he couldn't approach the laneway any closer than a few feet and couldn't see a thing on the other side of the bushes. And he couldn't decipher what the voices were saying. Frustrated and prickly, he made his way gingerly a little further along the path to where it led onto his road.

He stopped when he saw what was in front of him.

Seated on the wall just beyond where the lane exited to the road were Jayo, Washing Machine and Jesse. Mouse was nowhere to be seen but Sam didn't even register that at first. The trio were flanked by two large male gardaí, one of whom was writing down everything that Jesse said with a nod every now and again, his pen moving furiously. There were two police cars parked against the curb and an ambulance with the lights twirling dramatically. They had just closed the doors at the back so Sam missed seeing who was inside. The taller of the ambulance drivers walked over to where a third garda was walking up from the lane. They spoke briefly and then the driver got back inside the ambulance and drove off slowly with no fanfare or loud sirens.

Sam was confused. Normally the ambulance rushed off

in a flurry of burning rubber and ear-piercing noise, or at least that was how he had always envisioned it – that's what happened on television. Maybe the ambulance was taking it easy until it was out of the residential area.

The mystery of the ambulance was forgotten when he turned his focus back onto the lads. He stepped back behind the wall so that they wouldn't notice him and he could try and figure out what happening.

The taller guard had bent his head as if to give some encouraging words to Jesse, his hand clasping the boy's shoulder firmly. Jayo looked completely spooked, his face white, all the blood having drained from it, but Jesse looked like he might start crying so the guard was focusing his energies on him. Washing Machine never liked being around the gardaí and seemed tense, watching every move they made as if he was waiting for them to turn on him.

What had happened? Sam ached to find out.

"What are you doing, young man?"

The question was directed with disdainful authority at him.

He turned around and found himself looking directly into the stern face of the garda who had told him to go around the other way a short while before. He had walked up the laneway without Sam hearing him.

Shit, it was obvious he hadn't gone the other way. He became aware of the stolen magazines in his bag and hoped that he wouldn't get his bag searched, especially with the porno – because he was underage they would bring him into Easons as it was a serious issue to sell adult material to minors – and then they would discover that he'd actually robbed it. Every time he had previously met the gardaí he'd automatically felt guilty – even if he hadn't done anything he always felt like he must have done something. This man's eyes were a deep blue, cold and unreadable, and his skin was waxy with flecks of old scars around his cheeks. His stubble was coarse and he had that unenviable country accent that was heavily tainted with inner-city Dublin inflections from spending too much time there. Not the kind of garda that you wanted to mess with for he was most likely pissed off to be up here in the 'big smoke' in the first place. His small country village was most likely much quieter and filled with more buxom agreeable women who didn't turn their noses up at dating a garda. Sam just knew these things, like everybody else did.

"I asked you a question. Did I not tell you to go around the other way?" The garda was pretty fed up.

"I did go another way," Sam lied.

"I didn't want you on this side of the street."

"Look, I'm here now. I live just over there." Sam pointed to his house across the road.

"Well, you're going to have to go back the way that you came and come around another way."

"You're joking?"

"I'm not."

Sam looked at the guard, incredulous. This guy was just being a prick and normally Sam would tell him to fuck off but the bag with the porno mag was a dead weight against his back.

"Those lads are my friends – I just want to know what's going on."

"Go back around the other way and find out later."

"Listen. I'm not walking all the way around the other way – it'll take me twenty minutes and my house is just over there."

"I don't care – you didn't do what I told you."

"No, I did what you said and went another way which is exactly what you asked me to do if you remember correctly. I just went my own way."

"Listen here, boy, I'm not in the mood for your cheek."

Sam stared him down defiantly, the real drama unfolding a few yards away as Jesse burst into tears.

The guard's face began to turn a different colour, a deep shade of juicy red, when his radio crackled, taking him out of the impending violent trance. He shot Sam a look to stay where he was and turned away to answer the call. Sam took his cue and skipped by him and out onto the road where the lads saw him. Jayo nodded but then looked away. He made to move towards them but the other guard who had been talking to them stepped in front of him.

"Where are you going?"

Not again! Fuck, something serious must have happened.

"They're my mates." Sam replied curtly.

"They don't need to talk to anybody right now – they're going home once their parents come and collect them."

On cue Jayo's mum came walking across the road towards them, followed by Jesse's bewildered and bedraggled mother who looked shocked and the worse for wear. But Jayo's mother seemed resigned to yet another confrontation with the gardaí over her son.

"What happened? Will you just tell me?" Sam looked up pleadingly at the tall guard.

He sighed and bent down to him, too tired to really care. "Look, son, your friends found a dead body in the forest."

"No shit! Seriously, where?"

"Look, that's all I'm telling you."

"Was it close to here?"

The man sighed and rolled his eyes at the young boy's eagerness for gory details – it was always the same.

"Yes. The swing on the tree – do you use that?"

"Yeah, why?"

"He was there."

"What do you mean?"

The guard wouldn't answer any more and waved him on.

There was a small congregation of people outside their houses watching the commotion unfold. Even people from other streets had started filtering down, having heard whispers of something happening. Sam walked slowly backwards to his house, watching as the lads' mothers consoled them, were given brief instructions by the gardaí, and walked slowly away arm in arm with their sons. Jayo pushed his mother's hands off his arm and walked in front of her, putting on a show of strength that Sam admired for some reason. Jesse had collapsed into tears when his mother grabbed him and he allowed himself to be led away. Washing Machine's mother, who was the last to arrive, seemed to be on the same page as her son and appeared suspicious of the whole event.

A dead body, fuck, who was it?

Where was Mouse?

Fuck, what if it was him?

But it couldn't be?

Chapter 14

Things Are Subject to Change

He waited until the furore had died down and the police had finally left the street, which was long after darkness fell and neon lights illuminated the shadows. The eerie glow they shone across the empty road had an extra edge to it, a fresh danger on account of a lost spirit floating around in the vicinity. Not knowing what had happened was aggravating Sam no end. His parents didn't know any more than he did and had told him to stay inside this evening despite his protestations about needing to acquire information.

Was it Mouse? What had happened? He imagined Mouse climbing up the tree to untangle the swing and then falling to his death at the bottom of the gully, but that couldn't have happened as they would have removed the body from down by the street leading into the concrete dump. Thousands of possible scenarios flickered in and out of his mind, but he dismissed them all like waving at a fat bluebottle that just won't take a hint until you eventually squash it.

When he was certain that his parents were asleep he crept silently downstairs to the front door and gently opened it. It was too noisy to close it behind him so he left it on the latch. Once he was out the door he was free and determined not to come back until he knew what was going on. He simply had to figure it out because it felt like the sort of thing that a man should do. A man would go down there and find out for himself. If he didn't he would feel like a coward. He felt like a fugitive as he crept towards the dark lane, the blackness extending a colourless finger towards him enticingly. He reached the lane and peered into its depths but saw only solid black. The moon was sheltered momentarily from passing clouds, so he waited a few minutes for it to free itself and, when he could make out the shapes of the bushes and the line of the pathway, he stepped into the shadows.

He was acutely aware of how loudly his heart seemed to boom inside his chest, and of the heavy blackness that was all around him, suffocating his senses. The glow from the moon allowed him to see the vague outline of the path in front of his feet and he stepped forward tentatively. He could feel the darkness wrapping its cloying hands around his back, shrouding him from view, incorporating him into its terrifying mass.

There was a rustle in the bushes right beside him and he froze, too frightened to move. Nausea rose in his throat and his legs stuck to the ground with imaginary glue. There was a complete and deafening silence.

He began to have second thoughts about the merit of this idea. What was he going to do when he got to the swing?

He had to prove to himself that he could do it but surely there would be nothing left – the police would have removed everything so what was the point? The questioning and obviousness of his own fear subversively spurred him on. This was something that he had to do. It was only the darkness. He resolved not to look behind but broke his own rule immediately, for one last look at relative safety. The brightly lit street behind looked appetizingly warm and safe. He looked away and steeled himself but try as he could he was unable to release the tense weight in his shoulders that hunched him down like a creeping rodent.

Halfway down, the lane swung slowly to the left and the hollow shape of light behind and above him was sucked from view. The moon disappeared as the branches closed over from above in their familiar tunnel recreation. He gradually made his way through the heavy blackness by sense memory. He was almost there. He could see, as his eyes adjusted to the darkness, the beginning of the slope leading up to the swing where he hoped to find some clues.

A thought suddenly struck him and he had to restrain from slapping himself. Why hadn't he just knocked on Jesse's door? He couldn't call into Jayo – his family didn't like anybody – and Washing Machine and Mouse lived a quite a few streets up the hill. It had never occurred to him to do that – he just wasn't quite part of their group enough to feel comfortable knocking on any of their front doors. Maybe he could go back and knock in for Jesse but he'd been so pained when he'd left that it seemed inappropriate. He toyed with the idea of going back but it was just as black behind as it was in front of him and despite himself he couldn't turn around, because he was too afraid. The fear of there being something behind him, following him silently and waiting for the right moment to pounce, was overwhelming. If he turned around he would find himself face to face with some horrendous beast. He had to keep going because he was too fucking scared to turn around. He should be afraid of meeting one of the crazed alcoholics that speckled the woods, their lonely presence a warning to all those who failed in school and had violent tendencies, but he was more afraid of the supernatural.

His groin felt sore and he really needed to urinate but there was no way that he was going to unzip himself and be exposed here, making him more vulnerable than he was already. Ghosts. The ghosts of the dead. When people die unhappily, the ghost, spirit, or soul depending on what way you wanted to look at it, would traverse their old haunts until they were satisfied, until they had alleviated their pain and found happiness or until they had gained their revenge. What if it was a violent, unhappy, evil spirit that now waited there for him?

Man up, he told himself. He moved forward again.

At the beginning of the slope he could just about make out a line of police tape across the bushes, indicating to the general public that something tragic had taken place here. He could just about see its outline and he grabbed it to push it aside. It crackled violently in his hand, eradicating the calm silence. He immediately regretted the noise the tape had made and held his breath to hear if there was anything out there that had heard him. Silence. Complete silence, and near total darkness. He wanted to leave but a morbid fascination coupled with his pride wouldn't allow him. He had suffered enough blows to his self-esteem lately and it was easier now to just keep going. If he turned he knew the fear would overcome him and he would be forced to sprint as fast as he could and his body felt too tired for that exertion.

He began to climb up the slope, gripping stalks of failing saplings for support and wrenching them from their bed of soil when his balance threatened to fly from him.

He made it out of the bushes and to the top and looked around. He could see much better up here – the moon had some space to breathe. The outline of the massive oak was vividly highlighted against the dark sky behind it, like the cover of an old horror film where the tree would come to life, stretching ancient boughs forward to crush and maim. There was nothing around the clearing to indicate that anything out of the ordinary had gone on except maybe some extra churning of the dirt from more numerous feet than usual. He stepped closer to the tree and then felt very exposed away from the cover of the bushes which ironically held the most fear by concealing the unknown but could also hide him. Frustrated that he couldn't see anything that gave him any clues he stepped closer to the tree, resting his hand upon the cold pulsing bark.

Then he noticed it. The swing was gone! Where it used to reside hung instead a pitiful excuse, a few meagre feet of old rope sliced clean through close to the top of the bough. The rope had been cut. Why? It looked like a professional job as there were no loose strands hanging down like there would be if the lads had done it – it was a thick industrial fishing rope and they didn't slice easily. He wondered where it had gone, their swing. This rope that had seen so much had now seen something extra, and was holding a new secret that it wasn't going to give up easily.

Somebody was watching him. Or something. He could feel it, the eyes boring into the base of his skull. He had read that humans have an extra sense, one that tells you when something or someone is watching you – the way that a girl knows when you're trying to catch a peek of her ass under her short skirt so she will unconsciously reach behind and flatten it down over her bum and she might turn her head and look at you, not knowing you're looking until she sees you. It was an instinct that had saved people many times in a dark alleyway before an attacker hit his victim, giving them that extra second to respond, a second that might save their life.

Fear was overtaking Sam and these thoughts ran through his head as he felt himself being watched right now just like that, by something unknown and intrusive. He could feel the unblinking invisible line drawn through the cool muggy air straight to his shivering skin. What was it? He felt uncomfortably close to the edge of the gully. Ghosts, the malevolent ones who weren't destined to solve any great mystery in their life but were encased in a shell of pain and misery for all eternity, set out to inflict death and suffering. They could move objects and even push things. He was close enough to be pushed into the ravine. He slowly stepped to his right and reached out for the safety of the tree. He was further away than he had thought and had to take another slow gentle step.

The gaze was unwavering, like icicles on his neck, raising the hairs rigidly.

"Mouse, is that you? I'm not here to cause any offence. I'm sorry," he whispered.

He didn't know if that would help, but he hoped it would. He feverishly hoped, if it was Mouse's ghost, that he hadn't disliked him enough while he was alive to want to physically harm him in the afterlife. What if it wasn't

Mouse, but somebody else and he referred to them as a 'mouse' – would they take that as an insult? He steeled himself, or more correctly held his body in place like a mobile statue to keep his insides from slumping in on one another. And he turned around.

There was nothing there. The prickly feeling was gone. It had left, whatever it was. He had an active imagination but there had definitely been something there – he had felt the presence of something. A presence. He walked as coolly as he could back towards the slope, straining to keep his calm, his hands shaking from the effort. He forced down the impulse to run, dragging the revolting desire to scream back down his throat. It was like a thick lump of clotted mucous, needing to be spewed out, got rid of. But he held on. He almost slipped down the slope but found his footing, his hand digging into the muck by his head acting like a brake. Dirt dug into his nails but it didn't matter.

He reached for a branch to steady himself and was looking at where to best place his hand for support when he saw it. A face. It was only visible for a moment before it dissolved into the darkness. It was a man, achingly sad with deep rings ingrained like carved sculpture beneath his eyes, lips turned downwards, the cheeks sunken. It was only there for that split second but the greatest, most painfully cold shiver raped his entire body from the tips of his fingers to his toes, freezing every blood cell in his being and the mucous in his mouth launched outwards in a violent spew. He spat everywhere then screamed and lost his balance, falling to his knees and sliding down to the path. His knees sank into the vegetation at the bottom and he tipped forward, his hands just getting out in front of his face to break his fall.

He was up and on his feet in a second and he ran. There were footsteps behind him, he could hear them approaching, but they weren't running – they had a sad lonely gait about them, a solid clipping against the stone. They faded slowly into the background as he ran, but he wasn't going to stop and analyze why the steps weren't chasing him, or whether they really were receding or not. He couldn't breathe, the air didn't have any time to find its way into his lungs – he was inhaling and exhaling too quickly, regurgitating the air in his mouth, tasting carbon dioxide. The light grew before him and he burst out onto the road like an exhausted Olympic sprinter, arms flailing but legs powering him forward. He raced into the light as far away from the lane as he could before he dared to turn and look behind.

There was nothing. The black laneway was empty. His heart rate slowed and he loosened the collar of his shirt. He felt sore and drained.

"Sam?"

He spun around like a frightened deer at the sound of his name.

Jesse was sitting with Jayo only a few feet away from him on the wall, both watching him casually.

"What're ya doin'?" asked Jesse sadly.

Jayo's eyes were more curious. "Did ya see somethin'?"

Sam nodded, his throat too dry to speak. He opened his mouth but nothing would come out and he had to swallow five or six times first.

"Yep – saw – I saw – eh, a face."

Jayo stared at him. "A man?"

"Yeah."

"How old? Middle-aged? Sad-lookin', like?"

Sam was unable to hide his surprise. "Yeah. That was him?"

Jayo didn't say anything but acknowledged in the affirmative with a slow gentle nod of the head and took out a packet of cigarettes. They usually never smoked openly, especially not in the middle of the road in plain view of their own houses, because they were all afraid of their parents' wrath even if they pretended otherwise.

Jayo lit a cigarette and handed the packet and lighter to Jesse who accepted it gratefully. Jayo took a long painful drag, allowing the smoke to fill his mouth and lungs like a pufferfish, then he slowly let it escape through his nostrils. The smell of nicotine filled the air around them and was strangely comforting in the circumstances. Sam waited for Jayo to speak but he offered him a cigarette first. Sam was about to decline then remembered the intense face he just had seen and almost grabbed one out of the packet. Jayo didn't even react. Jesse handed him the lighter and Sam lit it the way he had seen them do. He felt closer to them, bonding over the shared ritual of smoking. It had a power. He felt calmer, more masculine and in control of his own destiny.

It was just the moonlight casting a shadow he had seen, surely not a face. Out here in safety it felt like a trick of his mind.

Jayo spoke clearly, his deep voice calming. "It was him. We found him today hanging off the swing. He'd wrapped it around his neck, dunno how, looked complicated – but he managed it."

"Fuck." Sam had seen him then.

"Yeah, Jesse was there first. We had gone to get smokes an' when we walked up Jesse was jus' sittin' there lookin' at him. Weird, huh?"

"Yeah, fucking hell!"

"Must have been his ghost you saw."

Nobody disputed that it had to have been the ghost of the dead suicidal man, it just had to be – and whether you believed in spirits or not was irrelevant. It just was and that was it. Jesse was completely silent.

"We called the pigs and they came down in a few minutes – called them from Mr Jones' gaff – his was the closest gaff we saw somebody in. Was strange, seeing a dead body. He looked in pain, his neck all twisted."

Sam didn't know what to say. "Where's Mouse?" It was the only thing he could think of to say.

"Dunno, he wasn't with us – ain't seen him today – haven't thought about that, ya know?"

Sam nodded and sat in silence. It was what they wanted, no questions, not having to talk about it. Jesse appeared to just want to sit in his own thoughts, dragging the life out of his cigarette in the company of his peers.

Sam tried to imagine what the dead body must have looked like and desperately wanted to ask for more details but it felt important to act morose with them. Solidarity in pain, like at a funeral. They stayed like that for almost twenty minutes, just sitting quietly. They never asked what he had been doing. They instinctively must have known, and respected him for it – it was dark and unknown down there. It was another step towards being accepted by them.

But he also knew that after this it wouldn't be the same – he had been late coming home and so had missed the event that would bond them for better or worse. They had experienced something together and he felt himself angry and jealous that he hadn't been there. He felt a little guilty that he wasn't sorry for the dead man, but he didn't know him. He felt guilty for not being sympathetic to Jesse's clearly apparent pain but he wished that he been there, to experience it with them: the shock, the fear, the pain. He even wanted to feel Jesse's pain, he was jealous that he couldn't have that. They had something that could never be erased for the rest of their lives and he would never be able to understand. He was more of an outsider now than ever.

Chapter 15

Everything Remained the Same, but Everything Changed

"Would you have liked to have been there?"

Sam didn't answer. He wondered how long he could sit there without talking, what would happen then.

"Shall I take your silence as a perverse answer in the affirmative?"

Don's languid voice slowly drew him back to the matter at hand. His parents, especially his mother, had requested this meeting, "as expediently as possible". Those had been her exact words. He had listened upstairs, hanging off the landing, as the conversation took place over the phone. It was ridiculous because he hadn't been through any trauma – well, he had but it was completely unrelated to this event. He held Don's look and for a second he felt like they had exchanged something meaningful, with their eyes alone conveying their inner thoughts. Only he had no idea what Don's thoughts actually were – the connection just felt like it had to hold some sort of meaning. It probably didn't though – direct eye contact simply felt important.

Don's cigar smoke was overwhelming today, and the room was stifling with the mixture of early summer humidity, sweat and that heat that emanates intangibly from smoke. Sam moved in his seat, shifting his weight from one buttock to the other – he tended to do that in this office, maybe it was the chair. Don's eyes narrowed for a moment with interest, almost imperceptibly. Sam noticed and waved him away.

"Don't worry, that doesn't mean anything – my ass is just sore."

"What doesn't mean anything?"

"My shifting in the chair."

"Then why would you think that I would think about it?"

Sam wasn't in the mood for this. He would have liked to tell Don all about Antoinette, and Daniel, about Greg and Darren or Jesse and Jayo, even about the girl at the campfire, but if he did Don would just draw it back to the dead body which he rightly or wrongly believed Sam was attempting to draw attention away from.

He hadn't thought much about the girl at the campfire over the last few days. He suddenly wanted to know her name – how could he find out?

"Are we going to talk about it?" Don pressed gently.

Sam had no choice, so he began. "I did have a nightmare about it last night."

A lie. He had begun with a lie again. He could feel the honest closeness that he had shared with Don over the last few years slipping away but there wasn't anything he felt that he could do about it. There was an inexorable force pulling at the bond. It wasn't his fault, he was being cornered, there must be blame elsewhere.

"You did?" Don encouraged.

"Yep. I dreamt that the man was in my room."

"Where were you?"

"I was in bed, under the covers, just watching. He walked around the room, didn't look at me. But the rope was around his neck. Then I blinked and he was in my bed and I was walking around the room. Only this time I had the rope around my neck."

"I see."

"Yeah, kinda fucked up."

Don took a longer drag from his cigar than he needed to and the ash almost burnt down to his fingertips. He would have to relight a new one soon but he never smoked more than one per session – why was that? Maybe it was etiquette of a sort for the benefit of a non-smoker. What would the campfire girl's name be – maybe Sandra? He would like if she was called Sandra – it was a nice name, reliable and cute.

"I don't believe you," Don said slowly.

Sam looked up sharply. Don was staring at him wearily. He had never looked at him that way before. His cigar was on the ashtray, its life dwindling, and with it steadily disappearing was Sam's time with Don. That's what the cigar was used for – it was to mark the time.

"Okay, you're right. I didn't dream of anything last night," Sam backtracked quickly.

"So why did you lie?"

"Because I felt like you wanted me to tell you something."

"You shouldn't feel that I *need* you to tell me anything. Or that you are *obliged* to tell me anything. That's the whole point of these discussions: you are free to tell the truth without recrimination or judgement. But if you lie then you're wasting your own time. Not mine, but yours – I'm here anyway."

"I'm sorry – I've been under some stress lately."

"I've noticed. I heard about Mr Cusack."

"Mr Cusack is an asshole."

He immediately regretted saying that. Don abhorred cursing more than anything else. It was odd, people's foibles. He could tell Don that he smoked hash, had stolen a magazine, got drunk and had under-age sex and he wouldn't bat an eyelid, but curse while doing so and he would be asked to leave.

"I'll pretend that you didn't say that."

"Thanks."

"No problem."

"Okay, what actually happened is that I went down to the swing last night, to see for myself, but there was nothing there."

"Of course not."

"But there was somebody watching me. I could feel it, and then as I left I saw a man's face, old and sad, and I ran because I was scared. When I got back to the road Jayo and Jesse, two of my friends from the road – they were the ones who found the dead man – they said that the face was the same as him, so I must have seen his ghost."

Don stared at Sam for what seemed an age, then swung his chair away and faced the window. There were no pigeons present, just empty space through the window and the sky blocked by ugly towering buildings opposite. The sun was hidden behind the clouds.

"You've never mentioned those two boys before."

"They live on my road – they're the ones that I play

football with at home. I'm in a gang with them, sort of. A group really. We hang out. Sometimes go drinking 'n' stuff."

"Oh, right."

Don's voice sounded betrayed, as if the lads were part of a grand secret that Sam had been keeping from him, and their inadvertent exposure was simply the tip of a lying iceberg that harboured deeper seedy secrets.

Sam suddenly felt for the first time in Don's presence that he was being judged. He didn't like it. "You don't believe me, do you?"

"I don't recall saying anything, either way," Don replied distantly.

Sam stood up quickly, a sudden immature anger coursing through him. "I don't need this shit off you – you said that you wouldn't judge me and that's precisely what you're fucking doing!"

Sam had never experienced what followed: the temper of a silent man. It was terrible simply because of its unexpectedness.

Don got to his feet in slow motion, seemingly much larger than his thin 5'9 frame should have allowed, and gracefully flung the ashtray against the wall, scattering shards of glass through air showered in a cloud of heavy dust. His face was calm, his features still gentle and soothing, but muscles shivered beneath his robe, and his teeth were pressed tensely together as he uttered one word.

"Leave."

He didn't turn his back like he usually did when a session was ended but stayed standing, staring at Sam's head until he had left the room.

As Sam walked down the corridor and back into his

class he found himself thinking about how the element of surprise was even more important than the action itself, that the violence Don had shown was actually quite pitiful but it was the sheer confidence in the absolute rage that he held that was so disconcerting, and more significantly that it was preceded by complete calm. He sat down and took out his French books, wondering how he could apply that to his own life. Could he be powerful by being silent and then suddenly violent? Would that earn him more respect? What if he did that with Greg and Darren the next time they bothered him on the bus? He imagined being in Don's vestments as Greg threw a Malteser at his head, catching it in slow motion, then turning slowly and while they were confused at his complete calm smashing the Malteser into Greg's skull. That would definitely surprise them, but he might need the correct clothes, and posture would be important.

His French teacher muttered something in French that broke his concentration, and he realized that he had spent the entire lesson with these thoughts. Sometimes time would just pass as he drifted around in his own head. He had to stop doing that. Maybe. There was nothing much happening in class, just some past-perfect-tense grammar stuff, so he began to try to analyze the argument that he'd just had with Don.

"I went down to the swing late last night, and I saw the man's ghost." The statement repeated itself in his head.

Don was a priest – maybe they didn't believe in ghosts and so he had been offended. Although that would be absurd as it went against their fundamental beliefs: the Holy Ghost, Jesus rising and all the other tales he had been forced to absorb, essentially stories about ghosts and spirits. But maybe they didn't believe in ghosts in everyday real life, or believed that if there were then they were a representation of the devil, and by seeing one it was some sort of joining, an admission of ugliness that allowed the ghost a way in past the holy barriers of your soul. It must be complicated being a priest.

"I heard you found a dead body yesterday?" Daniel was talking to him.

Sam swung around in his chair, his chain of thought broken again. Class was finished, in fact school was over and the room was emptying rapidly, bodies streaming through the door in unison like a wave of sardines moving as one. Everybody was leaving except Sam who was lost in his own thoughts.

Daniel was sitting behind him, waiting patiently for Sam to find himself again. Sam looked hard at him. They hadn't spoken all week. He wasn't in the mood right now, but at the same time everything suddenly seemed completely irrelevant. Not just with Antoinette, or the campfire girl, but with everything. With Daniel it was anyway.

"I didn't find the dead guy. My friends did."

Daniel didn't know about Sam's friends at home either, and the confusion in his eyes said as much, but Sam didn't really care.

"Oh, I heard that you did – that's what Greg has been telling everybody."

"Greg's an idiot."

"True."

There was nothing else to say on the subject so Sam turned away and began to pack up his things. Daniel moved out of his chair, already with his bag in hand. Sam stood up and they walked out of the room together in silence.

"I'm sorry about bringing this up, but do you want to talk about it?"

"Talk about what?"

"Look, I only know what she's been telling Catriona. She's a bitch really – wouldn't trust her."

"Who? Antoinette?"

"Who else?"

"What's she been saying?"

"Just about you not being able to have sex, that shit. She's been . . . harsh."

Sam digested this information for a moment, allowing it to sink in, waiting for something to resonate. Was that why she had stood him up, or did she think he had stood her up and was being bitchy since, or what could it possibly be? He was tired of thinking about it.

"It doesn't matter," he found himself saying.

"Really?"

The surprise in Daniel's voice made Sam stop walking and he turned to his friend.

"I was with this other girl on Saturday night, and she jacked me off. I came all over her jeans so I don't care any more about Anoinette, or what she's been saying to Catriona or you or anybody."

Daniel looked at him for a second, scrutinizing his face for anything that would give away the lie, then saw that he was telling the truth and broke into a beaming smile, his teeth filling his face like a grotesque wall of uneven stones.

"That's cool – why didn't you tell me?"

"Because I think you're being a prick."

Daniel's smile shattered and the stones were hidden by his wet lips. He shrugged. "Fair enough, you're entitled to your opinion, but I'm just telling you what I know."

"So you know what happened on Friday?"

"Yeah, I do. I don't know why she's telling, but like I said she's a bitch. For fuck's sake, she's a ride and she knows it."

Sam nodded – he couldn't argue with that. But he didn't want to think like that. She was still a goddess in his eyes and he had no wish to shatter the illusion – it was more romantic that way. Every poet they studied in English class paid homage to the wonder of the flawed female form and the illusion that was her eternal beauty and he wanted to remember Antoinette the same way.

"At the very least meeting her showed me how much of a dickhead you could be." Sam smirked at Daniel who took it on the chin admirably.

"Let's just forget about this whole thing, okay?"

Sam let the question hang in the air for a moment then he smiled brokenly and nodded. "Sure."

Daniel grinned and they began walking down the stairs.

"So are you still seeing Catriona then?"

"Yeah, sure thing."

"You had sex with her yet?"

"What kind of question is that?"

"Well, you seem to know all about my 'sex' life, in inverted commas of course, yet never mentioned what happened with you. I found two johnnies in my room though – thanks for that by the way – but you haven't mentioned anything. Or cleaned them up."

Sam didn't even break stride as he spoke.

Daniel did.

"Yeah, sorry about that. I thought she had got rid of them."

"Not a problem, but you see where I'm going with this."

"I think so, but I could be wrong."

"Go with your instinct."

"That I should share the intimate details of my sex life with you?"

"Don't be a smartarse."

Daniel stopped walking. "I think I'm tired of this conversation, buddy."

"Well, I'm not."

"This was a short-lived reconciliation."

"It would appear so.

Sam walked out the door alone and didn't look back to see if Daniel was following.

Some days they played pool down at the local amusement arcade before getting later buses home. Today would probably have been one of those days.

Sitting on the bus home Sam found himself becoming even more introspective than usual. The body was haunting him, but not in any morbid manner. No, it was much simpler than that. He had worked hard to get himself accepted by the lads and had again found the door closed in his face. Even thinking that thought without any form of remorse for the seriousness of the situation, for a person who was no longer on this earth, physically at least, didn't cause him any morality check. Maybe the arguments with Daniel and Don were all a result of that, and he was being unkind towards both of them. Maybe he had overreacted. But the more that he thought about it, the stronger his conviction became that he was correct in everything that he had done, especially towards Daniel, and he would do it again if he had to. Even if Daniel hadn't meant anything by his actions, his lack of understanding made them just as intolerable.

He got off at a farther bus stop than usual, which meant

a longer walk home but eliminated the need to walk up the laneway and past the swing area where the body had been. He justified it by telling himself that the police would have the area cordoned off like they do in films so he wouldn't be able to go that way in any case.

The night was long and it took him much longer than usual to drift to sleep and he was afraid of what he might dream.

Chapter 16

Trying to Redeem Is Harder Than Not Needing To

The week passed by uneventfully. One of those weeks in a teenager's life where absolutely nothing happens but it seems to never end. Football training was fitful. He felt a part of it only momentarily, his touch coming and going in unison with his own frayed interest, and he knew he wouldn't be picked to play at the weekend, for which he found himself surprisingly thankful. He didn't want the hassle right now. School drifted by aimlessly enough, despite an altercation with his maths teacher over forgotten, or more appropriately, not attempted homework. But he got off lightly and he immediately suspected that had to do with something Don may have said to all his teachers.

He hadn't spoken to the lads for the last few days. Without the communal swing area – it was cordoned off and the huge jutting bough which had so loving held the swing ropes for years had been abruptly cut down – and with the gardaí taking a more than avid interest in what went on around the general area, coupled with their parents showing a sudden interest in their offsprings' whereabouts, freedom seemed more like a luxury than a necessity.

On Friday evening Sam was bored. He had nothing to do, the lads weren't around and the only option was to sit and watch television so he went outside to belt a football against the wall at the other end of the street. This wall was at a cul de sac so it wasn't encroaching on anybody's property but the noise could be heard all over. A constant thump thump thump. This was always frowned upon by pretty much every household on the road, especially by Mr Atrix, the standard grumpy neighbour who ran the street council. He would constantly try and stop them yet this evening he had walked by with his dog and completely ignored Sam. This only made the morose air that hung over the area like a claustrophobic wet blanket even more uncomfortable. People were afraid of death and afraid of doing something that would be seen as insensitive. Sam wondered how far he could push the affected-by-death façade and if it could have benefits.

Eventually Jayo wandered out of his house to join Sam but didn't say a word – just sat there and slowly smoked a cigarette – he was smoking openly now. He eventually joined in but his heart wasn't in it.

Sam found it frustrating that Jayo should be so affected by the event – after all, it was simply a dead body he told himself, yet everybody seemed tamed by it, and this exacerbated the irritation for Sam. He wanted to say this to Jayo, to challenge him about how trivial it should be and to break everybody from their stupor but something in Jayo's face stopped him. Maybe he was avoiding contemplating the seriousness of it but then he wasn't a real part of it so how could he be expected to participate completely in this macabre game of sorrow? It seemed unfair.

Jayo grew bored with the wall ball game soon after he had begun and started to drift off up the road without a word.

"Where you going?" Sam called out after him.

"Have a smoke with Jesse, ya know."

"Have a game later then?"

"Not really in the mood for playing tonight – just going to chill out."

"Okay, see ya later."

"Yeah, sure."

Sam nodded and watched helplessly as Jayo moved away from him. He hadn't asked him to come with him and Sam knew instinctively that he wasn't invited. He wanted to go along, to just be able to sit with them and do nothing, but to do nothing together. For the hundredth time he wished that he had been there.

Once Jayo was out of sight Sam began pounding the ball against the wall violently, hoping that he would burst it with the sheer power contained in his ferocity. The ball flew high into the air on one bad kick, up and over the wall to land, lost, in the heavy undergrowth behind it. Sam stood in front of the wall and stared at it for a long time. He had no idea what to do now. The evening was still young, summer was approaching hand in hand with famished packs of roving midges, eager to feed, themselves pursued by the swallows that would fill the air in happy flocks. Swatting away the little insects Sam began to walk back home, suddenly completely cowed by virtue of having very little to occupy himself with. On a whim he turned and walked up the road, past Jesse's house and then headed to the other side of the harbour.

The sun was setting, casting a great orange cloud, mashed with pinks and blood reds, across the sky like a net, catching all living things in its undercoat. Antoinette floated back into his thoughts and after letting her drift around unmolested for a while he pushed her back into the atmosphere to taint somebody else's desires.

It grew dark and Sam got up from his resting place overlooking the harbour with its various boats that bobbed up and down like irrelevant bits of cork. The pier was oddly empty and the air felt heavy, weighing him down. There really was nothing more to do but go home and sleep. At least sleep offered the promise of a new day and possibilities of change – to stay awake overnight would ruin the magic of the night's transformative powers and everything would remain as it was. He scuffed his runner as he got up, and as he bent down to check the damage he lost his balance momentarily and had to reach out for a rock to grab and steady himself. A searing pain lanced through his palm. A fishhook was dug deep into his flesh. He pulled it out and began walking home, throwing the rusted hook into a bin beside the bus stop as he passed.

The blood had hardened quickly and he half hoped that it would get infected, a serious infection that would involve doctors and priests, maybe even somebody famous. Everybody would know about it and they would forget the fuss with the dead man. He would pull through day by day and be commended for his mental fortitude and physical strength. Stories of his bravery would spread and Antoinette would hear. Laden by guilt, and desire, she'd come back to him, tail between her legs, begging forgiveness. Which he would grant her without hesitation.

It took him a while to dissociate the intermittent banging and scraping at his window from his dreams and, when he rose groggily and peered out the window, he found the images of moving shapes more discombobulating than concerning.

"Get de fuck outta bed, ya dope!"

Sam opened the window to hear what was being hissed at him properly and immediately recognized the dull monotone of Washing Machine's voice.

"Come on, we're not going to wait much longer – in two minutes be out the front."

And then the figures were gone – well, it was just the one figure – Washing Machine's movements had been leant a much grander form by the halogens spraying interrupted light across the gardens.

Sam closed the window and fell back onto the bed, his head landing in his soft pillows. He needed to change his sheets, he remembered. And then he fell back into nothingness.

His dreams were fitful, flitting between grand schemes of wondrous ideas and tearful recognition to darker moments of violence and death, dirty sex and hard smells, treachery and debased affairs.

When he awoke it was still dark, and the light filtering in through the crack he had left in his curtain cast a dull shadow over his toes. He got up to relieve himself and then collapsed back onto the bed. His entire body felt heavy, his mind clouded with smoggy thoughts, none clear enough to discern any importance in them.

He slept again until the afternoon. It was Saturday.

Chapter 17

There Always Comes a Time to Make a Stand

Rain gently wet the windows with a soothing pit-pat-patter. Sam put down the book he was pretending to himself to be reading and went into the kitchen to make a cup of tea. The television flickered in front of him as he returned with a steaming drink, the sound on mute. Sunday late-afternoon television was possibly designed solely to test a person's resolve but it was all he had to pass the time, apart from Latin grammar, which could never appear attractive no matter what the circumstance.

He stood in the sitting room and stared at the outside world, sipping his tea and hoping for something to happen. The street was empty. He was about to sit back down and see who was going to win a trip to China on some inane television show when he caught sight of Washing Machine skirting furtively towards the lane. Making a split-second decision, he put down his tea and raced out the front door, following in what he hoped was Washing Machine's slipstream. The rain was soft but even still his T-shirt was quickly soaked through.

He ran quickly down the lane and just caught sight of Washing Machine scrambling up the slope to the where the swing used to be. It wasn't cordoned off any more, or more likely they had ripped the tape away. He clambered up the slope with enthusiasm, grateful to have something to do.

When he broke through the bushes into the clearing beside their maimed tree he fell over Mouse's prostrate form on the dry ground at the edge of the clearing, sheltered here from the rain by the overhanging oak tree.

"Watch it, ya fecking eejit!"

"Sorry, Mouse."

The smell of hash filled his nostrils within seconds and his eyes took a few moments to focus. The three other lads were sitting in a circle. They all looked up wearily at him, no greetings, and continued passing around the roughly made joint. Sam didn't know quite what to do so he sat down to Mouse's left on his hunkers and waited for the joint to come his way. When it was his turn he would be careful to do it properly without coughing. The smell brought back memories of soft-skinned Antoinette from that infamous night. She had been sweet with him about smoking then.

Jayo was closest to him but he didn't offer him the joint, instead getting up and handing it to Mouse who accepted it with his eyes closed.

Sam didn't say anything.

A few minutes passed like this, then a few more, the strange silent ritual continuing until a second joint had been consumed by the bleary-eyed pack, with Sam sitting innocuously beside them as if he wasn't even there.

Eventually Mouse sat up, finished the joint and looked him straight in the eye.

Sam looked back into his distended pupils and waited. Mouse took a long time to speak.

"You going to come with us?"

"Where are you going?"

"It doesn't matter. Yes or no?"

It wasn't much of a choice – in fact, not knowing made it even more certain that he would go. He couldn't miss out on any more events. The secrecy already made it exotic, even if it culminated in simply sitting on the hillock overlooking the harbour and drinking Bacardi Breezers it would have been worth it because of the anticipation.

Sam followed the lads as they silently rose and made their way through the undergrowth and around the back of the wall that led towards the Gravins' estate – a huge sprawling house and gardens that were out of place in the area. It took Sam a few minutes to realize where they were headed, and the thought of what they might do excited him. It was perversely enjoyable, this male camaraderie, bonding in a quest for something possibly illegal – they were all tied together, even just for these few moments in time.

Skinsers, Carney and six other lads from the roads above were waiting for them in the bushes at the back wall of Gravins' estate. They too were silent.

"We got abou' half an hour, but I'd aim for fifteen minutes tops, jus' in case." Skinsers spoke in hushed tones, flicking his eyes to Sam a few times as he leaned towards Jayo, their sally-fight scuffle obviously forgotten, or hostilities at least temporarily suspended.

Jayo nodded, and Carney led the way. The wall into the estate could only be traversed one at a time and even then with the aid of somebody at the bottom to give a leg up. This was done by crisscrossing the fingers together to give maximum strength and by then placing this hand-basket under a foot. At the same time as the foot's owner jumped the hand-basket was thrust upwards with as much power as could be mustered, much like the traditional log toss in the Scottish Highlands. One of the other lads, Git, got landed with that job and he couldn't contain his distaste for helping Sam and his stirrup lacked conviction which left Sam scrambling to reach the top with his fingertips cutting into the surface of the wall. It was only when he was safely up and over that he remembered that it was Git he had knocked down unawares in the sally fight. He made a mental note not to be dependent on him in any situation that might occur later.

Git had to be pulled up by his wrists at the end, painfully scraping his belly against the rough stone work.

Once they had all safely scaled the wall Skinsers took the lead with a bent-over run, constantly looking over his shoulder as if expecting a shower of bullets at any moment to come raining down on him in a tempest of furious anger. A blackbird sang its little heart out on the far side of the garden, oblivious to the carry-on of the small band of boys running through its patch. A massive glasshouse loomed up in front of them, appearing suddenly out of the shrubbery, a goliath. It was made of glass all the way around from top to bottom, the roof and sides constructed entirely of glass panes, with thin slivers of metal and plastic on the edge of each pane holding them together like a jigsaw. Nobody said anything but they all stopped in a broken regimented line in front of the shiny building, their reflections staring back at them mutely.

The rain had stopped and the sun peered through the clouds as if vaguely interested in this odd communion of teenagers. Sam stared back at the reflection of himself in the glass, standing side by side with the other boys whose company and respect he had yearned for since the halcyon days when he had first learned to ride a bicycle, and a smile flickered across his face. This was what it was to be part of a gang – exploring, adventuring, hurting and bonding together. Then his smile shattered into tiny minute little fragments as the glass pane containing his reflection was smashed into shards by a heavy rock. Sam turned in shock to his left and saw Jayo slowly retract his arm from the movement of the throw – he had followed all the way through like a true pro, sending all his power into the rock so that there was no chance of it not doing its intended job in front of so many of his peers. There was an approving murmur from the other boys, a silence when the world took its breath, and then bedlam broke loose. The group converged on the unwitting glasshouse with all the excited fury of a herd of hyenas, with the singular goal of destruction at all costs.

Sam didn't know what to do and remained rooted to the spot. Then Mouse emerged from the mayhem like a small vengeful god. Glass was shattering above his head from marauding rocks, sending crystalline sparkles around him like a diamond halo. He sneered at Sam and, hefting a rock, threw it at his head. Sam caught it, and for a split second considered launching it back at Mouse's own forehead, knowing that he would not miss at this range, and in that split second realizing that Mouse hadn't been trying to hit him but had been offering him a rock to join in. He nodded and, with Mouse watching, threw the invading rock right through one of the centerpiece window panes. It was one of the few that had a pretty motif drawn into the actual glass itself, painstakingly hand-created over many hours, destroyed in a whisper of time. Mouse smiled and turned on his heel back into the war zone. Sam's mind had been made up for him and he followed.

The glasshouse never stood a chance and was left as a barely standing spine in what amounted in real time to just over two minutes, but had seemed to the boys to be an infinite slow-motion montage of absolute bliss. Sam had found himself lost in the adrenaline as soon as the rock had left his grubby hands, the freedom to destroy without recrimination utterly irresistible.

But it wasn't finished. The pièce de résistance had yet to be surmounted. The band of brothers drew back from the carcass surrounding them and turned their dewy attentions inwards. There in the glorious invading sunlight, finally freed from its suffocating prison and allowed to breathe was a car. But not just any car. This was an antique Porsche. Maybe thirty years old, maybe even more Sam reckoned. Beautiful. It was and in all probability would remain the greatest feat of streamlined engineering to ever fall beneath these grimy fingers and each boy simultaneously resented and was overawed by that fact. Sam ran his fingers over the hood as its metallic skin eagerly soaked up the beating of the sun's rays. The warming paint gave him a pleasant tingle of electricity. He knew what was going to happen and this time he couldn't allow himself to be a part of it. He stepped back and watched, unable to prevent the event even on the many times that he replayed it like a television show in his mind. He observed with sad detachment as Jayo hefted a huge iron bar that he had discovered on the floor, raised it high above his head and held it for a moment, in suspended animation. The collective held their breath, all eyes on the glinting metal that winked at them with a knowledge of repercussions much deeper than they possessed. Sam turned away as the bar was brought down violently and he heard, rather than saw, the screeching sound of agony that the car made as its husk was pierced and pounded helplessly by its murderous cousin, the betrayal of metal the only way that it could be truly cowed. The boys attacked the car like animals and Sam picked his way out of the wreckage gingerly, careful not to stumble or touch the metal pylons that still held shards of vengeful glass. He stood on the soft forgiving grass, eyes downcast as the wanton destruction from his gang carried on around him.

There was a movement beyond the glasshouse, coming from the residence. The scream of a distressed man. It must be Mr Gravin. Instinct set in immediately – survival was all that counted and he broke into a run. Behind him he heard the shouts of the other lads – they realized the danger only seconds after he did, thoughts of empowering destruction segueing into fear. He had a good fifteen yards' head-start and knew that he would reach the wall first and no matter what they couldn't all be caught – he certainly wasn't going to be anyway. If they were caught the pain would be acute: this was a criminal offence. The car was but a hulk of heaving metal, unrecognizable from its original state and the owner would be sure to seek revenge. That would not happen to Sam.

His mouth exploded in riveting pain, and his front teeth held firm only from the pressure exerted by his locked lower jaw. The ground flew up at him and hit his face with a violence he had never known was possible. His body followed his face, twisting downwards and sideways to lie in a crumpled heap. A foot ripped into his ribcage, beating against his bones with a tremulous force so hard that all he could do was turn his body inward and protect his tender belly with his arms. Then the offending foot hit his face, the force whipping his whole body around and over in one seamless movement.

Skinsers stepped back, spitting on Sam's skin exposed under the ripped T-shirt. The group of boys stood silently watching the beating with the same dispassionate grimaces that had preceded the destruction of the glasshouse.

"Dat's fer running away, ya little cock! *And* not warning anybody!" Skinsers spat the words out with such force his lips trembled. "Yer lucky nobody got fuckin' caught or I swear I'd fuckin' murder ya myself. Who de fuck brought dis little fag here anyway?" he challenged the group.

Nobody said anything and as Sam opened his swollen eyes he saw Jayo's face blaze with anger. Once the other lads had gone, if he was still able to walk Jayo was going to make sure he couldn't.

Sam groaned and began to sit up.

Skinsers turned away from him and hopped up onto the small four-foot wall that separated them from the safety of Sam's road. His beating was taking place only a few hundred yards from his own house.

"Don't get fucking up or I'll knock ya back down, ya little prick!" Skinsers sneered.

Sam glared at him balefully through the blood swimming in streams through his teeth, the iron taste in his mouth strangely comforting. Rising to his knees he took a deep breath and then stood up uncertainly. Skinsers laughed at him and clenched his hands into fists, his sinewy body stretching as he readied himself for another all-out final assault. His mouth moved to say something but Sam couldn't hear anything. He couldn't feel anything either. It was if all the pain and hurt that he had suffered over the past few weeks, months, years had culminated right here. This juncture was the final resting-place for humiliation and no more could be endured. His mind felt clear for the first time in weeks. There was a plank of wood a few feet away from him, part of a pile of discarded stuff – pipes, rubbish, all sorts – and Skinsers watched in bemusement as Sam clasped his hands around the hard wood, lifted it up and then walked unsteadily towards the wall. Noises were being spoken around him, but they held no meaning for him – they were like ghosts speaking to him from beyond the grave, nothing to worry about. Skinsers turned away from him with a dismissive scowl as Sam stumbled, his knee breaking his fall on the hard earth. Then he rose abruptly and two quick steps took him to within swinging distance of the other boy. Skinsers noticed the threat and turned, but too slowly. There was a collective intake of breath that was matched by the air whooshing around the wood as it sliced through the thick atmosphere with a violence so smooth that it almost seemed soft and gentle. The wood wasn't. Nor was the nail that protruded abrasively from the side of the plank with a sharpened eye, hunting for a final place to bury into. It fulfilled its destined purpose deep within Skinsers' calf. He screamed with an agony so loud and shrill that even Jayo winced. Skinsers fell from the wall and landed flat on his chest, his hands clutching at his leg as if the intensity of his desire could remove the pain. Sam stood over him like the Grim Reaper, half doubled over, blood dripping down his clenched jaw. He reached down and with a sharp yank removed the wood and the offending nail from the other boy's stricken calf, ripping away a hunk of flesh as he did so. Skinsers wouldn't be running anywhere for a while.

As tears ran down Skinsers' face Sam stood over his fallen enemy and raised his foot, contemplating delivering a death blow like he'd just had released upon him. His foot pulled back and Skinsers' soft features rolled into view. His blurred wet eyes widened, expecting a blow to tear his nose from one side of his face to the next. But it never came.

Sam smiled sadly at him, threw the plank away and without so much as a backwards glance at the others headed home. Nobody followed him.

Chapter 18

Being Cocky Never Works Out

"What do you mean, 'you forgot it'?"

"I mean I forgot it."

"Don't get smart with me, Samuel."

"My name is Sam."

"'My name is Sam, sir'."

Sam was silent, unblinking. Mr Cusack towered over his desk, a volcano ready to erupt.

"Samuel? Did I hear you say 'sir'?"

Sam continued staring ahead. "No, you did not hear me say that, 'Martin'."

Students were never supposed to call teachers by their first name but if Mr Cusack was going to openly mock him by calling him 'Samuel' then fuck him. He felt different today. Monday was usually a bad day, the start of a long week but today it felt like a new beginning. He could still feel the adrenaline from hitting Skinsers with the wood, and his body was swollen to prove he had been in the wars.

He wasn't going to take crap from anybody any more.

"Samuel. Because you have obviously had a difficult weekend, judging from those bruises, I'll pretend that I didn't hear that. But that doesn't excuse you not having your homework, and if you ever speak to me like that again –"

Sam had had enough and interrupted Mc Cusack mid-flow. "Fuck off and go teach the class like you're paid to."

Nobody moved. Nobody was prepared for that. It was simply not done. Sam didn't regret saying it.

Mr Cusack admirably took it in his stride. "You can leave my class now, please." His voice was unexpectedly calm.

Sam stood up. He regretted it now. Shit. Mr Cusack's voice followed him as he left the room.

"You can wait outside the principal's office and we will sort this out after school. For now I don't want your behaviour to disrupt this class any further."

Sam closed the door behind him and stayed there, taking in what had just happened. He knew he had crossed the line unnecessarily. More hassle. Then he decided that he'd had enough of everything. Walking back into class he made a beeline for his desk. Mr Cusack watched him without saying a word as Sam gathered the belongings off his desk efficiently and threw them into his bag. Then he walked out.

As he closed the door behind him he heard Mr Cusack continue teaching the class as if nothing had happened.

It was actually quite difficult to leave school. It was like a strange prison in many ways, Sam thought. You could leave whenever you wanted and do whatever you wanted when the official school day was finished, but during school hours your every movement was scrutinized – you were their responsibility until 3.30 p.m. A note was required to leave before then or a prior arrangement approved with permission. The front gate was locked and to get out you had to go past the office where the secretary, an unnecessary bitch, would only buzz you out if she absolutely had to. Or you could leave via the service entrance and nobody would be any the wiser, which Sam did.

He wandered around town a bit, just watching people. He took up his inner-city Dublin 'walk' where he knitted his eyebrows together and bobbed his head. He felt invincible now, after the weekend when he had proved himself as a man who was not to be trifled with. He stared down anybody who caught his eye, his shoes scuffing the ground as he walked. Apart from that there was nothing for him to do. He considered robbing something but wasn't in the mood – it felt like too much effort. He wished he had been this renegade when he had been on good terms with Antoinette – then he could have arranged to mitch off school with her. He had always been afraid of the consequences, but not any more. He spent some time watching people, daring them to hold his eye contact, then finally just headed home.

He made sure to leave the house before either of his parents got back from work so that he could come in afterwards and pretend like he had been at school all day. This was all much easier than he'd thought it could be. He was sitting half hidden behind the wall far across the street so he could see them when they came back. As they pulled into the driveway he slipped behind the wall down the laneway and went down to the slope area. He needed to wait a little longer. He was going to wait for the lads but he'd been hanging around enough all day so once it was late enough for him to have conceivably got the earliest bus from school he sauntered casually back.

It was only when he was closing the front door behind him that he realized he had left his schoolbag and jacket on the floor in the hallway. They stared at him accusingly. His heart sank because they would surely have noticed. How had he been so stupid? Shit.

He sidled into the kitchen where his mother was busily preparing dinner. She didn't look up when he entered and seemed cheery. His father was engrossed in the newspaper.

"Had a nice day at school?" his mother asked.

"It was fine."

He stood there hesitantly, waiting for her to comment on his bag but she didn't. He must have got away with it.

His father finally looked at him.

"Are you going to tell us how you got those bruises?"

"I was in a fight."

They had seen him come in yesterday but he had refused to talk about it, and because he hadn't seemed that distressed they had left him alone. Now, though, his father seemed to be taking in every detail of the cuts on his face.

"Did you win?"

"I guess."

"Okay then."

That was it. His father went back to the paper and Sam felt a little silly.

"I'm going to do my homework in my room."

"To catch up on the work that you missed today?"

There it was – she had noticed. He tried to think of

something to say back to her but couldn't think of anything so he left the room. He knew they would bring this up later. They would always allow things to settle first. It made it worse because he would be on edge until finally confronted.

He had only gone halfway up the stairs when the doorbell rang. Maybe it was the lads.

"I'll get it!" he shouted to the kitchen.

It wasn't the lads. A tall garda stared back at him with the look he usually reserved for criminals. It was one of the same ones who had questioned Jesse and the lads after the suicide on their swing.

"Are your parents in?"

Sam's mouth was abruptly dry and his hands were clammy. "Why?"

"Can you get your parents for me?"

"Yeah. Okay."

There was some comfort because the garda was outside and he was protected within the house. If he remained in his house then nothing could happen to him. Or at least it felt that way.

He closed the door to the man's obvious surprise and walked to the kitchen. He stood in the doorway until they both looked at him expectantly.

"There's a garda at the door – he wants to talk to you both."

His father stood up quickly.

"Is there anything that we should know, Sam?"

Sam was quiet. His father stepped near him and put his hand firmly on his shoulder.

"Sam. What should we know?"

"Nothing. There's nothing to know."

His father stared at him and Sam looked at the floor, unable to hold his gaze. His father strode to the front door with giant steps. After a moment Sam followed in his slipstream.

His father opened the door and the first thing he did was apologize.

"Sorry, I'm not sure why he closed the door on you. Kids get nervous around policemen."

"It's fine, I'm used to it. It's boring by now."

"I'm sure. Would you like to come in?"

"No. I'm sorry to bother you but I need to ask about your son."

His father shot Sam a look and he leaned against the wall, wishing that he could dissolve into it and disappear. Mr Gravin must have gone to the police. He couldn't have seen their faces though and he definitely didn't see Sam, so what proof did he have?

"What happened?" his father asked.

"There was an incident, and a lot of criminal damage yesterday at Mr Gravin's estate. A car was destroyed. A very expensive car, and a greenhouse and some other property. There was an awful lot of damage. He saw a group of teenage boys doing it and he chased them away. He's going to press charges."

"Press charges against whom?"

"Against all the boys who were involved."

His father didn't miss a beat, replying smoothly, "Well, it couldn't have been Sam – he was with us at his grandparents' all day yesterday."

The garda looked past his father and directly at Sam.

"Where did you get the bruises, son?"

"Football."

The garda arched an eyebrow. "Football? Was it a violent game?"

"I had a violent row afterwards."

"With whom?"

"Another kid. He's not from around here."

The garda nodded. It was clear that he didn't believe him.

"A kid from up the street was in hospital this morning with an infection in his leg, from a nail that was embedded in his shin. Did you hear anything about that?"

"Nope. Sounds awful."

"It is."

"Who was it?"

The garda suddenly smiled. Maybe he respected how Sam and his father were playing this game, or he just didn't really care that much.

"A kid you probably wouldn't know – hangs around in bad circles. Can't say that I'm surprised that he's in hospital."

"Right."

"So you don't know anything about the damage yesterday?"

"No. I don't even like cars."

"Me neither."

His father watched the back and forth between Sam and the garda with interest.

"Does he have insurance?" he interjected then.

The garda thought about it. "I guess he probably does."

"Mr Gravin can afford it, if not, anyway," his father quipped.

The garda laughed. "Yeah, I guess he can. Right, I'll be on my way. Sorry to have taken up your time."

"No problem."

The garda turned to leave then had one final thought. "What did you have for dinner at your grandparents'? Sunday dinner is always my favourite."

"Stew," Sam answered, at the same time as his father said, "A roast."

There was an awkward silence until his father corrected himself. "Sorry, yes, stew. Food all becomes the same to me at my mother's."

The garda nodded, his smile fading. "Of course. Have a good evening."

"You too."

His father shut the door and turned to Sam who was relieved that it was over. He looked at his father hopefully.

"That went well."

"You're grounded for the rest of the week. Now go to your room."

"What? Really?"

"Yes."

He wasn't fucking around. Sam had foolishly thought, because his father had so carefully and quickly defended him, that they were in cahoots together, but he was sorely mistaken.

And his father wasn't finished yet.

"I don't want to know what you did yesterday, or how you got those bruises. I don't want to know if you were there, or if you know the kids who were there and I certainly don't want to know if you were involved in that kid going to hospital. I don't want to know anything because I've already lied for you and I'm going to keep doing so unless I think that you deserve to be punished, but I'll be deciding that, not some stranger. So it's better if I don't know what happened and I can pretend that you're innocent. It's better for you and for me."

His father was a man of few words so this diatribe left Sam slightly shaken. He would never raise his voice, he never needed to – he just had to have the look in his eyes that he had now, for Sam to do exactly as he was told. Fear. Respect.

Sam nodded and went up the stairs two at a time. He knew that this wouldn't be the end of it but, out of all the possible scenarios, he had got lucky. Secretly he was proud that his father had defended him. In a way they were in it together, the two of them against the law.

He waited in his room for one or both of them to bring him up some dinner but they didn't. They were leaving him to starve and stew in his own thoughts.

Eventually the night came and they were going to bed when his mother walked in without knocking. Knocking was a privilege only afforded when you were deserving of it apparently. Sam was sitting on the floor aimlessly reading some comics and looked up her hopefully. She wore that pained look that wasn't just disapproving but was genuinely disappointed, the kind of look that only a mother has. He wished that she would be angry. She looked at him sadly, as if she didn't recognize him any more.

"Please go to school tomorrow – don't disappoint your father any more."

"Of course I'll go to school."

She hesitated. "Your father got a call from the principal today. Apparently you left school sometime today and didn't come back. You were supposed to talk with him over your behaviour in class, something that you said to a teacher."

Oh. Shit. There was no way out of this.

"Yeah, that was just a misunderstanding."

"Will you fix it?"

"Yep."

"If you don't then your father will. You don't want your father to have to do that."

"Nope."

"Okay. Goodnight, Sam."

She said 'goodnight' so softly it was like he was leaving tomorrow, being emancipated and never coming back, it had such finality to it. Fuck, she was dramatic.

Once she shut the door his entire body deflated. He had been on such a high. He had felt like a new person, strong, powerful, generally not giving a fuck any more. The way he had acted with Mr Cusack, then left school, and just felt completely in control – he had liked that feeling. He had imagined not going to school for the rest of the week, just doing whatever he wanted. Not any more. He would have to face up to his actions tomorrow and apologize. He simply couldn't catch a break at the moment. Common sense said that he was lucky to get away with the events on Sunday but that was no consolation.

He got into bed, pulled the covers over his head and tried to think about the campfire girl – that might cheer him up. She had been beautiful in the firelight. You could do a lot with memories.

Chapter 19

Leaving One Shore Behind to Conquer the Next

The gardaí had knocked on the door of every house in the area with a boy between the ages of twelve and eighteen. That was a lot of doors. They had mainly received short shrift as expected.

"My ma told them to fuck off an' jus' closed the door," Mouse said proudly.

"Didn't they just keep knocking?" asked Sam.

"Yeah, but she turned on the telly real loud until they went away."

It seemed that Sam's father had actually been the most distressed over the whole affair. They had left Jesse, Jayo and Washing Machine pretty much alone on account of the dead man. All they had done was make a quick courtesy call to ask their parents to watch who their kids associated with, but nothing more. This was another reason for Sam to wish that he too had witnessed the suicide – it would even have given him an excuse not to go to school. The gardaí had nothing to go on except Mr Gravin's wavering account of seeing a bunch of boys in track suits destroying his property, but they pretty much all looked the same to him and he was getting on a bit in years so his eyesight wasn't to be trusted.

"The insurance will pay for it, fuck it," Mouse announced sagely, as if he'd had some experience in that area before.

The others nodded in agreement.

Without the swing the slope didn't have quite the same appeal but they were sitting there nonetheless. Their focal point might have gone but it was still their hideaway, even if it had been tainted by the presence of the pigs.

Mouse coughed as he got to his feet. He seemed excited.

Jayo looked at him wearily. "What now, Mouse?"

"I got it."

"Got what?"

"The boat. I got the boat."

Now Jayo was interested. "Fuck off?"

"Yeah, I did."

"Deadly."

Jayo stood up and high-fived him. Washing Machine and Jesse looked pleased but Sam had no idea what was going on.

"What boat?"

"None of yer business, Samantha."

He had thought that almost cleaving Skinsers' calf in two would have garnered him some more respect but apparently not with Mouse. Nothing he did ever seemed to change anything.

Jesse pitched in. "Sam should probably come, in fairness."

"Why?"

"He can sail."

Jayo looked at Sam curiously and nodded. "Yeah, you're right. Sam, you're coming to the island with us this weekend. Mouse got a lend of a boat."

"What type of boat?"

"Doesn't matter. A little sailboat or some shit. We need somebody who can sail."

Mouse was pissed off. "I can sail."

"Yeah, but if you die out there we're fucked. And you can't really sail – you just like to think that you can."

"Fuck you! *You* can't sail!"

"I never said I could. Sam, you're coming." Jayo was strangely adamant about Sam coming.

Jesse and Washing Machine high-fived Sam who ignored Mouse's cutting glare.

Sam then stood up to high-five Jayo. "Why are we going to the island?"

"Why not? To get hammered."

"Cool."

Seemed as good a reason as any other. Sam looked at his watch and saw that it was almost five. He was grounded all week and being late on the first day that he was expected home on time wasn't such a good idea. Now the weekend sailing trip gave him a solid reason not to test his father's wrath.

"I gotta go, lads."

"You really grounded?" Jesse asked.

"Yeah."

"Shit buzz. Later."

He turned to go but Mouse reached a hand out to high-five him too. Sam put out his hand and Mouse slapped it so hard that it stung. Sam pretended that it didn't. Mouse leaned in.

"Skinsers is going to come looking fer ya, just so you know, and when he does we're not gonna help ya."

Sam stared Mouse right back in the eye in a way that he wouldn't have dared before.

"I'll be fine."

He wouldn't be fine. He would be far from fine if Skinsers did decide to come after him, but he had to keep bluffing from now on. The moment he shirked from a confrontation any credit he had gained would disappear.

Jesse called out as he left. "Saturday morning meet here around two – then we head down to the pier."

"Cool."

His meeting with the school principal had been brief and painless, insofar as he didn't get to say a word and was simply told what to do in no uncertain terms. He was informed that he had two weeks of detention and had to write Mr Cusack an apology note. He had also been banned from attending Mr Cusack's class until Mr Cusack saw fit to reinstate him, despite the note, and the rumour around school was that he was lucky not to have been suspended. However, Sam thought that the principal really didn't seem that bothered about the whole event. He wondered what his father must have said over the phone – he imagined it was probably something about punishing Sam himself.

The rest of the week was a grinding bore – with detention and being grounded there wasn't very much he could do except actually study and wait for the weekend.

He didn't talk to Daniel all week. He wanted to ask

about Antoinette but decided that she was probably best left in the past. He was most likely never going to see her again. The weekend loomed achingly large in the distance as the week dragged by with lead in its hours and then suddenly it was Saturday afternoon.

He was late and they weren't at the slope when he got there so he ran for the pier as fast as he could, hoping to find them, but Jesse hadn't specified where exactly. After searching frantically all over the East Pier he found them in an alcove of the West Pier near the entrance to the trawlers' port. They were sitting by a small ostensibly three-man dinghy when he got there. They had already launched it into the water off a rusted little trailer and rigged the sails. Mouse had made a decent job of it.

They were setting up to leave, clearly not bothered about waiting for him despite the fact that he was the only one who could really sail, although Jayo was to one side smoking quickly, almost frantically. It was patently obvious that he was nervous but everybody was pretending that they didn't notice.

He looked at Sam with a smile, seemingly happy to see him.

"You're late. We were gonna leave without ya."

"Sorry. Slept in."

"Whatever."

Mouse was already stepping onto the boat. Mouse's father was a fisherman, which meant that he should have a deep and trusting knowledge of the ocean. Or a fearful respect, depending. Sam genuinely had no idea what Mouse was like on the sea, which struck him as odd – he couldn't even recall a moment when the sea was mentioned by

Mouse. Usually anything Sam had to say on the subject of sailing drew irritated groans and jealous glances. Sam always did the local sailing course each summer and the lads resented him for it. It was too posh an activity for them.

Sam was staring out to sea when Jayo stood in front of him.

"Jesus, fuck, if ya do this shit out der I'm fuckin' ya overboard."

"Do what?"

"This space cadet shit ya keep doin'? Can ya fuckin stop? It's weird."

"Yeah, sure."

He hadn't realized that he was zoning out again.

Mouse was the only one in the boat. The others stared at it like it was a foreign object.

Sam took control. "Get in the boat – I'll get in last and push us off."

"Fair enough."

Jayo made no movement towards the floating dinghy but found a sudden interest in his sock and the skin underneath which seemed to be covering an important itch. Jesse and Washing Machine clambered onto the boat with all their bags containing alcohol, spare clothes, some cooking supplies and other general things, probably way too much stuff. Sam hoped that they didn't capsize and lose everything. Mouse looked as if he was fighting the temptation to rock the boat as they got in but kept it relatively balanced as he held onto the dock.

"You gotta get in." Sam looked up at Jayo who suddenly gave him a clip across the ear. 'Don't push it' was the silent warning, and they all got it, except for Mouse who smiled secretly.

Jayo placed his white runner on the gunwale and tested its balance, the boat swaying gently underneath his tentative touch. Then he put all of his weight on it. There was a second where everything was in perfect harmony, with the boat at a perfect angle to the water's surface, Mouse holding on to the land and Jayo balanced with one foot on dry safety. Even the breeze held off out of respect. Then Mouse pushed into his wrist ever so slightly. It was just enough to send a tremor through the wood which vibrated against the water like a pulse from one side to the other, pushing then pulling the gravity of the little dinghy's weight against itself. The boat rocked away from the shore and then back into Jayo's foot as it moved underneath him. He was caught off guard and instinctively leant into the movement, his body toppling downwards and away from the dock into the unforgiving cavity of the boat's skeleton. His arms flailed around him like a clipped duck and he smacked against the gunwale with a thud. His body weight completely threw the precarious balance of the boat and it swept up and down in a motion akin to that of a theme-park ride. Washing Machine and Jesse held onto the gear so it didn't fall out as the boom whipped the sail from side to side. Jayo's body careened to the other side, but mercifully Jesse whipped a free hand out to devour a lump of Jayo's jacket and pulled him back into the middle of the bulwark, his head just avoiding a smack of the boom by millimetres. Mouse couldn't conceal his disappointment that Jayo hadn't fallen in.

Sam rolled his eyes and, before there was any time for recriminations, pushed the boat away from the jetty with his toe and stepped lightly onto the gunwale. His balance was perfect, the ball of his foot finding its place on the wood of the gunwale. Here on the boat Sam was the master. He whipped in the mainsheet with his left hand, and with his right directed the humming little boat through the water with the tiller. You weren't technically supposed to stand up while steering but Sam wanted to look cool. The dinghy was overcrowded with five of them anyway so standing up created more space.

The weather was clear and the sea was flat with a southeasterly coming in off the ocean, creating minimal waves against the steady breeze. The tide was with them so they would broach the short distance on a convenient tight reach within less than half an hour.

Jayo was in obvious discomfort and his knuckles gripping the stanchion betrayed his nerves. At one stage Mouse stood up as they were leaving the harbour entrance, clasped one hand around a single stay and leaned his head backwards, arching his body like a bow towards the murmuring water. He kept flicking his eyes at Jayo, challenging him to watch what he was able to do, but Jayo ignored him. After he had done it a few times Sam caught Jesse's eye, then casually let the mainsheet drift out of his fingers. The tension was released from the sail which immediately billowed out rapidly without any pressure to keep the wind inside its curled body. The boat fell in on itself towards the water on the opposite side of the sail where Mouse was hanging himself out extravagantly. His weight pulled the little dinghy to fall in on top of him and as he felt the gunwale move away from under his feet he had to quickly readjust his body and reach desperately for the sail itself to avoid falling into the water.

Sam winked at Jesse and readjusted the tension on the sail to even out the boat.

Mouse had just barely avoided falling in.

Jayo laughed heartily and nodded approvingly to Sam but Mouse glared at him under his heavy eyebrows.

The little boat admirably ate up the sea and Washing Machine began singing songs to pass the time.

When they were nearing the island, Mouse suddenly asked if he could steer for a while.

"Let me do it, Samantha."

"But we're almost there."

"Yeah, but it is my cousin's boat, so if I wanna sail it then I will."

He had a point so Sam reluctantly relinquished the helm to his antagonist.

Mouse gestured for Sam to move further up the boat as they swapped positions because there wasn't enough room for them to sit at the stern together. Sam allowed Mouse to move behind him and, keeping hold of the mainsail, he tentatively released the tiller to Mouse. The next thing he knew he was toppling backwards, the sky moving around him in a bewitching circle, and then suddenly the water was where the skyline should have been. The icy-cold sea hit his entire body like a vacuum, sucking all his energy into it greedily, and for a few seconds he couldn't move from the shock as his prone form slid into the darkening depths head first like a discarded toy soldier. Then the freezing rush was countered by instinct and his muscles screamed out in pain. He was on the surface with one quick kick of his limbs and took a deep breath, experiencing a momentary joyous rush when his lungs filled with fresh oxygen again. The rush was fleeting as his blurred salty vision saw the boat circling around him with four bobbing hysterical figures doubled over. Despite the shock he had managed to keep his wits about him just enough to keep his hold on the mainsheet. More likely the shock of the cold had frozen all his muscles and, similar to what the body does in death, his fingers had refused to loosen their grip on the rope. By keeping a hold of the rope he had worked like an anchor when he was tossed into the heavy sea and his dead weight had dragged the little boat backwards to a spinning stop. He grabbed the rope in both hands and pulled himself steadily through the water and back into the boat. Sea salt crusted around his eyes and stung a small ulcer under his tongue.

Mouse grinned as Washing Machine recounted the dexterity he had shown in simultaneously pushing Sam overboard with his free arm and leveraging his feet from under him with a quick kick to his left shin, much like the technique used for striking a rugby ball.

Mouse then offered him the tiller. "I changed my mind – you can do it again."

"No, you can do it now."

"Nah, I've had my fun."

Mouse stepped away from the tiller and, out of control, the boat flapped and spun in the wind.

Jayo didn't look happy with the boat rolling from side to side and pointed at Sam. "Just take the fucking tiller or steering wheel and that poxy rope or whatever."

Mouse exacerbated the rolling motion by moving up the boat and Jayo tensed. He was in no real danger of being thrown into the sea but he had seen how Sam had fallen in so easily.

"Take that fucking main rope!" he snarled.

"It's a mainsheet."

"Whatever the fuck!"

"Mouse wanted to helm – let him do it." Sam was soaked to the bone and being petulant.

"*Just fucking do it, Sam.*"

The boat lurched to one side from a rolling wave and Jayo lost his shit.

"*I can't fucking swim so if you don't sail this fucking thing in to that island I'm gonna lamp ya so fucking hard that you're gonna wish you were in the sea!*"

It was news to everybody that Jayo couldn't swim. Sam had just presumed that they all could. If you couldn't swim then why get into a small dinghy and sail to an island? None of them were wearing life jackets so Sam took responsibility. He sheeted the boat and got her on a steady course for the island again within moments. They had drifted a little off course so their approach was now a little tighter. He had to be careful not to bring the boat too close to the wind because there was so much weight in it that it would quickly begin to keel over. He watched Mouse carefully as he propelled the boat forward. Mouse must have just guessed that he was a strong swimmer – otherwise it was dangerous to have dropped him in the middle of the sea in his clothes. If he hadn't kept hold of the mainsheet would Mouse have come back for him? He had the feeling that he should watch his back this weekend: Mouse wasn't to be trusted.

Sam piloted the dinghy in to shore with great dexterity and here he readied himself for some revenge as he instructed both Mouse and Washing Machine to leap into the water to stop the boat grating against the sand.

"On my count jump in," he ordered.

"Fuck off, you do it!" Mouse replied.

"I'm helming."

"Well, stop helming and you jump in and stop the boat."

Sam was determined so he kept the sail taut and their speed up. The shore was approaching rapidly.

He shouted at Mouse. "Jump in or we're going to hit the shore too fast!"

"Then let the sails out!"

"I will when you jump in!"

"No, we can just hit the shore – it's only sand."

"If we scrape the bottom and get a hole we're all swimming home!"

This alerted Jayo and he boxed Washing Machine. "Get in," he growled.

Washing Machine got ready to jump in first so, much as it pained Sam, he had to be fair about it and didn't instruct him to do so until the timing was right and the depth correct, which he might have been premature about if Mouse had had the stupidity to go first. Mouse was too smart to fall for that, however, and with Washing Machine suffering more than enough abuse on an ongoing basis it just didn't seem right to take advantage of him.

Sam let the sails out, and the boat slowed down, coming to a stop when Washing Machine jumped into the water and held it tight, followed by Mouse when the boat was in the shallows.

They duly beached the boat, dropped the sails, or more accurately Sam dropped the sails and then, assisted by Jesse, tied the painter to a nearby tree. Mouse seemed to have lost any interest in the boat now that Sam was there to do all the work.

Jayo had got out of the boat quickly and gratefully planted himself on dry land with the air of Columbus discovering new territory. Assuming control now that he was once more on familiar ground that didn't threaten to swallow him into its murky depths, he set about finding a suitable place for a fire, and sent Washing Machine off in search of wood and tinder.

Chapter 20

Fire, Fire, Burning Bright

The heat from the campfire was scalding, so they had to keep moving their bodies, shifting constantly so that one side turned to face the fire and then the other. The dusk had swept up on them remarkably fast as the day had drifted away, but the moon was in full bloom so they were not in any fear of being cast into total blackness. It wasn't particularly cold so the fire served the dual purpose of fulfilling that atavistic human urge for security and comfort as well as satisfying the pathological male desire to watch something burn. Nobody had thought of bringing a bottle opener and with Bacardi Breezer the poison of choice along with a few meagre rations of cheap Russian vodka, Washing Machine again helpfully volunteered his teeth to prise open the bottle caps. Drinking began in earnest once the fire was in full show, the boys having waited patiently until sufficient stocks of wood had been gathered and sausages had been cooked – or more precisely, blackened.

Remarkable restraint was shown to wait to drink until everything was set up, exposing some semblance of civility. Then they began to devour the little bottles of sugared alcohol. Sam relaxed in the simple camaraderie, his friends, his group. Teasing was rife of course, but the atmosphere was easy and he felt sufficiently uncompromised to be able to deal out as much gentle abuse as he received, even to Jayo. At one stage he even aided Jesse in dragging Washing Machine through the sand by his feet, though Jayo then subjected Sam to the same unfortunate horseplay and it wasn't as enjoyable.

The banter was in full flow when Mouse turned to Sam and when he did there was something more than just drunken bemusement flickering behind his eyes.

"You never saw a dead body, did ya?"

The question caught everybody by surprise, and the murmuring that tickled the underbelly of each conversation trickled away as if a tap had been turned and fastened with a vise-grip.

Sam swallowed a mouthful of Blackcurrant Breezer and turned his head with a gentle swivel. "What are you talking about?"

"A dead body, have you ever seen one?"

Sam paused for a moment as he tried to exactly ascertain what was beneath Mouse's tone. "I have, yes."

"In a coffin at a funeral doesn't count," Mouse scoffed.

"Well then, no, I have not."

Mouse took a long swig of his freshly opened bottle and bobbed his head, his neck slipping into the realm of skin between his shoulder blades like a fattened pig.

"So what makes you think you're on the same level as us here?" He gestured with the hand holding the bottle for emphasis at the boys sitting around the fire.

Sam's back was cold from facing the sea breeze and his front was too hot – he needed to turn to one side or the other, but didn't want to move or squirm lest it be misinterpreted as discomfort at the rising confrontation.

"I don't see what that has to do with anything."

"Do you think we are all on the same level here?"

"The same level as what?"

Mouse rolled his tongue around his teeth and licked his lips before replying. "As in, to break it down to basic fucking English here for the dumb private schoolboy, do you think that you should be able to hang around with us? My point is that you haven't experienced what we have, so you can't understand what we've been through, and so can't understand us. How can we respect you if you aren't on the same level?"

Whenever an individual confrontation began, no matter how trivial, Sam had long since noticed that the others rarely if ever interjected, even if they felt uneasy or disagreed. He often wondered how it must look to an outsider when the others sat through abuse of their peers, keeping quiet lest the focus be switched onto them. Occasionally Jayo would intervene but usually only to assert his authority, never for any altruistic reason.

Jesse mumbled under his breath once Mouse had finished his monologue on this occasion, however, much to Sam's surprise, and everybody else's.

"That's enough, Mouse, we don't need to go there."

Mouse ignored him and actually increased his questioning, as if spurred on by the intrusion and Jesse sank back into the shadows, having satisfied his conscience.

"What do you think we know that you do not?" Mouse persisted.

"About what?"

"About death, and life."

"Well, you weren't there either, Mouse – the lads here were but you weren't."

"I found my uncle in his bath having slit his own wrists when I was twelve, Fuck-face!"

"Explains a lot." Sam muttered the riposte under his breath as he took a swig of alcohol and unwisely turned his head dismissively.

Mouse immediately launched his own half-full bottle at Sam's head, but managed to miss, inconceivable at such close range, and almost hit Jesse who only just moved his shoulder out of the way in time. The bottle disappeared into the blackness.

Jesse swore and re-engaged. "That's fucking enough – there's no need for this shit." Discussion of the dead man was the only thing that seemed to raise Jesse from his ever-increasing daily stupor.

Mouse was now facing Sam head on, having positioned his body squarely in front of him.

"Go get my bottle – you didn't catch it."

Sam looked at Mouse, incredulous. "You're joking me?"

"Do I look like I'm fucking joking with you?"

"Depends."

"Well, I'm not, so get the fucking bottle." As he spoke he smacked his hand against Sam's knee like a man might do to a brassy dog. "Go on, get it, hurry up!"

"Fuck off, Mouse!"

"I said get the fucking bottle, prick."

Sam stared him down and then immediately regretted it as Mouse hit his knee again but harder this time, and then began to hit it repeatedly as if knocking out a solid beat on a drum over and over, harder and harder, the slap morphing into a fist that found the soft flesh on the side of the joint.

"Get it, get it, get it, get the fucking bottle, get it, get it!"

Sam shook his head and pushed Mouse's hand off his leg, rising smoothly to his feet as he did so, then swayed as a wave of dizziness from a blood rush to the head swept over him. They all watched him intently while he regained his balance and retrieved the by now empty bottle to prevent anything further happening. Mouse just opened another bottle and smiled at him, the shadows and blood-orange glow from the fire giving his face a demonic look, ignoring the bottle Sam dropped dutifully at his feet.

The damage had been done and there was an intense energy in the air now that Sam wasn't comfortable with. He sat down again and sipped at his bottle as the darkness of the night closed around him closer and colder than before.

Sparks flared in the blackness as little hazes of flame spat out angrily from the firebrand that Jayo lifted carefully above his head, holding it out so that the breeze didn't carry any of the burning fire onto his body.

They were drunk by now. Washing Machine was spinning around like an inbred dog chasing its own tail repeatedly until he got dizzy and fell down in the soft sand, laughing. Jesse and Jayo were finishing each other's sentences with the worst swear words possible that began with the last letter that the other ended with, and Mouse was surveying all from a small stumbling trek he was making around the fire.

Sam threw some more wood on the fire and missed. The branch flopped pathetically on its side and he laughed, his tongue catching in his throat. Mouse stopped stalking around the fire and opened his arms like a grand vizier making an announcement.

"It's time."

The lads all stopped what they were doing solemnly and looked at him knowingly.

All except Sam. "Time for wha . . . what?"

Mouse turned and looked at him. His eyes glowed black like coals. He swaggered over to him, theatrically drunker than he was.

"You haven't seen a dead body?"

"You asked me that already."

"And you haven't?"

"No. That's what I said earlier."

Mouse nodded and swept his arms through the air like he was conducting an orchestra.

"Well, you are going to see a dead body then. Tonight."

Sam sipped his drink, waiting for the continuation of Mouse's thought process. There was none. So he asked. "How?"

"This island is haunted to fuck. My dad said it's filled with the spirits of sailors and raped women from the Viking days. Evil fuckers these ghosts, the lot of them."

"So?"

Mouse gestured to the surrounding darkness. "So, we are going to find one of those ghosts of the dead, and you – *you* – are going to . . ." His voice faltered in his throat, dying like the embers of their smouldering fire. His eyes blazed, flickered, closed and opened and he spat some of his drink on the ground. "You are going to talk to it."

Sam wanted to laugh at the ridiculousness of it. If he was in the comfort of his own environment he would have, but out here everything seemed all too vivid.

"Why?" he heard himself asking without actually physically forming the word.

It was ignored as Mouse grabbed him by the shoulders, pulled him to his feet and marched him out into the darkness.

Jayo and Washing Machine each outfitted themselves with a low-burning stick that cast an eerie hazy light.

"I thought these things burned better than this, like," said Jayo.

"Yeah, we need petrol or something."

On cue, Mouse, now the de facto leader, splashed some vodka on the end of the branches and fire leapt up, twisting angrily. Taking the branch off Washing Machine, he led the way.

"You know where you're going?" Jesse sounded as unsure as Sam felt as the posse was led off into the enveloping blackness, leaving the false safety of the fire behind.

"No, but we don't need to – the dead will find us."

There was something ominous in Mouse's tone and Sam found himself shrinking nearer to the stolid figure of Jayo until he was uncomfortably close. Jayo didn't comment.

The suffocating blackness was cloying, like a thick mud slithering in at all angles and suddenly nobody was talking, every movement loud and emphasized.

Minutes passed as they stepped tentatively into the future. The waves could be heard greedily lapping the shore somewhere in the distance. The wind whispered dirty secrets around their heads, and their feet made insensitive crunching sounds beneath them. It was surreal, and everybody felt it, the calm before the storm. Something was building and it wasn't just the fear of being alone in the night. It was something more.

Mouse abruptly stopped walking and held up his hand, illuminated by the flickering flames.

"Here."

Sam looked around him. All he could see was blackness. He looked behind and nothing but thick suffocating darkness groped back at him. Peering deep in its depths it got blacker and blacker, devouring him eagerly. He stepped forward.

"Where?"

Nobody answered and turning around he found that he was alone. The flames gone, his companions disappeared. He instinctively froze, awaiting the joke he knew would come. That he hoped would come. Nothing happened. He was completely alone. There was no sound and no movement apart from a cloying darkness that seemed to grow thicker around him like a floating quicksand. He shivered and stood still. His breathing seemed strained, his heart like a beating drum. His limbs suddenly felt heavy and all he could hear was his own pumping blood. He couldn't move. There was something behind him. He could feel it, a presence. It was the same feeling he'd had the night of the suicide. His heart began to beat faster, his muscles tense. It was directly behind him, he could almost sense it touching him. He wanted to curl up into a ball. He wanted to run. He wanted to disappear. He spun around to face his tormentor and faced up to a thick wall of solid night. There was nothing there. It was behind him again. He twirled on his heel again but missed it – it moved too fast, toying with him as a cat with a mouse. Adrenaline pumped through his body, and he wanted to scream. Where was it? What was it? He twisted around again, but kept missing it – no sound, no shape, just the presence. His head was about to explode

– he couldn't handle it, the unknowing, what was around him.

A scream had built up in his throat and desperation clawed inside his chest, when something blew gently into his ear.

Time stopped.

He couldn't move for what seemed an age as a voice licked his skin.

"*I'm here.*"

The syllables lapped against his lobe as if the voice was savouring each sound.

He bolted. His ankle almost buckled as he hit the ground hard, bouncing off the mixture of grasses, sand and uneven rise. He stumbled and rolled with the movement, his momentum taking him back to his feet. He knew it was behind him, he could feel it, and if he stopped it would catch him. In his irrational imagination it kept getting bigger but had no semblance of shape or form. It was just something.

Suddenly a light danced before his eyes, then another, bouncing up and down like yoyos. He slowed, focused, and saw the torches stuck in the ground, his bobbing head making them seem to move like the roll of the sea. He ran for them and collapsed, arms spread out in submission. The lads turned and looked at him groggily.

"Stop being a twat!" Jayo said.

Then he looked away from him and back to the centre of the rudimentary circle where Mouse had taken up a position as Head of State.

Sam looked behind him. The blackness was still all around him, but it was held at bay by the flickering torchlight, afraid to encroach upon its brightness.

Jesse and Washing Machine didn't move, their attention held by Mouse.

They were on the other side of the island now, far away from their campfire. It was so calm that Sam was confused, but they paid him no attention so he drew himself up onto his hunkers and followed their gaze, the creature in the darkness a fading memory. Mouse was on his knees with a small wooden board and was whispering to himself. A foreboding counter piece sat on the board like a little figurine. Mouse leaned in and whispered to it, then leaned back and closed his eyes. They sat there in rapt silence, eyes rooted to the board. Nothing happened. Then the piece moved forward gently, as if being pushed by an invisible hand. If Jesse hadn't jumped backwards instinctively Sam would have figured that he had imagined it.

"I'm not doing this, this is fucked," Jesse whimpered.

"We can't stop now." Mouse stared gravely at Jesse as if to stop was to invite disaster.

Jesse continued. "This is too weird though."

"Of course it's weird – we're trying to talk to a spirit – what did you think was going to happen?"

Sam's blood went cold and he shivered.

"What are we doing?" he asked, his voice still shaky.

Jayo looked at him sharply. "It's a Ouija board. Don't say anything unless Mouse asks you."

Jesse looked at him, his eyes wide, and Sam felt very afraid. Not the fear of the unknown that he had felt in the shadows, nor the fear in the laneway that night, but a deep bellyaching fear of something spiritual and potentially evil. The Devil always scared Sam more than he could countenance and here they were, alone on an island in the dead of night, trying to drunkenly call upon the spirit world. He tried to speak but fear held him down, as if the Devil himself pressed his hands upon his shoulders and pushed him deeper into the earth. He found himself speaking without making any movements of his lips.

"Something just spoke to me in the darkness."

They all looked at him.

Mouse looked afraid and squirmed unconsciously. He stared at Sam. "Where?"

"Out there, when you left me."

"We didn't leave – you just ran off into the darkness." Mouse was hesitant now.

"No, I turned around and you were gone."

Jayo shook his head slowly. "We were standing there watching you. You stood really still, then turned and walked off into the night. It was really weird. We thought you were just drunk."

Sam's mouth went dry. "But, no, I couldn't find you, I didn't . . ."

"What spoke to you?" Mouse looked earnestly at him.

"I don't know – a voice."

"Man or woman?"

"Man. But it was soft, like, I dunno, quiet."

"What did it say?"

They were all looking at him. Nobody moved, not even a blink.

"It said . . . 'I'm here'."

Jesse shrank back from him, and even Jayo shifted uncomfortably.

"Fuck." Mouse looked at the board as if it were a viper poised to strike him. "That's what I asked him – was he here?"

He stared around at the others for confirmation, and Washing Machine nodded slowly as he put down his

Breezer bottle. Now was no longer the time to drink.

Sam felt very sober. "You asked who?"

The wind moved between them, like a silk scarf brushing their skin, but it was cold as ice. The torches flickered and they all felt very exposed. The blackness closed in on them and their isolation was very real.

Jayo sort of half stood, half crouched, clearly unwilling to rise fully for fear of being too exposed. "We should stop this and go back."

Mouse nodded.

"Who did you ask?" Sam had to know. He knew he shouldn't, that he should just pretend it had never happened, but the ignorance seemed worse than the knowledge.

Mouse looked at him without malice, more like a soothing mother at a tormented child trying to conceal a lie.

"There was a murderer who died out here. About fifteen years ago. He killed eight people in one night, moving from house to house. They chased him and he swam out here to escape. They chased him to the cliffs and he fell into the sea and disappeared. They never found his body, but people have seen him. And everybody who's seen him has died within a week."

Sam held his breath. He scanned the others for any sign of a joke, any sign that he was being toyed with.

Washing Machine looked away, unable to hold his eye.

"That's bullshit. No way, not true."

"It is," Washing Machine said, his head held down to the ground.

"My cousin saw him and it freaked him out so much that he got hammered drunk down by the harbour alone.

There was a storm and he got swept out and drowned . . ." Mouse's voice trailed off and he looked at Sam. "Did you see him?"

"No, I just heard him."

"You sure?"

"Positive. I kept looking around but there was nobody there."

"If you didn't see him maybe you're alright."

"What happens if I saw him? Is it certain?" Jesse mumbled under his breath and kept his eyes on the ground.

Sam noticed that they all did, as if they were afraid that if they looked up then the ghost would be there before them, forcing them to see him and begin their doom.

Mouse spoke to Jesse gently. "Everybody who has seen him has drowned."

"Everybody?"

"Usually sailors fall off the boat drunk into the sea, or people have fallen off the cliff for no reason."

Sam recalled all the unexplained apparent suicides off the cliffs and wanted to vomit. The acrid taste of bile spread through his sticky mouth like a plague. He resisted the urge to retch.

"I'm sure you'll be okay." Washing Machine looked up at Sam as he said this.

All humour was long gone. They all believed this quite sincerely. Jesse was shaking and the group looked at him.

"Nobody has ever seen him on the island though. That's fucked up. This is fucked up." Jesse looked up at Mouse as he spoke and then down at the Ouija board. "Why the fuck did you bring that thing? That's fucking stupid."

Jayo reached out to Jesse who was by now shaking uncontrollably. His hand touched the boy's knee and Jesse jerked away to his feet. His eyes were wide like a frightened rabbit – he was losing it.

"Jesse, calm down – nobody saw him." Jayo was firm.

Jesse looked at him sharply and his fear spread through them like a cloud. "I did. I thought that Sam was beside me all the time. I didn't look at him properly. It was just a figure, but I thought it was Sam."

There was silence. Even the wind stopped moving.

"What do you mean?" Jayo asked.

Jesse was talking faster and faster. "Sam wasn't with us. All the time we stopped here and Mouse took out the board and you were all in front of me I thought Sam was sitting beside me, but it wasn't him. Because then Sam came out of nowhere, and he came from my right."

"So what?"

Jesse could hardly speak he was shaking so much. His teeth chattered and his hands quivered violently as he indicated the blackness.

"The figure was to my left."

Chapter 21

Fear Breathes Madness

Sam screamed until his vocal chords strained like dried twigs about to snap in two. Jesse ran in front of him, a darting ducking weaving figure. Sam and Jayo raced side by side, the flickering flame from Jayo's torch giving just enough illumination to keep track of Jesse's desperate shadow. Jesse stumbled and in the moments it took him to regain his balance they were upon him like jackals. Jayo leapt forward first, grabbing his friend's arms behind his back and dropping his brand to the ground where it snuffed out. In momentary darkness, while their eyes adjusted to the sliver of light from the moon, there was a scrabble of motion and limbs. Sam reached out to help Jayo and Jesse's flailing foot smacked him on the side of the head. He went down hard, and came up dazed.

Jesse began screaming like a dying animal. It was so primal that it chilled Sam and he stood back, but Jayo held onto his friend with great conviction, eventually forcing him to his knees in a lock with his arms held behind him.

"Calm down, calm down." Jayo's voice was powerfully soothing. He spoke with an aggressive confidence as he pushed Jesse down roughly, letting him know that he wasn't able to physically move, but simultaneously placating him with his tone.

Jesse stopped howling and let Jayo take control of him.

"There you go, it's okay, it's okay."

Jesse began to inhale and exhale rapidly, like a panting dog, and Jayo looked at Sam sharply.

"He's going to have an attack – hold his legs."

"What?"

"Just hold his fucking legs!"

Sam grabbed Jesse's sandy ankles as Mouse and Washing Machine finally caught up with them. Mouse moved close with his torch so that they could see what was going on. Jesse was frothing at the mouth and his eyes rolled around his head like a dying horse.

"Gimme the fucking stick!" Jayo ordered.

Washing Machine picked up the brand Jayo had dropped and shoved it between Jesse's teeth to stop them biting down.

Sam looked away but held onto Jesse's legs tightly as they violently flapped about.

After what seemed an age Jesse let out a deep sigh and his body shivered and slumped. Jayo held onto him until he was certain he wasn't going to shake again, then he lowered him to the ground, cradling his head. His voice was soft.

"He hasn't had one of those in a while."

Washing Machine looked stunned. "He's quite religious, isn't he?"

"His uncle was a priest. His mum goes to Mass every

day. I never trust those religious-heads – they get too passionate about some shit."

"Yeah, it's odd, the whole religious thing. I mean, who knows, right?"

There was no appropriate response to that so nobody said anything.

The last few minutes had been a whirlwind. In the split seconds it took them all to realize what was going on Jesse had raced into the darkness screaming murderously about ghosts, not letting the Devil get to him, and chanting paragraphs from the Bible. Jayo had been the quickest to react and Sam had followed in his slipstream. All thoughts of the ghost and the Ouija board had dissipated as Jesse screamed about getting "the fuck off the island" and swimming home to go to Confession. Knowing that Jesse wasn't a strong swimmer and would most certainly get swept out to sea with the current had propelled the other two boys frantically forward and they had caught him just as he had reached the far sea.

Now, with a momentary respite, the absurdity of the situation hit them all. Washing Machine slumped to his knees and Mouse looked sheepish.

"I left it there."

"Left what?" Jayo replied.

"You know, the board . . ."

"Leave it."

"It's not mine."

"Just fucking leave it, you gobshite!" Jayo was in no mood to be trifled with.

"It's not mine, it's my brother's."

No one responded to him and Mouse gazed wistfully back where they had come from, deep in the middle of the island's undergrowth.

"Then go get it if you care about it," Sam said under his breath.

"Anybody want to come with me?" Mouse asked.

Nobody looked at him.

"It's fine. He can get another one. It's all bullshit anyway." Jayo was getting angry.

Sam looked up. "What do you mean? It's not real?"

"No. Of course it's not."

"But I saw the piece move." Sam looked at Mouse – had he been lying?

Mouse didn't answer and Jayo shot them all a look to indicate that the conversation was over. "Let's get back to the fire."

Sam nodded and gingerly wiped the sand off his face where Jesse's boot had hit him.

The dawn began to quietly break over the horizon and the lads waited impatiently for Sam to finish the rigging of the boat so that they could get home as quickly as possible. It wasn't yet six so there was still a good chance that they would make it back to their beds before their parents even knew that they had been gone. A brisk wind began to pick up from the east with the tide, strong enough to carry them back at a good pace.

Jesse sat alone on the rocks a few yards away the group. He had gradually risen from his fit, vomited and since then had been very quiet.

The embers of the fire still smoked sporadically until Mouse walked over and trampled them deeper into the blackened sands.

Sam pushed the little boat out into the sea once everybody was on board, pulled in the mainsail and the dinghy began to stumble through the water. Each was lost in his own thoughts.

The night had been cold. Washing Machine shivered in his wet shoes and Jesse looked as grey as the clouds filling the packed sky overhead.

The boat pulled away from the island and, once she was on a solid beam reach, Sam looked back over his shoulder. The sickle shape of the beach made it a perfect tourist spot, with the north side protected by the cliffs, and the natural bay protected by the jut of the rocks on the east and west sides. He wondered what else had taken place on that beach over the years, what stories had taken place that were far more disturbing than a few boys and their superstitions.

There was a tower on one end of the island that they hadn't explored that night. It was a remnant from the Viking invasions hundreds of years ago, and it had been a great vantage point to espy attempted sorties of bloodthirsty Scandinavians. It had long since been blocked up by the authorities after a fire had made the inside too dangerous to enter and, with little rational reason to renovate it, the tower had stood firm but desolate on the far corner. Maybe that was where the ghost had lived. In the breaking light of day such thoughts seemed childish but, as he turned back to guide the craft towards the harbour, Sam couldn't help but feel like something was watching him. He resisted the urge to turn back and kept his focus on the little boat's taut sail.

When they had dragged the little vessel safely up the slipway, they sat on the wall and lit some cigarettes. There was something desperately melancholic about the whole affair, like the last vestiges of a funeral. It reminded Sam of when he had come across the lads sitting on the wall after the suicide, only this time he was involved. He perversely took some pleasure in this. He duly accepted a cigarette and looked down at his feet, simply so that he wouldn't have to look anywhere else. But covertly he watched the others. Washing Machine picked at a lump on the side of his neck. Jayo pursed his lips in sombre reflection then he finished whatever he was thinking about, tossed the butt into the water below and stood up. The others rose in unison and they gradually filtered off back home.

Back on the road, Sam nodded to Jesse but he hardly acknowledged him as he went into his house, head bowed. Jayo lived closest to Sam and they walked side by side in silence to the mouth of the cul de sac where Jayo's house was. Jayo nodded to Sam at the corner with a masculinity that was not affectionate, but firm, an indication of acceptance. This was what Sam had imagined might have happened between them all after the dead body and he couldn't suppress a tingling feeling of elation at having joined the lads in some sort of emotional bonding. It didn't matter that all hell had broken loose, or that they might have disturbed some crazed ghost – at least he had been a part of it and more than anything else that was worth something.

Watching Jayo wander home, Sam scuffed his shoe against the curb with a sigh, not wanting to go inside and end the night. He looked around him, more for something to do than for any specific reason. A fox slipped out of the hedgerow and darted silently across the path towards the forest, giving him a dismissive glance along the way. Everywhere looked different in the soft morning light, like a televised dream. When he realized that nothing was going to happen apart from the odd bird drifting lazily across the sky he made his way inside. He was careful not to wake his parents, taking great precautions not to let the door groan or the floorboards creak, which he achieved successfully by stepping on the sides of the stairs balancing on his toes.

Once inside his room he collapsed onto his bed exhausted and had barely pulled the duvet over his body before he had fallen into a deep sleep.

Chapter 22

Moving and Changing

"I was quite worried. I thought that he might die."

"Okay..."

"I felt elation for a moment, and then I felt guilty."

"Why did you feel guilty?"

"Because it was exciting."

"Was there a part of you that wanted him to die?"

Silence. Then there was a shifting of uncomfortable buttocks, a shuffling of claustrophobic feet.

"I didn't want him to die, of course not, but I wanted... I can't say."

"Go on, take your time, I actually understand what you mean."

"You do?"

Sam looked at Don hopefully. He could feel tears in his eyes. He hadn't understood the feelings that he had experienced that night, the sense of belonging on the sail home. He had awoken to a slight depression, the aftermath of an event that you wished would never end. It made no sense – Jesse would actually have been on the brink of death if he'd had that fit while swimming, which was apparently a distinct possibility as he had somberly announced to the lads on Sunday evening.

Jayo had stayed with Jesse by the slope area for hours that evening, not talking, the two of them just sitting side by side. Sam didn't understand and desperately wanted to be included, yearned for Jesse to confide in him. It was obvious that he wasn't welcome though so he had left with Washing Machine and Mouse, neither of whom seemed to care that much.

Now that he was sitting in Don's office, explaining what had ailed him in class with Mr Cusack, he found the story just gushing out, and when it manifested itself verbally he was ashamed.

"It's a natural reaction," Don said gently. "I'm not saying it's something that you should crave, or be entirely comfortable with, but being able to understand it is very important."

"Why?"

"Why what?"

"Why is it important to understand? Am I not simply a bad person?"

Don stood up languidly. He never expended any unnecessary energy – every movement was certain and economical. His loose frame moved in front of Sam and he looked down at him.

Sam averted his eyes. His palms were sweaty, his body numb.

Don reached down and grasped his shoulders, pulling him to his feet. Then he hugged him. Sam didn't respond and Don just held him. Then the tears flowed. Sam didn't understand what they meant, or where they came from, but he couldn't stop the tide once it swept outwards. Don's smoky frame felt comforting. He felt safe, if a little embarrassed that such a small human gesture as a hug was making him feel that way. It was the closest that he ever physically been to Don and it made him a little uncomfortable.

Don patted his head, stood back and went back to his sitting position. He just knew things, that wily old Jesuit. Without looking at Sam, he took out a cigar and began to light it. His heavy thumbs handled the cigar with a rough dexterity and Sam found himself focusing on the movements avidly, subconsciously removing himself from the situation.

Don looked at the wall and indicated a black-and-white photograph. It was of two young men smiling by a canoe. It could have been Don but much younger, maybe early twenties.

"That's my brother and me. He was eighteen when he died."

"I didn't know. I'm sorry."

"Thank you. At first I hated him. All the attention from the family went to him. Everybody kept recalling his achievements, how wonderful he was, how he was essentially the perfect son. Nobody seemed to recall how he was a complete tear-away and very selfish. I had hated him for that."

Sam shifted his hands, unclenching them and putting them respectfully on his knees, palms down. Hearing another person open up made him remarkably self-conscious and he wanted to project the correct body posture. He wasn't sure why he did this, it just happened naturally.

Don continued. "The thing was that I didn't hate him per se. I actually adored him, but he never gave me that adoration back and I hated him for that lack. Looking back I now see that he never did anything wrong – he was too young to understand that I might have needed his affection back. When he died I was angry at how nobody gave me any attention. I kept getting good grades but my parents hardly noticed. So I deliberately stopped working and my marks slipped. They still didn't notice. Without Matthew their world had been turned upside-down and nothing else was important any more. So I did the only thing I could to get their attention. I tried to kill myself."

Sam nearly fell off his chair in shock and he had to close his mouth tightly to stop it lewdly hanging open. He stopped breathing, trying to figure out the correct response to this information.

"It's okay – you don't have to be so tense." Don looked at Sam and smiled gently to reassure him. The smoke was beginning to fill the room again, and the smell was soothing.

"I didn't get the reaction I expected. My parents knew it was an attention-seeking mechanism, and my father was disappointed in me. That was worse than anything. I realized then that I just wanted to be loved, and accepted, and all my actions were geared towards that."

"Is that why you became a priest then?"

Don chuckled, a deep throaty laugh that reverberated in his throat and vibrated down his chest. "No, no, no. I finished school and went travelling, and whilst traversing the Pyrenees I met a woman, this incredible Spanish girl.

We went to Africa together to help with a charity distributing aid, rebuilding villages, volunteering. I found myself wanting to understand people. There was a missionary there, a wonderful man who told me about God. He was a Jesuit. We spoke every day, and when I finally came back to Ireland I knew there was something missing so I joined. She wasn't very happy!"

Don laughed again, and Sam relaxed and laughed with him. A smile creased Don's face and the joy was infectious.

"Don't tell anybody. I never told the others about the girl part."

Sam nodded. He felt elated. Don had shared something important with him – he had given him something priceless and intangible, a very important truth. He trusted Don now more than ever. He knew that had been Don's intention but he loved him for it.

Neither said anything for a moment and Don slowly smoked. Sam knew that it was time for him to continue.

"I guess that's all I wanted, to be included. To have an event to bond me with them."

"You can't force something like that – it will either happen or it won't, and if it doesn't it's simply not meant to be."

"I know." He didn't really know, but he wanted to pretend that he did. He was young, the here and now was everything, the future was unfathomable. He carried on. "I didn't really want anything bad to happen, but because I partly did I feel so guilty. How could I wish something negative on another person for my own gain?"

"You didn't. You had an instinct, a survival instinct, because you knew what would drive you closer into the bosom of the group. In times of strife and hardship or extreme events the strongest bonds are formed. Sometimes these bonds are unbreakable. But the bonds formed over time through genuine warmth and trust are just as important."

Sam nodded passively – he was drifting deep into his own thoughts again. The pigeon by the window was watching him with its head cocked to one side. How often did pigeons experience life and death? Every day most likely – and did those experiences bond them closer together or did it mean nothing to them? Maybe if it was an everyday occurrence it ceased to have any effect.

"You're drifting again. I'll have to get a cat for those pesky pigeons." Don was examining him quietly.

Sam smiled and felt grateful for Don.

Chapter 23

The Benefits of Detention

The cathartic conversation with Don that morning had assuaged Sam's guilt completely and he felt content again. He scratched himself absentmindedly as he watched Mr Dwyer teach another rudimentary history lesson that was only made mildly interesting by his obsession with constantly changing coloured markers to emphasize each point. If Sam squinted his eyes at just the right angle the board looked like a multicoloured rainbow. He was doing this when Mr Dwyer looked at him.

"What are you doing?" Mr Dwyer raised his hands in exasperation.

"What, huh, nothing?"

"If you can't see the board then maybe you should move closer to the front?"

Sam hated sitting at the front because it seemed so exposed. He liked his corner by the window where he could rest at an angle against the sill and let his mind drift away with the birds that flitted from rooftop to rooftop.

"Sorry, sir, I was just trying to see."

Sam's tone was conciliatory but Mr Dwyer had the bit between his teeth and wasn't going to let go. He had been getting a harder time than usual off every teacher, which he knew must be because after the Mr Cusack incident he was being marked out.

"Come sit up the front and swap with John."

"I'm okay – I can see now."

"You clearly can't so come sit up here, please."

"I really don't want to, sir."

Mr Dywer glared at him so Sam reluctantly got up and swapped with John who was equally irritated at having to move.

Sam was now directly in Mr Dwyer's eyeline.

"It's probably best if you sit there for the rest of your classes this year, so you don't have any problems with your eyesight again. I'll mention it to the rest of your teachers."

"Yes, sir."

Mercifully the bell rang shortly afterwards and Sam began gathering his things to leave. John came back to swap seats and looked at him.

"You still banned from Cusko's class?"

"Yeah."

"For how long?"

"Dunno."

"Cool. Can I keep my seat for the other classes? I like sitting up here."

"Yeah, course. And tell Dwyer you wanna stay up here and maybe he'll let me sit at the back again."

Why somebody would want to sit at the front of the class was beyond Sam but that's what John wanted.

The next class was Mr Cusack so Sam was trying to leave before he entered. Unfortunately he ran into him at the door, almost knocking the books out of his hand. Cusko stared at him and Sam averted his eyes.

"Sorry, sir." He was on thin ice.

Mr Cusack nodded. "Can you wait outside, please, Sam, and I will come out and talk to you in a moment."

"Okay."

Sam waited for almost five minutes outside the door as Cusko gave the class an assignment, then the door opened and the irritating gangly frame of his adversary appeared.

Cusko closed the door behind him and stood facing him with his arms crossed.

"I don't want to continue this feud, Sam." His voice was steady and superior.

"Neither do I, sir."

"But I can't have you challenging my authority or speaking to me with the disrespect you have been showing."

"I understand, sir."

"I want you to get a good education and get good grades this year. You're lucky it's not your Leaving Cert year or you'd be a long way behind."

"Yes, sir."

"You need to pull your socks up and start working if you're going to catch up."

It was hard to respect somebody who said 'pull your socks up'.

"Sam?"

Mr Cusack was staring at him.

"Yes, sir."

"Are you going to pull your socks up?"

"Yep."

"Okay. Good."

There was an uncomfortable silence between them for a moment as if neither knew what to say.

Mr Cusack broke it. "I appreciated your apology note."

"I am sorry. I was having a hard few weeks."

"We don't have to be in conflict, Sam. I am your teacher but I can also be your friend."

Sam looked at him. Was he being serious? It appeared that he was. This was awkward.

"Yeah, I'd like that, sir."

"This all started when yourself and Daniel were going to meet those girls – that's when you and I first started having issues. You've always been a good student and I see a lot of potential in you."

This was getting way too pally for Sam's liking. What the fuck did Don say to him to make him act this way? It must have been Don's doing. Goddamit.

"I guess," was all that Sam could muster.

"So what happened?"

"With what, sir?"

"Those girls? Did it work out, were they cute?"

Fuck, he really wanted to go there. Sam had no idea how to respond.

"It was fine. Yeah, they were."

"I thought they must be. Daniel hasn't been in school much, so it must be a girl."

He was actually right. Despite being a complete twat Cusko was actually right about Daniel. Maybe he wasn't such an eejit after all.

"I would never have missed school for a girl though when I was your age."

No, he was still a complete eejit.

"Right, course not. Study is more important, sir."

"Exactly. Okay, you can rejoin my class now."

Sam nodded and moved to go inside but Mr Cusack was holding his hand out for him to shake.

Sam took it and Cusko stared at him.

"Friends now, no more rivalry. We are both dominant males – let's respect each other."

There was nothing Sam could say back to that without being mocking, so he smiled weakly and went back to the most boring class on the syllabus. He had been sort of enjoying his exile. Ah well.

The only positive about having detention for two weeks running was that because the days were getting longer it was still bright when he began the walk back down to the bus stop and he had his homework already done before he got home. There was nothing more disheartening than leaving school to a sheet of rain against the backdrop of quivering black gloom, and still knowing that you had work to do.

As he passed the council flats he adopted his perfected gait of aggressive agitation. A few edgy-looking boys walked past him too close for comfort, but he held his ground. The nearest brushed his shoulder and Sam held his breath. Then they were gone. He had never deviated off course and kept his head held straight. He was proud of himself.

"Hey, Sam!"

He froze. He knew that voice, those dulcet tones that had so captivated him. He didn't want to turn around. His body began to disobey him.

"I didn't expect to see you here!" he exclaimed, turning in a painful circle.

Smiling tightly, he was now face to face with Antoinette. She looked beautiful.

"Yeah, well, I'm here," she said, stating the obvious.

"Yeah, true, wow, so how you are? Jeez . . . ?"

He had no idea what to say and his smile hid the inane thoughts floating around belligerently inside his skull.

"I'm great, thanks – you looked a bit intense dere – bad day?"

"Oh no, that's just what I –" He caught himself before he came out with it, realizing just how ridiculous he would sound. "Yeah, I had detention so it was a rough day."

He cleared his throat because it was drying up quickly. He needed a glass of water. Or a kiss, a kiss from her would help. He stared at her. She had such gorgeous lips. He forgave her – right then he would forgive her anything – it didn't matter any more. Why was she on this side of the city, and next to his school? Had she come to see him? She must have. He moved closer to her.

"Hey, man!"

A figure appeared to Sam's right and he reluctantly tore his eyes off the most beautiful girl in the world to see who it was.

"Daniel?"

"Still called the same name, yes," Daniel replied in good spirits.

It took him a few moments to begin to put it all together, and when he did it took him even longer to actually assimilate it properly as a potential reality. It was only when Daniel took Antoinette's hand in his own possessively that it was confirmed in the literal world. She at least had the grace to seem embarrassed and shook his hand away gently, prising his fingers off with a little twist.

"Right, so you two, together, that's great, but what, you know, what about, em, what was her name?" Sam was trying not to freak out even though Daniel was touching the love of his life.

"Catriona?" Daniel looked awkward.

"Yeah, sure, Catriona, that was her name."

Daniel shook his head. "Catriona and Antoinette aren't friends any more."

It was odd how everything that needed to be said was explained in that simple sentence. There didn't need to be an extended commentary on why the girls were no longer on speaking terms, nor for that matter why Sam and Daniel didn't speak the same way any more. Mr Cusack was also far more prescient than he appeared, as judging from their casual clothes and Daniel's lack of appearance in today's class, it was easy to pinpoint the precise correlation. Daniel was skipping class because of a girl . . . only for Sam, and maybe for Catriona, it was the wrong girl.

"We were just going to go get a burger or something and then go play pool, if you want to come?" said Daniel.

"With the two of you?"

"Well, yeah, there's nobody else here."

Sam was tempted to make a smart remark but held his tongue.

Before he could answer Antoinette interjected, "I need te run to de toilet."

He suddenly found her accent very irritating. It was so common he frowned. She saw the face he made and gave him a quizzical look before moving off to a pub to use the bathroom.

Daniel watched her appreciatively, his eyes devouring

her. Sam waited until he turned back to him. He was so oblivious, Sam thought, or he didn't give a fuck.

"So, you and her, that's, well, great."

"Yeah. Ah man, she's so fucking gorgeous. We've been having sex almost every day – we skip school and go to my house, then before my parents get back we come into town so it looks like we've just come back from school."

"That's very clever of you."

Daniel nodded like an excitable dog. He clearly had nobody to share this magical experience with, and either didn't understand or didn't care why Sam would be uncomfortable. The first time a boy has sex with a girl is supposed to be life-changing, but it almost negated the impact if nobody knew about it. Sam wasn't going to let him boast about it. Fuck him.

"You haven't been in school much, I've noticed," was all he could muster.

"Yeah – I was gonna ask you for the notes."

"Of course you were."

Daniel suddenly looked shocked, as if he had been hit with some eureka moment.

"Shit, this is a bit weird for you, isn't it?"

Sam laughed despite himself. "A little . . . yeah."

"I'm sorry, I should have called you."

"No, you shouldn't have called – you just shouldn't have started seeing her in the first place." He smiled casually at Daniel, surprising himself with his searing honesty.

Daniel's expression hardened. "What are you talking about?"

"You know what I'm talking about. I was kissing her, and then she didn't turn up for me – nothing to do with you, I imagine?"

"No, of course not."

Sam shrugged his shoulders.

"You think that I had something to do with her standing you up that day?"

"Well, didn't you?"

"No, of course not."

"So how come you knew all about it?"

"We would talk. Catriona would tell me anyway."

"Right, and then it just happened that after this girl stood up and embarrassed your best friend you just happened to kiss her and then just happened to have sex with her?"

Daniel shook his head and did the only thing possible to deflect from his own imperfection. "You don't get it, you're still quite immature. It's cool."

"What?"

"When you meet a girl and manage to actually have sex with her you'll understand."

Sam wanted to hit him and Daniel knew it so he took a slight step back and tensed up, waiting for the blow. It never came. All the emotion of the experience with Antoinette came flooding back at Sam, and he didn't know whether to laugh or cry.

Antoinette re-emerged at precisely the best or worst moment and the spell was broken.

"What's goin' on wit ye two?"

Daniel moved to her quickly, giving her a kiss on the lips that she half turned away from.

"Nothing, babe, just having a chat."

"Are ya gonna come te get some food wit us den, Sam?"

Sam answered before Daniel could. "I've got better things to do. I have to get home and do some homework.

Got exams coming up and I don't want to fail." Daniel ignored the barb and Sam continued. "I would give you those notes, Daniel, but I don't think that you'd understand them – too mature for you."

It wasn't the greatest riposte – the last part was an extension too far – but it got the message across.

Before either of them could say goodbye Sam turned and strode off, quickly adopting his indignant walk. He really hated her accent actually, and her nose was far too small for her face – it made her look like a bland china doll. She wouldn't be good-looking when she got older, he reasoned happily.

The bus was on time, which was nice – it continued the rapidly changing effects life was having on his reflected mood today. A pretty girl walking past him for the next bus gave him a darting smile that helped mollify his anger, but no sooner had his rage ameliorated than he saw them.

Barry, Darren and Greg. They saw him at the same time, and they waved sarcastically. It was the last thing that he needed.

"You don't catch any breaks with Cusko, do you? Two weeks of detention?" Greg's tone was cheerily amused as always.

Sam smiled back tightly. "We seem to have differences of opinion."

"Sounds like it, alright."

The bus arrived and they all filed on, with Sam inadvertently finding himself at the centre of their little group. He moved with the tide of their movements to the back of the bus and with relief remembered that the other schools wouldn't be getting on today as it was a much later bus than the usual one. The trio wouldn't be as driven to humiliate him without an audience, he hoped.

"Why are you three getting the later bus? You weren't in detention."

Darren smirked at him and opened a packet of Maltesers, popping a few into his mouth with a loud smack. "We go play snooker some days. Greg's dad gets us free membership to this private place."

It was amazing how such a simple response could have such a degrading effect. It basically informed Sam that he wasn't hip enough to have partaken in such a cool social activity and couldn't get into a private-members club. A wave of red mist began to flush over him, but as always happened around these three his brain froze up and he couldn't think of anything to say. He turned and looked out the window, deciding to ignore them.

It worked. The bus journey passed uneventfully. The three boys drifted into their own thoughts and a less than stimulating conversation. It was as if Sam's lack of interest and the paucity of any audience bored them.

When they got off Greg actually gave Sam a nod, and he nodded back quickly, immediately irritated at himself for capitulating so easily and being friendly.

It was still bright when he got home and his mother was in a good mood. They had an engaging meal and Sam's spirits lifted again. A new family had moved in today only a few doors up the road, with the prime source of interest according to his father being a striking brunette precisely Sam's age. His father seemed especially interested in Sam meeting this girl – maybe he thought it would calm down his recent rebellious activity. The new family had already come by to introduce themselves but Sam had missed them because he'd been late home.

He took a wander later that evening, hoping for a quick peek at this new girl, but the curtains were pulled and the lights off. The moving van was still outside, so they obviously weren't settled yet.

He went to bed early, his thoughts jumbled again – would he now be fighting the affections of the lads for a brunette girl on his own street? His street had always been frequented solely by boys – there were no girls their age who hung around. This could change the dynamic. Life was getting complicated.

Chapter 24

Thou Shalt Not Steal and Get Caught

Jayo was getting stranger without question. The events of the past few weeks were visibly affecting his behaviour. He had always worn an introverted almost philosophically violent air about him but now he had taken to attending Mass every second evening with Jesse, something that he had never previously done. Seeking solace in religion hadn't made a difference to his mood, however, and he was becoming distant and irritable which made Sam uncomfortable. The general vibe between the lads was now one of distinct unease, as if some sort of calamitous event was inexorably approaching.

They had stopped playing football entirely because Jayo and Jesse weren't in the mood any more, both seemingly devoid of energy in homage to their melancholy. Instead, whenever Sam joined them after school lately they would huddle behind a broken-off section of wall nearer the top of lane where the woods were at their deepest and smoke for hours on end without really saying anything. The area here was far more claustrophobic than the slope area, and seemed to exacerbate the depressed mood.

Sam had always wanted to be accepted in the group, and now when he finally felt a part of it he was bored and unhappy. As a group they had always been prone to just hanging around aimlessly but now they did even less than before. He remembered reading about some pattern that develops in teenagers after puberty where alcohol, suppressed sexual desires and loner tendencies would manifest as a precursor to social deviancy.

They did go to the slope one evening later that week and Washing Machine proffered an idea about a new way of making a swing from some planks nailed to the tree and a new rope, or even using a branch even higher up, but it fell on disinterested ears and instead they just lay there smoking and carving their initials in the bark of the tree. Jesse was smoking less and less but only because everything he did had a depressively languid air and he simply moved about less. At one point he sat up suddenly and stared out into the distance, and Jayo reacted almost immediately, like a loyal dog poised and alert. Sam waited impatiently for Jesse to say what had caught his attention, maybe something profound that would jolt them out of this turgid cycle, fucking anything really, but he just squinted, shook his head and then lay back down. After a minute he began to cry, tears drifting down his cheeks in lazy patterns. Jayo clasped his hand and he stopped. Then they left abruptly.

Sam suddenly found himself alone with Mouse and Washing Machine, and the silence was deafening. They had never been alone, just the three of them before, and there was no precedent as to how they should behave. Sam felt an unexpected urge to go and study for his summer exams.

Washing Machine interrupted his thoughts. "Want to go rob something?"

Washing Machine had at least offered an activity. Neither Mouse nor Sam could think of any viable alternative so they got to their feet and strolled down to the shops. At least it got them moving. Everything caught their attention along the way – things always got more exciting when summer was approaching. They momentarily paused at various intervals to scratch a telephone pole with Washing Machine's knife, fling some rocks at a passing cat or at one stage even retie Mouse's laces. It was incredible the lengths that apathetic boredom would drive one to.

They finally stood across the street from the local shop, a ramshackle little trio on a mission.

"Who's gonna go first?" Washing Machine asked.

"Are we taking turns?" Sam responded.

"Dunno. I guess."

They hadn't thought much about what it was they were actually going to do, let alone who would go first, last or not at all. There wasn't exactly a plan. Without Jayo to lead them or approve of an idea, they all seemed a little lost.

Sam spoke up. "What are we going to rob, and why?"

The other two sniffed at him for trying to formulate a plan, the chance to denigrate him giving them sufficient cause to bond, and so the hierarchy was formed, two against one. It meant that Sam was now going to be doing whatever it was they were going to be doing.

"The football magazine. Let's get that," said Mouse.

"Which football magazine?"

"The big one, the one with free stickers 'n' shit, who cares what it's called."

"Okay, fine, whatever."

"You know which one?"

"I guess. It doesn't matter anyway."

"The one with the free stickers."

"Okay."

There wasn't any rational reason to try and steal this particular magazine – it was simply a point of interest. Robbing a magazine meant the stickers that came with it were 'free' anyway.

Sam entered the shop as casually as possible while his two comrades-in-arms stood outside the shop watching as casually as possible, which made them very conspicuous. He nodded to the two shop assistants, trying to appear boring as possible so they wouldn't notice that he was there, like a lizard thinking it was camouflaged because it wasn't moving. What a stupid thought. He picked up a different magazine, something about home improvement, and began reading it to throw them off the scent of his end goal, not that they could possibly know what it was. He looked back and saw the lads watching. The audience made it more difficult. He felt a pressure now rather than his usual air of detachment. His fingers were sweaty and they left wet smears on the pages. He put the magazine down and moved to another one, moving closer to the target – he could see the free stickers stuck to the front of the magazine like a bright colourful beacon. He looked back towards the lads and saw that they were openly staring at him without any concealment. It was painfully clear what was happening but Sam couldn't back down now.

One of the assistants noticed Washing Machine and gave him a look but Washing Machine ignored him and kept staring at Sam. Sam finally picked up the magazine of choice and fondled it carefully like it was fragile and alive. The pages felt sticky and heavy under his fingertips. He looked back at the lads once more and Mouse gave him a thumbs-up. He was a lamb for the slaughter and he couldn't do anything about it. Holding the magazine behind him, he turned and looked at the counter. They were busy serving other customers. He didn't know what to do. Should he just walk out clutching the magazine, should he pay for it and just pretend to rob it, or should he place it under his jumper and buy some chewing gum so that it would throw them off the scent?

"What are you doing?" a voice asked from behind him.

He turned sharply and found the imposing figure of the shop owner, a friend of his father's, staring at him. He tried to remember his name but couldn't.

"What do you mean?"

The owner indicated the magazine with his eyes. "That. You gonna steal it?"

"No. I'm gonna buy it."

"We have cameras here – you would have got caught."

Sam stood there, dumbfounded. He looked out the window again and saw Washing Machine gesticulating wildly to get out quickly. The lads couldn't hear what was being said.

The owner glanced at them covertly and seemed to realize what was happening. He kept his back to them and focused on Sam. "I'm going to turn my back, so you should wait a moment, and then walk out, son." His tone was warm.

Sam stared at him in utter bewilderment.

The owner's mouth creased with the hint of a smile as he began to act as if preoccupied with some shelves beside him. "I was fifteen once – a long time ago, but I was, so I'm going to help you out. A one-time deal, okay?"

Sam nodded meekly. This was far more degrading than being caught in the open. The shop owner, Gerry was his name he recalled, turned so that his back was to him. Sam hesitated, acutely aware that it could be a ruse, that the minute he walked out the door he would feel Gerry's rough hands around his collar. Then Gerry inclined his head slightly to him, and winked.

Sam nodded and walked out the door, the magazine clutched so hard that his knuckles were white from the pressure.

Exiting the shop, he turned sharply around the corner into Washing Machine's waiting arms. Washing Machine clapped him on the back and laughed, taking the magazine off him. Mouse kept staring back at the shop, as if he was hoping for somebody to come out and catch Sam. He seemed disappointed when nobody did.

"Good job, that was cool!" said Washing Machine. "I thought that you were gonna bottle it when that guy saw you."

"Yeah, I just waited for him to turn away."

"Ya got balls of steel."

"Thanks."

Sam turned to Mouse who took the magazine off Washing Machine and ripped the stickers off.

"This is the wrong one," he said.

Sam gave him a look. "Well, it's your turn next – you go get the one you want, or are you too chicken to do it?"

He made a grab for the stickers but Mouse put them in his pocket and then looked over Sam's shoulder back to the shop as if he saw some incoming activity.

"Shit, we should get outta here in case they realize," he said.

"Quick, run!" Washing Machine agreed.

They both took off and Sam followed – not having any reason to run didn't lessen the illicit excitement that coursed through his body. He even found himself semi-convinced that he had robbed the mag. After all he had kept it pretty well concealed under his arm, and he was a very cool figure. It was more fun to believe that he had robbed it if only because it allowed him to keep up the façade with the lads.

They made it to the pier front, panting from their exertions, but in better spirits for having done something illegal. They sat down on a wall overlooking the sea and Washing Machine took out some cigarettes and a small plastic packet with tiny white tablets. He opened the packet and put one on his tongue, balancing it on the tip then swallowing it. He held the packet out to Mouse who took one and then passed it on to Sam.

Sam held the packet in his hand.

"Are you going to take one or not?" Mouse needled.

"What is it?"

Washing Machine grunted, taking the packet back and putting one of the tablets into Sam's outstretched palm. "It's just a pill. Gets you happy, that's all."

"You don't have to take it if you don't want to."

Mouse looked at him, and after a pause Sam put the pill on his tongue and closed his mouth. He was becoming accepted so if he wanted to cement his place now was the time.

It was an odd thing to do – fake swallowing drugs. The others didn't notice – why would they? Sam sat there a moment until they weren't looking, then he turned his head to the side and gently pushed the pill out of the side of his mouth into his hand. It hadn't really dissolved that much but he still felt a bit odd. He had no idea what effect the pill would have but just the idea that he had taken something mind-altering made him feel impaired. He sat with them for a while, trying to pretend like he was enjoying the experience, then he suddenly felt uncomfortable and abruptly got up. They looked at him lazily.

"I'm going home," he announced.

Mouse giggled and ignored him. Washing Machine was already falling into a trance-like state and he just raised his hand in salute.

Sam nodded and walked off, hands in his pockets, clutching the pill tightly. Once he was out of sight he dropped it into the first gutter that he saw.

He took his time going back home and had just reached the entrance to the road when he saw movement up the road at the new girl's house. Her father, he assumed, was clearing out the front of the removal van. Sam walked past his own house and sat down on the wall a few yards away, observing and trying to figure out if he should do anything – go over and introduce himself perhaps. He was so completely lost in his thoughts that he didn't realize he was staring until the man coughed loudly. He was looking directly at him questioningly. Sam hadn't done anything wrong but when an adult directly or indirectly questioned his behaviour he invariably felt improper no matter what the circumstances. He pretended to be interested in the weather and scanned the sky for clouds.

Sam was painfully aware of the vague aftertaste of the pill on his tongue, which may have explained why he was staring so intently. It might have affected him just enough to cause him to subconsciously drift. He got to his feet as smoothly as possible, trying to make his movements sleek which made them even stiffer, and walked in the opposite direction to his house, deciding to take the long way home so he didn't have to pass the man. He could feel the man's eyes boring into his back like a steady pressing into his spine until he was hidden from sight by the slope of the road. Then he relaxed his bunched-up shoulders and took deep gulps of air all the way home to ensure he was fully sober. He wasn't sure why he did this but it seemed to help.

He wondered how long Washing Machine and Mouse would sit there. Should he have stayed? Without Jayo there seemed little reason to hang out with them. He felt very alone. Without the lads or Daniel he didn't have anybody to really talk to. He began to look forward to his appointment with Don next week: it would at least give him somebody to talk to. It was Saturday tomorrow and he needed to think of something to do – it didn't seem like the lads would be doing anything. Maybe there would be something good on telly, and he always had his football match – that would pass some time.

Chapter 25

Fresh as a Daisy

"I'm Sam."

"Fran. It's short for Francesca. Francesca Baker."

It was Saturday morning and Sam had been walking to the shops because he had nothing better to do when he had walked past her driveway and she was standing there. They had caught each other's eye at the same time and said hi.

Sam could think of nothing to say beyond his name. He realized that he was smiling at her stupidly. So he stopped. Then realized he was just staring. She was very pretty. Sam found every girl pretty, each one was fascinating. Girls just looked different – their eyes had a nicer shape, their lips were juicier, their hips appearing to slot into their bodies like dancers and when they giggled it was like music, not the rough uncouth sound boys made which usually coincided with a fart.

He tried to make small talk. "So . . . you live here?"

"Well, yeah."

"Me too."

She shook her head and pushed him back gently with the palm of her hand against his chest. "You don't have to stand so close."

"Shit, yeah, sorry, I mean – fuck!" He had been moving closer to her all the time without noticing.

She giggled then, a soft sound much like a stream happily gurgling down a gentle mountain, all cascading bubbles and reflected sunshine.

"Well, thanks for introducing yourself. I'm sure that we'll bump into each other if we live on the same street."

There was an awkward moment where they both just stood there so Sam simply nodded and turned out of her driveway.

"It was nice to meet you!" she called out.

Sam looked back and she waved. He watched her for a brief moment and wondered if she was as nervous as him. She couldn't hold his gaze and she shifted her weight from one foot to the other and wrung her hands in front of her, having the effect of making her seem a little shy. This made him feel better. He smiled back at her, his skin stretching against his teeth. He was suddenly aware of how unnatural his smile felt. It was like when you stopped and thought about breathing, and it became difficult and almost worrying how hard it was, until you forgot about it again and it just happened. He was still smiling like a weirdo psycho when she went inside and closed the door. He walked a short distance until he was out of sight and then sat down on the opposite side of the road.

He began to replay in his mind every last detail of the interaction, how she had responded, what she might have meant. There wasn't a lot to analyze from such a short conversation. He had thought that after his experiences with Antoinette he would either know exactly how to act, or that he would be scarred for a long time. He felt neither. He just felt blank and clueless, as if he had learned nothing about girls.

It was a weekend and it was sunny so he got to his feet, and scuffing his runners against the concrete a few times to keep their compulsory lived-in look, he ambled towards the village.

How would he meet Fran again? What if she never walked past his house, or they came back from school at different times? Or if he was never outside when she was? It seemed so obvious that they'd meet again as she lived on the same street, but he never saw any of the other neighbours who lived between them – just saw their cars in the driveway which indicated that they were home or not. This was worrying.

As fate would have it Sam bumped into Francesca only days later. She was coming back from school in her uniform late in the afternoon and he was casually dressed which gave him a slight feeling of superiority. They passed each other in the laneway, both waiting until the last possible moment to acknowledge each other's presence, those fifty yards before you actually walked into somebody being so interminable. She blushed, and he saw it so he immediately felt empowered.

Sufficiently emboldened, he asked her if she wanted to join him.

"Where are you going?"

He wasn't actually going anywhere, he realized – he had been running an errand to the shop for his mother. Without the lads to hang out with, he'd been hanging around at home more often after school. This week his mother suddenly seemed to have numerous errands for him to run, which was frustrating. It almost felt like she wanted him out of the house.

Fran was looking at him so he answered before his silence became weird.

"I was just going to go and hang out by the pier."

"And do what?"

He blinked. She smiled.

"Let me go home and change. I'm a bit sweaty in my uniform."

"Okay."

She looked at him, a little insecure. "You do want me to come join you, right?"

Sam wanted nothing more in the world right now. "Fuck, yeah! I mean, sure, if you want?"

"I do. Okay, cool. I'll be five minutes."

He nodded as nonchalantly as possible and leaned against a tree to wait for her. She walked quickly up the lane, glancing back over her shoulder once and then disappeared into the belly of the street.

The tree he was leaning on had numerous little bumps and nubs digging into his back so once she was out of sight he looked for a better tree to lean on. It had to be close to this one in case she didn't see him and thought he had left. There didn't appear to be any trees of sufficient comfort nearby so he just stood there, sucking in his stomach for better posture.

He was in the process of dislodging a particularly sticky lump of snot from his nose when she appeared beside him. She had been much longer than five minutes, so he had eventually got tired of holding his back straight and being cool and just sat on the ground. Her footsteps had been so light that he hadn't heard her, or else he was so engaged in the extraction that he hadn't noticed. He immediately took his finger out of his nostril, leaving the lump hanging for a moment awkwardly against the bridge of his nose, and wondered how much she'd seen. If she had she didn't say anything, so he scrambled to his feet and they began to walk without saying anything.

They quickly found each other's stride – it was cute and she giggled. He liked it when she laughed, it made him happy, so they made a silent game of matching each other's gait. It was partly because neither knew what to say or where they were actually going so this was the only thing they could control, and it felt comforting.

Eventually he broke the ice.

"How was school?" he asked politely.

"Great."

"Really?"

"No. It was school."

"Oh. That was a terrible question, wasn't it?"

"Pretty bad."

He grimaced and she laughed, but it wasn't a teasing laugh, rather it was warm and welcoming and he began to relax. This was much easier than when he was with Antoinette. It just seemed simpler.

"It's nice living here, it's a nice place." Her voice was like silk.

"Yeah, it is. Why did you move?"

"My mum grew up here years ago and she always wanted to come back apparently."

"As good a reason as any."

"I guess."

They reached the end of the lane and faced a decision: cross the road and then onto the pier or turn right and towards the village. The lights were red so they had to wait for the traffic to stop for them. Sam looked at her for the first time without her looking back at him. She was pretty though not beautiful. Her face was too angular and her eyes were too small. She seemed more imposing and confident in her jeans and sweater – the school uniform made her appear more of a girl and her casuals gave her the impertinent stance of a real woman.

The little man went green, the traffic reluctantly halted and she looked at him.

"You're staring again."

He nodded and they walked across the road. "I have a tendency to do that."

"Why?"

"I don't know. I just start thinking about things."

"Fair enough."

It felt easy to talk with her – there was such ease in her presence, something calming.

"Where do you want to go?" she asked.

"I hadn't thought about it."

"Well, I'm new here so how about you give me a tour of the area?"

"I can do that."

He had to really think about where to bring her. When you're on your own or with a group of people who know the place, coming and going seems as simple as breathing. You just know where you like to go subconsciously. But when you are asked to specifically show somebody around nothing seems interesting or good enough, so he momentarily struggled for the correct places to bring her. What to show her? What if she didn't like what he showed her and thought him uncool?

He glanced at her and she smiled shyly back, the breeze blowing her hair so that it was half covering her face and just her eyes peeked through. Strangely her smile made him calm and he just walked with her, not even thinking about it.

It was over two hours later when he walked her home, the dusk having long since settled and given way to the initial vestiges of night. They paused at her driveway, their ease in each other's company suddenly broken. In the ensuing awkwardness he began to speak and then stuttered.

"It was – well – I'm glad that, you know, you moved here."

"Me too."

They smiled at each other, then they both looked away. So he did it. He had no idea what came over him and if the opportunity arose again he probably wouldn't have the courage but he leaned forward, grabbed her, a little too roughly perhaps, and placed his lips against hers without thinking about it. It was only when he found his lips pressed against hers that he became aware of what he had just done and shame flooded through him. He would have pulled back but time seemed to slow down and he froze. She didn't react, initially too surprised to comprehend what had just happened. It was a terrible moment, the fear of having crossed the line and undoing everything good. Then her lips parted ever so slightly and she kissed him back. They both paused, holding that position for a moment, eyes closed, not breathing, each unsure what to do next. He kissed her again and their tongues met gently.

Then it was over. He opened his eyes and she was looking at him timidly. He wanted to scoop her up and put her in his pocket forever.

"I guess I should go inside." Her voice was quiet and uncertain.

"Yep. They might think that you're lost."

"Or abducted."

They laughed then and it was easy again, the shyness gone. It just felt nice and normal and exciting.

He watched her go up to her door and take out her key, then he scampered away before she saw him staring.

His mother wasn't very happy with him for forgetting to bring back milk and butter but he accepted the scolding because it was more than worth it. She had only fabricated the errand to get him out of the house anyway, he figured.

"Where were you anyway? What was so important that you forgot my milk?"

"I was just out, you know."

"No. I don't know. I don't want you gallivanting around until all hours."

"Why?"

"Because I said so, that's why!"

"Sorry."

His father looked at him, raising his eyes from above the paper, and there was the smallest of smiles, a little twinkle that if he didn't know him so intimately he would have missed. Sam smiled back. It was a male thing, a bonding moment, his father just knowing what had happened and approving and as such he cherished that almost as much as the kiss. Almost.

Chapter 26

Handcuffed for Attention

The next few days passed by in a gloriously self-imposed social isolation as he waited expectantly to see Francesca again. He had no reason to speak with anybody else – they were boring to him because what could they possibly add to his life if they weren't Francesca? He certainly wanted to keep away from the lads so he avoided them, and it was easy to disappear in school as he wasn't associating with Daniel.

Days passed though, then the weekend slipped by, and in the blink of an eye it was already Wednesday of the following week and he still hadn't seen her. There was no specific reason why they didn't meet immediately but he hadn't seen her on the street, and when he had wandered by their house to try and casually bump into her it was empty. Her house was empty for the entire weekend and he began to worry that they might have moved back to where they came from, deciding that they simply didn't like the area.

On Monday her parents' car was back but he didn't have the nerve to knock on the door. He didn't know what to do and she was all he had been thinking about. He cursed himself for not having the foresight and courage to organize seeing her again. What if she had met somebody else? Maybe he was the first boy in the area that she had seen and now she had met others and wasn't interested in him any more. Fuck. He needed to see her.

He was getting fidgety and on the verge of getting obsessive – the initial euphoria crossing that dangerous threshold into seething self-doubt – when he passed her by with her mother in the laneway. She saw him just as he saw her and they both smiled uncertainly. He was in his school uniform, on his way back from school, but thankfully she was still also wearing hers. They stopped to greet each other and he couldn't breathe.

"Mum, this is Sam. Sam, this is my mum."

"Hi, Mrs Baker." The words felt heavy on his tongue. He rocked on his heels, slightly unbalanced whilst waiting for the etiquette to reveal itself: should he stand there and chat, turn and begin to accompany them wherever they were going or just carry on about his business with a short polite greeting? Should he ask her to join him? What the fuck should he do?

Francesca seemed equally uncertain and she began to blush.

Her mother noticed this with a disdainful scowl, obviously not of the temperament or disposition to indulge two lovelorn teens.

"It is lovely to meet you, Sam – tell your mother thanks for the flowers and the card welcoming us to the area." She began to walk on.

"Oh, okay, of course I will."

"Bye, Sam," Francesca purred.

He wanted to breathe in her breath. "Bye, Fran. See you later?"

The last part just stumbled out of his mouth before he could catch it and stuff it back inside his eager throat with a chiding grimace.

She looked back and gave him the sweetest smile and a brief nod, then trotted along to keep up with her mother's searing pace.

Sam watched them go until they had turned the corner and allowed himself a smile, enjoying the moment of elation that swept through his body. He was getting accustomed to those fleeting spurts of heady joy that electrified him when something offering boundless optimism occurred, so he let it happen and cherished it. It was bound to be deflated sooner rather than later anyway.

He bounded up the lane with an extra spring in his step until he was passing the slope. There was a movement in the bushes and he stopped. His gut told him to keep moving but he hadn't seen the lads in over a week. He started up the slope.

"Jayo, Mouse, Washo? You lads up there?"

"Shut up, ya dope," Mouse responded.

They were there. He had to go up. He was nervous for some reason – it felt like a bad idea but he didn't understand why.

"What should we do wit 'em?" Washing Machine asked the group.

"Hand them in?" Sam offered.

"To where?"

"The gardaí?"

"The pigs? You think tha' we should hand dem in to the pigs?" Jayo snapped.

"Well, yeah. I mean, no."

Jayo clipped him around the ear contemptuously, his nail scraping the soft skin on the edge of the lobe. "That's fer being stupid."

The excitement from the handcuffs he was holding seemed to have awakened Jayo from some of his stupor.

It was only the four of them – Jesse was absent again.

When Sam had scrambled up the bank Washing Machine was holding up a set of handcuffs like he had just been presented with an Oscar. His hands clutched the rusted metal hoops carefully, his fingers intertwined between the rings. He had found them in the bushes near his house an hour ago. For the first time in what seemed like an age there was a spark in Jayo's eyes as he took the handcuffs off Washing Machine with casual ownership.

"Well, what should we do?" Washing Machine needed instruction.

"What are handcuffs best used for?" Jayo asked the group.

Mouse had that glint in his eye that always made Sam uncomfortable. He hadn't had to deal with it in a while, not since the island trip, but it was back again.

Mouse spoke up. "For handcuffin' things."

"So let's find something to cuff," Jayo commanded. He was in charge again.

Jayo looked around at the other three who all seemed to be in on some sort of jape from which Sam was excluded and he felt distinctly uncomfortable. Maybe he should have gone home. He didn't want Francesca to see him with the lads, running around like gurriers with a set of handcuffs.

"Let's go get some fags and figure something out," Jayo decided.

There didn't seem to be much to figure out from what Sam could see. They had a set of handcuffs but nothing to handcuff and in his mind that was where it ended.

Jayo moved off down the slope though and the other three obediently followed him.

They walked down the lane and when they reached the end they headed towards the shop by the pier.

Fran and her mother had gone in that direction. Sam didn't want to run into her with the lads because he wouldn't be able to say hi to her without them noticing, and he couldn't pretend to ignore her. Shit.

"Shouldn't we go to McKeogh's?" Sam asked, in a weak attempt to deflect them to another shop.

"Nah, Jayo's brother is working in the Centra today."

"Yeah, but then, if we went to McKeogh's instead, we could, eh, head up past the village towards the summit maybe. There's nothing going on down the pier today. I'll pop into my gaff and get some money and get the smokes this time – it's probably my turn."

Jayo looked at him, trying to figure out what he wanted, but free cigarettes were free cigarettes in anybody's language. He nodded.

"Yeah, sure, smokes on you then."

They turned and walked up the road to the village, away from the laneway.

Sam took up a brisk pace and strode ahead. He was in and out of his house with some money by the time they caught up to him. Hopefully they would all be gone off the street before Fran and her mother walked back this way.

The lads were taking their time today, affecting a leisurely pace which was excruciating for Sam when he wanted to get away quickly. He looked over his shoulder to check Francesca wasn't approaching and Mouse caught him.

"What ya lookin' for, Sammy?"

"Nothing."

Mouse didn't believe him and looked back himself for a clue. They were only halfway up the road when Mouse stopped abruptly and looked to his right. He was looking at Francesca's house. The twinkle was there again.

"That's the new bird's gaff, right?"

Washing Machine stretched out his arms. "Yeah, that's it. She's pretty fit."

"Looked a bit rotten to me. What do you think, Sam?"

"I dunno – she seems alright."

"You spoken to her then?" Mouse smiled at him as he spoke in that achingly patronizing manner that he had perfected.

Jayo didn't say anything but looked bored.

"A few times."

"A few times?" Mouse whistled and raised his eyebrows for dramatic effect. "That's a lot . . . how come?"

"Just, well, you know . . . why?"

"Chill out, Samuel, I'm just askin'."

Washing Machine suddenly had an epiphany, or what passed for one in his narrow world. "You kissed her, didn't ya?"

"No!"

Sam's response was too rapid and defensive and Mouse laughed wickedly.

"He did too. Sammy and Franny up a tree, K.I.S.S.I.N.G!"

"You're a bit old for that song, aren't you, Mouse?"

"That's why you wanted to go this way – to walk past her gaff?" Mouse stared at her house and grabbed his balls in one hand.

"Does she look out her window and wave at ya? That's cute. Can she see this?"

He fondled himself lewdly and Washing Machine laughed.

"Does she blow kisses at ya, Sammy?" Washing Machine offered.

"She can blow this!" Mouse continued fondling himself.

"Fuck off, lads. C'mon, let's go. Jayo?"

Jayo didn't say anything. He simply watched what was happening approvingly like an overseer.

Sam made a grab at Mouse. "Stop doing that!"

Mouse ignored Sam and began dancing around him like an eviscerated chimp. He moved behind Sam as Washing Machine did an inane dance body-pop imitating kissing and sex. If Sam had been a little more streetwise, or maybe if he hadn't been blinded by concern for getting out of the eye-line of Fran's house he would have sensed what was about to happen, or at least reacted to the underlying vibe and the lads' over-enthusiasm, but he wasn't, and he was, and so he didn't.

Mouse grabbed his arms in one smooth motion, whilst Washing Machine pushed his shoulders in and down and before Sam could even exhale he had one cuff firmly around his right wrist. He didn't retaliate to the physical molestation until it was too late and Jayo had joined in – the incident clearly igniting his recently repressed masculinity.

He was half dragged, half carried into Fran's driveway

by the three boys. They had him splayed against the glass porch door in less than a few seconds. Washing Machine opened the porch and the other two manipulated the struggling Sam up to the front door. It had a big ring knocker, so it was easy for them to twist his arm behind his back, slipping the other end of the cuffs through the big loop and closing the cuff tightly. He was now handcuffed to the front door of Francesca's house.

The lads stepped back from their handiwork and doubled over in peals of laughter. Ignoring the pain and the slight humiliation at having been so easily overcome, Sam joined in to be a good sport, hoping it would be over soon and they could leave. But his hope was short-lived.

"Okay, cool, very funny, now unlock me, c'mon."

Mouse giggled as if that was a novel idea.

Sam's eyes opened wide and he looked at Washing Machine in despair. "There isn't a key, is there?"

Washing Machine paused, and even Jayo hesitated in order to take stock as the implications of this sank it. Fuck. Sam was handcuffed to what appeared to be a very expensive solid teak front door with a large silver-embossed door knocker and they had no way of getting him unlocked. The absurdity of the situation overwhelmed Washing Machine and he fell to the ground in a second fit of giggles, his fists beating the soft grass.

Mouse grinned at Sam as if to say 'I've won' and Sam grimaced.

"Seriously, you have to get me off this, Mouse, please."

"What's wrong, Sammy boy – do you not want to be close to your new girlfriend?"

Mouse walked closer to him, mocking him with every deliberate step. He stopped a few feet away and Sam felt a flush of anger and reached sharply out for him, stretching as far as he could with his free arm. His fingertips brushed Mouse's cheek then the snap of the cuffs yanked him abruptly back. Mouse smiled at him, revelling in the moment. It was then that Sam realized that Mouse genuinely hated him. It might have been jealousy or it might have been teenage male rivalry but, whatever it was, it was deeply seeded.

"Just tell your new little girlfriend that you missed her so much you couldn't bear to be without her, so you wanted to stay stuck to her doorway forever," Mouse mocked.

Jayo broke into a loud guffaw. He didn't give a fuck about Sam either. It was then Sam realized he had been blinded to his indifference by a desire for acceptance.

Mouse skipped backwards. "Right, I feel like a walk and a smoke, lads!"

"Would love one," Jayo agreed. "You got money, Washo?"

"Yep."

Washing Machine waved goodbye sarcastically as the three lads sauntered off cheerily.

Sam's heart dropped as he slumped back against the door. He couldn't think of anything worse. The door was solid, newly installed at great cost judging by the finish, and the centrepiece was the large antique door knocker. This was a family who clearly took pride in the appearance of their home. Running his fingers over the rusted metal rings didn't reveal anything of use – they were solidly built, and despite their aged appearance they were in good condition. The cuff was tightly closed around his wrist, thankfully not so tight as to cut off the circulation, but he had no chance of slipping through the circle. The only way to get out of them was to cut the metal, remove the door knocker, or find a key. He looked back out towards the street, half hoping to see the lads return with a wink and a nod and produce the key with a flourish. He knew they weren't going to, though – there had been something about their actions that went past simple playing – there was a burgeoning malevolence that worried him. This time felt different. He should have trusted his gut instinct and gone home when he had the chance.

His wrist was beginning to hurt, the skin reddening from the pressure of the metal where it grated against the bone.

Suddenly without warning a car sped down the road, slowed and then began to turn into the driveway. Sam looked on in horror, hoping against hope that it was just a misdirected car turning around. The car inevitably kept turning and parked in the driveway, stopping only a few yards from the porch he was standing on. He felt his heart drop and he lowered his head, averting his eyes, almost hoping that if he couldn't see them then maybe by extension they couldn't see him.

"Sam? Is that you?"

Francesca was staring at him in astonishment, her parents looking equally perplexed. Her father must have picked them up – the lads could have gone to the shop and the pier and probably never have bumped into her. He had brought this upon himself. He couldn't lift his head. He felt his cheeks get hot, the mortification overwhelming him, and a sudden urge to piss swelled in his belly.

"Sam – is that your name?"

He finally looked up, face to face with the imposing figure of her father. He did not look amused.

"Oh hi, Francesca, and eh, hi, Mr and Mrs . . . em, nice day."

Francesca's father eyeballed him. Clearly he wasn't in the best of moods.

"What are you doing at my door?"

"My good knocker, oh lord!"

Francesca's mother had only just noticed that he was actually handcuffed – beforehand she had merely thought he was waiting on her daughter in some bizarre fashion, an overly eager young suitor. Being attached to her newly burnished door knocker was a different story.

"Oh, get off that knocker! You'll scratch it!"

Without waiting for Sam to speak, her father grabbed roughly at the cuffs, trying to see if there was a click switch to unlock them.

"Okay, son, where's the key? I'm tired of this."

Sam mumbled something incoherent under his breath, trying to avert his gaze away from Francesca's scolding eyes.

"I didn't hear you, son. Speak louder." He lifted Sam's face up with his hand roughly. It smelt of sweat and lightly scented soap.

"I don't have a key."

"What do you mean you don't have a key?"

Sam nodded to reaffirm what he had said and looked down at his feet again, unable to take the glare from the imposing figure gripping his jaw tighter with each passing moment.

"It didn't come with one."

"So you thought that you'd cuff yourself here as a practical joke, did you now?"

"No. I mean, I didn't do it, it was the lads."

"Get him off my door knocker – it's going to leave awful markings. I had to order that antique – it took three weeks!" Francesca's mother mewled.

"It's okay, Vera – just relax and go inside and I'll sort it out."

Francesca's father opened the front door and Sam found himself awkwardly half swinging, half scuttling inside the first few feet of their elegant home. Mrs Baker passed him by with a snide mutter, then the door half swung closed again and he was pulled back face to face with her father who glared at him.

"I'm tired, I'm not in a good mood. I'm going to go inside and I expect you to figure out how to disentangle yourself pretty rapidly."

Sam nodded, turning his head to avoid the stale breath emanating from the older man's mouth that was not soap – more garlic and cabbage.

Mr Baker marched inside.

"Don't be too long, Francesca, I don't want you entertaining this idiot."

"Yes, Dad."

She waited until the door was closed and it was just the two of them. He avoided looking at her for as long as was possible, and then finally, eventually, he caught her eye.

She looked devastated, about to cry. Her lip quivered.

"What are you doing?" she implored.

He swallowed, hating himself for making her cry. "I'm sorry, I didn't – I mean, it wasn't me."

She shook her head. "You have embarrassed me in front of my parents, Samuel. How could you?"

He had no answer and she continued using his name in its fullest form like when he was being chastised by his parents, tears forming in her eyes. His heart sank.

"Samuel, how can I ever invite you in for dinner now after this? I'll have to feed you in the corner or something

– how awful!"

He looked up at the change in tone, and she hesitated. Then she looked up at him, eyes fluttering, and smiled coyly.

"Oh Samuel, how could you?" Her voice turned mocking and she giggled, the whole thing a façade. Her dimples leaped off her face excitedly. "I'm good, right?"

"You had me fooled."

"I want to be an actress, I think."

"Really? You'd be good."

"Well, I've only decided now just this minute, but it was fun fucking with you. Maybe I will. I'll probably change my mind later."

He smiled, the weight of the world lifted off his shoulders. She leaned forward and gave him a gentle kiss on the lips.

"I'd better go inside to appease my dad, pretend that I hate you."

"You don't, do you?"

"Oh no, this is very cool – my dad's such a grumpy old prick so this is great, and my mum, well, she'll be moaning about the knocker for weeks, and it'll do my dad's head in – it's going to be brilliant."

Sam had his doubts about how brilliant that could be, but she was happy so nothing else mattered.

She opened the door and he had to step inside and press against the door to allow her to pass. Their bodies squeezed against each other and she smiled like a temptress.

"Oh, following me in now, are you?"

He shook his head with a grin, dropping it only when her father appeared in the hallway.

"Close the door, Francesca."

She nodded, gave Sam a covert secret glance and closed the door, leaving Sam back out on the porch alone. It wasn't so bad this time. Now he just had to figure out how to get out of these handcuffs.

Chapter 27

All Good Things Should Get Better

It had all ended well, which was surprising really. Francesca's father had found a bunch of keys in his garage – it turned out he was a handyman geek – and, subsequently trying out each one, had found a key that was sufficiently similar to be able to force the lock. They had even had a joke about the ease with which he could help people escape from jail.

Sam still wasn't asked in for dinner but he had inadvertently endeared himself to Francesca and that was priceless. They had agreed to meet up over the weekend, setting firm plans this time, and he left with a bounce in his heels.

The lads were waiting on the wall just inside the lane when he got to his driveway and they called him over. He shook his head. Mouse actually stood up and beckoned him.

"Oh come on, Sammy, get over here!"

"No, I'm going home!" he shouted back.

"Don't be a twat, c'mere."

He found himself wandering over. It wasn't often that Mouse would be enthusiastic for him to join them. The handcuffs event had worked out in his favour so no harm had been done – and maybe they had just meant it as a joke. They were his friends after all.

"Cheers for that, lads," Sam said, trying to be cool.

Mouse eyed him as he approached and once he was beside them he grabbed Sam's wrists to see if he had hurt himself getting out. He seemed disappointed that there were no bruises or markings. Sam pulled his wrists back but Mouse held on to them for just a moment longer than he needed to.

"Were you gonna come back for me?" Sam asked hopefully.

"Probably not.' Jayo smiled.

"Okay." Sam didn't know how to respond to that.

"Well, ya got out fine, didn't ya?" Mouse was obviously annoyed at the fact.

"How did ya get out?" Jayo asked coldly. "Did ya use yer dick as a key?"

Sam knew he should be wary of Jayo when he was in one of these 'dangerous' moods so he just shrugged.

Washing Machine grinned like an idiot. "His dick is certainly small enough – maybe he did use that! Show us your dick, Sam!"

"Fuck off, Washo."

"Don't talk to me like that." Washing Machine had his tail up.

"Right. I'm gonna go, lads. That wasn't sound, what you did." Sam had had enough.

"Stop being a baby." Mouse glared at him.

It felt like the appropriate time to leave, the energy wasn't right.

Sam turned to go but Mouse's voice followed him.

"Oi! What about the cuffs?"

"What?"

"The cuffs – I want them back!"

"I don't have them – they weren't yours anyway."

"They were mine. And if they weren't mine then they were Jayo's."

Mouse looked to Jayo for confirmation of ownership and he nodded sternly. They stepped off the wall and fanned out around Sam. Like a pack of hyenas, Sam thought, with Washing Machine an eager jackal drifting around the outskirts waiting to pounce on scraps.

"You left me stuck in them," Sam said defensively.

"So you should have brought them back – we let you borrow them." Mouse threatened.

"That doesn't make sense."

"I want the fucking cuffs back, Samantha."

For the first time with the lads Sam felt threatened. They were far too highly strung right now. Mouse and Washing Machine only ever needed a little nudge to do something stupid and Jayo was acting very aggressively, his recent mood swings a precursor to this behaviour. With Jayo leading them, the other two would do anything. They never thought before they acted and they felt safe with Jayo behind them.

"Well, her dad has the cuffs now."

"Get them back." Jayo responded with a snide smile.

"I can't."

"She's your girlfriend – go back and get them off her!"

"He won't! He wants to keep them to play with her, I'll bet!" Washing Machine said.

"No, no, he's gonna use them in school with his gay mates tomorrow." Jayo wasn't blinking. He looked psychotic.

The banter was escalating, becoming more sinister.

"That's it – Sammy has kept the cuffs for some gay bum stuff when it's dark – that's why he's always late from school," said Washing Machine.

"Eww, gross, faggot!" Mouse jabbed his finger into Sam's chest roughly so that he had to take a step back.

"Fuck off, Mouse!"

Mouse pushed into Sam abruptly, his face inches away. "What the fuck did you say to me?"

"Just leave me alone, okay? I don't have the cuffs."

"That's not what you said."

"It was."

"No, it wasn't. Say it again."

Sam was silent. Mouse waited momentarily then pushed him so hard in the chest that he stumbled but he kept his balance.

"Come on, fag boy, say it again!"

"Oh, fuck off, Mouse, just fuck right off!"

The words had barely left Sam'smouth when Mouse swung his fist in a blurring arc. It sliced through the air with a whoosh and smacked him solidly on the side of his jaw. He staggered from the momentum, then lost his balance and fell to the ground. Mouse stood over him like a prize fighter, willing him to get to his feet so he could inflict more pain. Washing Machine giggled inanely and Jayo stood silently watching, biding his time.

Sam waited a moment to get his bearings, then rage took

over and he dived at Mouse. His body slapped into the other boy and he took him down to the ground with him. The impact of their bodies pushed them down the path a few feet, and they broke apart. Sam was first to his feet, and he gathered himself like he had seen boxers do on television. He suddenly wished that he had spent more time watching those Bruce Lee movies with Daniel to have learnt the moves.

Mouse looked up at Sam with complete hatred. This was more than just some internal gang rivalry – his eyes were explicit in their complete hate. He despised Sam, and they could all feel it in the emotional wave that smashed around them all.

"You shouldn't have done that!" Mouse whispered.

He stood up slowly. The slow motion made it worse as now Sam waited for what was about to occur. All those times that he had considered and subsequently dismissed the idea of taking Mouse on in a fight had now become a reality. This reality. Sam's hands felt heavy and sweaty and his arms leaden. It was hard to keep his fists balled up tight. Sweat pooled upon his brow as Mouse advanced on him slowly like some god of war. There was a dangerous intensity in his eyes.

"Protecting your little faggy girlfriend is so sweet, Sammy."

Mouse always spoke to reassure himself, Sam noted. It was his defense mechanism. He would taunt and tease to reinforce his own self-belief. It was odd how he had never really seen through this bully before. Mouse needed the assurance of the others. On cue Mouse flicked a glance at Jayo, desiring his approval, and probably his support.

Washing Machine clapped his hands like an idiot in

anticipation of the fight. Mouse was simply feeding off their energy, and without it he wouldn't do anything.

Sam stood his ground, testing this theory, fresh as it was.

"Well, come on then, you little tosser!" said Mouse.

He was waiting for him a few feet away. He wasn't attacking.

Sam was right in his assessment. Mouse was just a bully, and he was going to wait for Sam to attack him – he was too afraid to do it himself.

"Just fuck off, Mouse, and go home."

Goading him wasn't part of the plan but it just slipped out. Mouse didn't say anything but took a step forward and suddenly it all became a slow-motion blur. Sam moved as quick as he ever had, which was fast enough to move beyond Mouse's swinging arm and his own fist found the soft flesh below Mouse's ribcage. Mouse gasped in pain and then Sam slammed his other fist into his head. It became a mess of jumbled limbs, jutting elbows, grappling fingers and kicking legs. And Sam was winning. It was surprising but he knew the exact moment when he was. He couldn't say what had happened, but he felt Mouse wilting underneath him. Finally Sam pushed Mouse to the ground and he stood there panting and knew that it was over. He had survived. Mouse stared up at him balefully.

"Go fuck yourself, Mouse." Sam rolled each word with his tongue, taking great pleasure in each syllable.

He had barely enjoyed the moment of victory however when he felt the tiniest flicker of movement to his left. He turned and saw the darkened face of Jayo only inches away. Jayo whipped both of his fists out rapidly in succession, barely licking against Sam's face but causing maximum pain and damage. Jayo could definitely box. Sam felt himself falling to the ground even as Jayo's fists still rained down upon him. He could see knuckles slamming into his face and they looked painful but he didn't even register the pain. Then his head hit the ground and he bounced back into the air for a moment. More fists came down upon him. Then everything seemed to shatter around him in a sudden moment of searing agony, like a ceramic vase exploding in a fire, and the world went black.

"Sam, hey, Sam, can you hear me?" A voice floated around him.

He was surrounded by huge mountains of black and green. Massive steep ripples of heavy rock protruded from fissures in the ground at his feet like giant daggers trying to touch the sky. Swirls of mist coiled around him, drifting between his fingers like fanning smoke. He trod on uneven clumps of yellow flowers, each one more translucent than the last. His skin felt clammy, his head ached.

"Sam!"

He heard something in the distance but ignored it. Before him a shaft of bright light bit down through the clouds, illuminating a distant glade like a beacon. He felt an inexorable pull towards it, gravity dragging him like a stone on a string.

"Sam!"

The voice seemed fainter now, so he blocked it out, letting the drifting movement take over his body. It felt nice. The flowers were no longer touching his feet and he was floating.

He could hear the voice again, and he looked for it lazily. There was a rumble and then an image projected across the glade. He could vaguely see Washing Machine staring at him, eyes and mouth moving frantically. Washing Machine's fingers reached for him and touched something. The image flickered. Behind Washing Machine he could see Jayo standing like a statue, fists still cocked. Sam wanted to wave to them both, to show them that he was floating. They wouldn't understand and he didn't want to share this serenity with anybody so he turned away from the image and back towards the glade. He was almost there.

He stopped just in front of the light, where it was burning at his feet, and looking down he saw a never-ending black hole that was being hollowed out by the light acting as a searing bore. The heat emanating from the light was overwhelming and he felt sweat running down his shoulders and forehead in thick rivulets. It didn't matter though – only the light mattered, the warmth, the beckoning blackness that looked so comfortable. The mountains had closed in now so that he was in the centre of a great pit. It felt safe here. He took a step forward.

"Sam, wake the fuck up!"

The voice seemed to echo around the valley, giving him momentary pause, but it was from beyond the mountains, high up at the top of the hole, too far away to go to any effort to search out. He was comfortable here before his friendly band of light that was almost touching his toes. He held out his hand and his fingers penetrated the beam. Pain shot through his system, but joy in equal measure dispelled any doubts he had. He felt purified. He felt content.

"Sam!"

He felt a pain on one side of his body, then he tumbled away from the light all the way out of the hole and across the valley like a rag doll in the wind. It hurt. His face and fingers hurt. The light was far away. He tried to float back to it. Then another violent force smacked into him like a gale-force wind and he was whipped up over the mountains and into black again.

Sam's eyes opened. He became aware of Washing Machine slapping his face frantically. It was stinging. He wanted to tell him to stop but couldn't move his mouth. Then an angel pulled Washing Machine off him and grabbed his body protectively. Everything was hurting. He wanted to find that nice light again. He closed his eyes and willed the light to come back.

The angel smelled so nice though and her hair was soft against his face.

"You scared us."

"What happened?"

"You don't remember?"

"No."

"Nothing?"

Sam took the melting ice pack off his swollen face and put it on the table. His mother helped him hold a cup of steaming tea in his hands, more for comfort than anything else. He was aware that they were talking but it didn't sound like his voice. He motioned to the ice pack.

"The heat off that tea is melting this ice too quick. It's annoying, but I like it." He wasn't sure what he was saying.

His mother put down the tea, held his eyelids open and stared into his pupils. "You were in a fight. Why, baby?"

Sam shook his head. "I don't know."

"You remember being in a fight?"

He did now. It was coming back in pieces. He had an image of watching Jayo hitting Sam – him – as his body fell backwards through the air. Jayo was quick. He winced as he saw his body bounce up in the air and Jayo hitting him again as he seemed to float. It looked sore. Then he saw himself hitting Mouse triumphantly. The time line felt wrong.

"I fought Mouse and Jayo."

"Yes, honey. It looks like you got him good though." She was smiling.

Her voice was approving and he stared back at her in surprise while she elaborated.

"He had more cuts than you."

"Who?"

"That 'mouse' boy. He looked beat up bad. You had to fight two – that was unfair." Her smile faded as she saw his creasing grin. "But don't ever fight again, understand?"

He nodded. He couldn't remember that much of what had happened, but if he had confronted and beaten Mouse that was good enough for him. Jayo was a different proposition – he wished he could remember why it had started.

The doorbell rang and she went to answer it. He could hear her pleasant voice greeting somebody. Another younger female voice filtered through.

Sam didn't even have time to stand up and run his hands through his hair before his mother let Francesca in through the door to the kitchen, winking at him.

Fran smiled shyly and held out her gift of chocolate for him. Then she stood awkwardly by the counter.

"You feeling better?" she asked softly.

Sam winced. It wasn't so cool when the girl you liked saw you massaging your head after a beating. His mouth felt stiff and the left side of his face was swollen. He could taste blood gently trickling into his mouth from his enlarged lip.

"Yeah, well, um, I didn't see him coming at me. Them, there were loads of them."

"But you still beat that one guy up. I saw what happened."

"You did?"

"Francesca brought you here – she woke you up," his mother said as she put an extra cup on the table for Fran and poured some tea for her..

"Thank you, Mrs Leahy," Fran said to his mother.

"You're welcome, honey."

It was surreal watching his mother talk with this angel.

His mother smiled knowingly at him as she left, shutting the door to the kitchen, giving the two of them privacy.

"So you saw?" Sam continued when they alone.

"Yeah, I did. I was following you to give you the handcuffs – I figured you might want them. But it was just an excuse to follow you."

"Oh."

"You babbled a little bit when you were out, but you were cute, something about mountains . . . and my hair."

"Your hair? Why?"

"I don't know. I do have nice hair – maybe you just like it."

Sam shrugged, speechless.

"Do you want some tea?" he asked then.

"I've got some." She indicated the cup his mother had already poured for her.

"Yeah, of course."

She was still standing in front of him, shyly shifting her weight from one foot to the next.

"You can sit down if you want?"

"I was just waiting for you to ask."

She giggled that delightfully cheeky smile of hers with the husky laugh. She was perfect. He smiled back at her and it was all so easy.

Chapter 28

And So

His mother wanted him to stay home and recuperate until the weekend, but it was already Thursday and now that Francesca knew what had happened he decided that he had to be a man and face up to it. So he went to school with a badly bruised face for the second time in a month. This time he made sure to wear his bruises with pride. It was surprising how respectful people were when you had been visibly fighting. Each of his classmates wanted to know what happened, and he felt like a celebrity. He was now the kid who fought with rough kids outside school that nobody else knew, which was exotic. This made him dangerous because nobody knew what he was capable of.

On lunch break he regaled an eager circle of his classmates with the story of besting Mouse and then getting attacked from behind and seeing a white light. He had never liked being the centre of attention before but he almost had no choice so he began to enjoy it. It coincided with this being one of the few days that Daniel was in attendance and he watched Sam with an obvious hint of jealousy. Fuck him, Sam thought.

On the way home from school that day he got the same bus as Greg and Darren and they pretended that he wasn't there. They knew stories of the lads from his area and had obviously decided to give him a wide berth in future – who knew how he might react next time they riled him? He enjoyed being left in peace and even took some pleasure in their bollicking of one of their minions instead. He inwardly reproached himself but it was nice to see some other kid get picked on for a change. Sam felt he had deservedly earned this guilty pleasure.

The lads were making their way up the slope at the same time as Sam was making his way up the laneway. He stopped when he saw them. Jesse was back with them. There had never been a more awkward moment between them all before than when they stood and stared at each other. A stand-off. Sam wasn't sure if there was going to be another fight but the lads seemed inhibited and uncertain how to act.

Then an older man hurried behind Sam and there was silence as they each waited until he had gone before anybody spoke.

Mouse sported a large black eye and a cut lip but Sam's injuries were far greater. They seemed surprised to see him, as if they had expected him to stay away from school for a while.

"Hey, Sam," Jesse said weakly.

"Hey, Jesse, feeling better?"

"Yeah, thanks, just you know, been thinking, you know, it's been rough . . ." Jesse trailed off.

Sam nodded.

"Does it hurt?" Jesse asked.

"Yeah, like a bitch." Sam said these words while he stared at Jayo who didn't look remotely remorseful.

Washing Machine tried to lighten the mood. "You drifted off for a while. Thought you might have done something to your head, like?"

"No, saw a bright light and some talking mountains, nothing too mad." Sam found that his voice was steady. He stared at Jayo, but he didn't feel any fear. "Do yours hurt, Mouse?"

Mouse sneered at him – flanked by Jayo and with Jesse to impress he was back in his element. "Fucking less than yours, you gimp. I slipped, you got lucky."

"Yeah. Okay."

Mouse took a step forward. "Ya wanna go again?"

"Without Jayo helping you this time?" Sam felt brazen. His face hurt like hell but the day in school had made him feel like a hero. Being in fights got you respect, he knew that now.

"Don't need Jayo, do ya myself." But Mouse didn't move forward.

The tension was broken again, this time by Mr Atrix, their neighbour, ambling down the lane with his dog. He clearly could feel the potential violence in the air and saw Sam facing the other four. He slowed his pace and looked at them all in turn.

"Don't do anything stupid now, lads. I know where you all live."

"Fuck off!" Jayo sneered at him.

Mr Atrix looked at him casually. "Don't think I will, Jason. But say that again and I'll be calling the police about you threatening an old man."

"Yeah, whatever."

"Your choice."

Mr Atrix gave Sam a look and continued on his way.

The event wasn't major but it was enough to diffuse the tension. Jayo seemed suitably chastened – he wasn't used to being told off so bluntly.

Washing Machine had had enough.

Then Sam noticed that he had a rope and new swing in his hands.

"I wanna get this up on the tree an' have a few smokes, lads, yeah?" Washing Machine said.

Sam was surprised by what happened next.

Jayo stepped forward and then offered his hand for Sam to shake.

"I'm sorry for hitting ya like that."

He seemed genuine. Sam didn't take his hand immediately but waited for the contrition to be a ploy, a masquerade for some new trick. There was none. Jayo's hand remained in the air.

"Shake on it or not?" Jayo was serious.

Mouse looked apoplectic behind him. "Fuck sake, Jayo, seriously?"

"Shut the fuck up, Mouse, and stop being a prick." Jayo looked back at Sam. "I'm not sorry for hittin' ya, but I'm sorry for hittin' when ya were down – poor show on my part. I was angry."

It wasn't a complete apology but it was enough.

Sam took his hand and they shook firmly. His hand was dry and his handshake was firm and he was proud of that. He didn't need to say anything. Jayo took the handshake as an acceptance. He inclined his head towards the others.

"We're puttin' up a new swing in honour of the dead

bloke. Jesse is gonna break it in with the first swing. Ya wanna come up an' join us, no more bullshit?"

"No, thanks. Not this time."

Jayo was still holding his hand. He wasn't expecting a rejection but he wasn't going to beg. He took it in his stride.

"Fair enough."

They released hands and for the first time Sam genuinely felt like an equal. He nodded to Jesse and Washing Machine, ignored Mouse and continued up the lane home.

"Did you forgive them?"

"Of course."

"Okay. Good."

"You sound surprised?"

"Not surprised, but glad. I would have hoped that you would, but it can be hard to forgive when you're betrayed. It's a great sign of character when you can see somebody's mistakes and move past them."

Sam was sitting opposite Don in their Monday morning meeting. There had been a lot to discuss. Sam nodded now because Don was right somehow.

He had forgiven Jayo but hadn't forgiven Daniel quite as easily as he had made out. In fact he had ignored his initial apologies, making him squirm. But when he had seen how disconsolate he was, sitting alone in class and eating inside when everyone else sauntered to the yard, he had succumbed. He had been best friends with Daniel after all, and had come to realize just how important that was. Daniel had suffered himself: Antoinette was a dark girl and had spread rumours about his lack of sexual prowess which had blossomed like spreading wildfire. Even to boys who had no experience or had never kissed a girl of her calibre, it had resonated simply because another's misfortune was a great source of amusement, some of which bordered on sadistic. So Sam had accepted Daniel's apology, and they were friends again. It would take a while, but he had come to see the transient nature of most things in life, except friendship.

"Two apologies in one week – I must be doing something right – maybe there's something to this religious forgive-and-forget thing."

"That's awfully philosophical of you."

Sam had been mumbling out loud again, half aware that he was talking to Don and half speaking to himself.

"Yes, I guess. Is it?"

"Yes, it is."

Don took a drag from his obligatory cigar and Sam waited until the smoke had cleared sufficiently so that he could make out his face clearly again.

"You're not going to stop smoking those, are you?"

Don chuckled. "These are one of the few pleasures that I allow myself. Being a priest mustn't be too tough – there has to be some benefits. Mine are a constant source of cigars."

Sam didn't bother asking where he got them; he sincerely doubted that Don, ardently religious though he was, would ever deny himself simple pleasures. It was important to have balance, he said. It made sense.

"The vision you had . . ."

"It wasn't a vision."

Don shrugged, and paused before continuing.

"Okay. The non-vision vision that you may or may not have had. What else did you see or feel?"

"You mean apart from the clouds and the smoke and sunlight?"

"Yes, apart from all those things?"

Sam had had a scan just for safety on Friday which revealed nothing was awry, but he had been out cold for a few minutes dreaming of being in a different place and Don had an obvious fascination with the afterlife and the potential crossover that had occurred.

"Well, I didn't see any person, or have any voice of God talk to me or anything."

"Forget voices or people. The feelings, what did you feel?" Don was getting more animated now, his excitement betraying him.

Sam smiled, enjoying how passionate he got. He momentarily toyed with the idea of making something up for him, then dismissed it for there was shame in that deceit. So he was honest, even if at first it didn't feel like it was enough.

"I had this feeling of joy, pure bliss and contentment. I didn't want to leave. I was just happy."

Don nodded, satisfied with the answer. He sat back in his chair and took one final affectionate drag from his cigar.

The youth sat on the other side of his desk watching his every move, watching and learning, eager.

"Sounds just perfect to me."

"I guess it was."

Daniel walked alongside him for the bus after school that afternoon. It would take a while, but Sam decided that he would entirely forgive him. Daniel had professed how much he had adored Antoinette from the start and hadn't meant for it to happen, but it just did and he was truly sorry. She had also left him heartbroken, even more than Sam had been which made him feel a little superior. They had something in common now, a mutual heartbreak which Don had confirmed was strong for bonding. Daniel then confessed to not having had sex as much as he'd bragged. He had slept with her, but not that often. They were almost at the bus when Sam stopped listening to his ramblings and looked around.

"What are you doing?" Daniel asked.

"Do you see a girl, a pretty girl . . . ah, there she is!" Sam saw Francesca across the street and waved to her.

She saw him and waved back, immediately coming towards him. They had hung out that weekend and she had suggested meeting him in town after school. He had never met a girl in town before. It felt real.

"Who the fuck is that?" Daniel asked wide-eyed as Francesca trotted over in her casual clothes.

"Francesca."

"Who?"

"You wouldn't know her." Sam winked at him.

Francesca took his hand quickly and spoke rapidly and nervously. "We're going to be late – the film is on at four thirty – we'd better hurry cos I want ice cream."

"Okay – sure."

She looked at Daniel who put out his hand – still as smooth as ever.

"Hi, I'm Daniel."

Sam stepped in front of him, half joking, but half very serious. "You don't want to talk to him, Fran – he's not very interesting."

Daniel took it well. "Hey, yes, I am. I'm your best friend – I'd want to be interesting."

"Well, he is a little then, but he's in a rush for his bus, aren't you, Dan?"

Daniel smiled at Sam, gave him a friendly punch and bowed for Francesca who curtsied in return. Then he took off without a look back.

Sam turned to the beautiful girl in front of him. She smiled shyly and touched the bruises on his face.

"They're healing quick," she sighed at him.

He hoped they would stay. He felt tough.

"Fran?"

"Yeah?"

"Would you be my girlfriend?"

She bit her lip, making him wait, then giggled. "Only if you buy me ice cream at the cinema."

"I'll buy you ten ice creams."

"No, just one."

"Deal."

She kissed him then and it just felt easy.

He Could Smell Her

He could smell her
Where she stood.
Her sweat like warm vanilla.

She didn't look at him
But his eyes never
Left her. Not for a moment.

His shoulder was jostled heavily.
Once. Then over again
As people moved through the crowd.

His vision was blocked
And he panicked.
Searching for a glimpse of her.

Blonde hair flickered
Like a refracting shimmer
Between heaving bodies.

Then she was before him.
The greens of her eyes
Stopping him still.

She moved past him
Without a glance,
And he turned his head after hers.

Her suitor placed his hand
On the small of her back,
Guiding her forward.

He watched as she disappeared
Into the peopled mess
And was swallowed.

He was again jostled roughly
So he faced into the crowd.
And tried to fall in love again.

Acknowledgements

I would like to especially thank Josh Pearl for helping this book become a reality. He has been the most ardent supporter of my writing, and without his encouragement I would never have tried to put this out into the world, nor might I have continued writing.

Thanks to Caroline Grace-Cassidy, without whom this book would probably not have found a home in Poolbeg, and to Paula Campbell for enthusiastically supporting it there.

To Kendall McKinnon for having such belief in my writing and this book, and to all the supporters of my blog who read an initial chapter and gave me the spur to continue writing it.

To Gaye Shortland, my wonderful editor, whose ideas and expertise helped me shape this motley collection of words into something approaching a readable linear story.

To my late English teacher Mr Gerry Haugh who first introduced me to Steinbeck and pushed me to write with great ebullience, and to my parents who exposed me to so many great works of literary art, and to my sisters for always forcing me to try to make cool stuff to impress them.

Finally to everybody I've met personally whose creativity in some form I have admired and aspired to emulate.

Interview with the Author

What was your inspiration for the book?

The book was inspired by some casual reminiscing with friends from my area over some of the crazy stuff we used to get up to. I think possibly it was when I was making a film with one of the guys who lived on my street, Franco. Then I began thinking about the idea of making a film about some young teenagers. I think I had watched a French film about this young boy experiencing sex for the first time, although I can't remember what it was called. So I began to write down some stuff that happened to me, or from stories that I had heard, and I gradually began to create this character of Sam and then drew characters around him. The more that I wrote about him and the other characters in the story, such as Don and Jayo and Daniel (who were all amalgamations of people I knew growing up in a way), the more I fell in love with them. It wasn't a conscious decision to actually write a book – I was just writing for the enjoyment of it, and to try and not let the feelings of being a teenager disappear from my memory.

You have a successful career in acting and screenplay writing – why did you feel such a strong urge to write a novel?

I have always wanted to write novels, ever since I first read *The Hobbit* and then *Great Expectations* in school. Writing a novel seemed so exotic and impossible however, and I never believed that I was capable of either putting so many words on a page, or of creating something that people would have any interest in reading. Screenplays are much shorter and are grounded in visual and musical cues, in my head at least. A novel has nothing to fall back on to rescue it if it's failing, or a cut to change the pace if something isn't working, and you're either attached to the story and the characters or you're not – so it feels even more exposed as an art form. Also the only people reading a screenplay are the ones you're making the film with, or hoping to make it with, and you select those people, and they can have their own ideas in their heads for the creation of the film. A novel is finished and there's nothing to add to it apart from the reader's imagination. I can't underlay scenes with music, or get a wonderful actor to play out a scene. That's scary.

It must be hard to juggle your various interests and commitments. What's your writing day like? Do you have a set routine for writing? Or must it happen whenever you can grab a moment?

I like to write on the move, I like coffee shops, or environments with lots of activity where I can have a quiet corner in the middle of it all and listen to music. The energy of being around people and commotion inspires me. However, I do prefer to write at night-time – I wrote the first half of an entire screenplay over a year ago in a late-night bar in London, drinking coffee and whiskey. I usually write in blocks for a few hours straight, and then feel exhausted because I invest myself into the characters and what they're feeling, and writing itself is very taxing – for me anyway! But I always feel content when I've written something. Quite often it's after seeing a film, or some music, or having been social, that I have ideas and need to write them down. I did start writing this book when I was alone for a week however, and probably wrote at least forty per cent of it in the week because I didn't do anything else. Forty per cent of the first draft, that it.

Was acting your first love or were you always focused on being a writer?

I always wanted to write, but I was afraid of it. I wasn't sure that I had anything interesting to say. I've never been somebody who was convinced that what they were doing was correct or brilliant, although sometimes I wish that I was. Acting also scared me, and still does, and I grew into myself by forcing myself 'out there' as an actor, and then by making films and having no choice but to be criticized and rejected, so now I'm used to it. If I could never act ever again, or make films but I could write, I would be happy to be honest. I'm not sure if I'm good enough as a writer to do that. For me at the moment my writing is an incredible freedom which I'm just humbled and thrilled has been read by anybody at all. Honestly, having my writing created into a book and having that book read by people is the proudest I've ever felt about anything that I've ever done.

Would you consider writing a screenplay of the story?

I would, and will, and have already begun drafts of variants of the story. It won't be the exact same as the book, or follow the exact same journey but it will have the same characters. Where it's going to go I'm not sure yet. Maybe some of the events will feature but I haven't decided what the central journey of Sam and the lads and Don and Daniel or Antoinette will be. I think that when I'm writing it the story will just happen. Then a producer will hopefully come on board, and probably want me to change it!

With reference to what seems to be perhaps the central theme of the book, why does Sam need to be accepted by the local gang so much?

I think that, at the age Sam is, he needs to be accepted into the gang because it gives him some form of reference and justifies who he is. As a teenager it's so important to be accepted by your peers. The gang offers support, maybe not emotional but physical, through protection by weight of numbers. The age Sam is at is when there is always the possibility of violence every day – boys are filled with confusion about who they are and have confused energies and emotions and often lash out at each other. Being in a gang offers some support. It's also natural to want to be a part of something, to be a part of the group. Sam is quite lonely in school, and so the little group of lads where he lives is what he naturally gravitates to. I think that Sam gradually begins to realize by the end of the book that being accepted by this gang, and by people he's not even sure he likes that much, is not so important.

To what extent do you identify with Sam?

Well, I created him, and part of Sam's experiences are my experiences – from my past but also because I have now lived with Sam the ordeals he's gone through in the book. Maybe not quite directly, but I remember feeling some of what Sam felt in many of the scenarios. I think every man has had some similar experiences at some stage as a teenager – through the desire to be cool and accepted, to not understanding sex, to being rejected by a girl, or by a friend, or a group, to being bullied, to those exultant feelings from small victories.

Though Sam doesn't seem to be aware of it, is there a class conflict underlying the boys' behaviour towards him?

Yes, definitely. I think the other boys are aware of it, but are maybe slightly afraid of addressing it for fear of what it may mean for them. I remember how class played such a big part of my own childhood, and most of it was ridiculous, but I imagine it's still as prevalent now. When I was younger it was class, and being Catholic or Protestant – there's always something. As teens it's so important what car your parents drive, what school you go to, what clothes you're wearing – I didn't want to delve too deeply into that because it didn't interest me enough – but I can only imagine how PlayStation, iPhones and gadgets have created even more pressure on teens to conform and be considered 'cool' by their possessions and social status.

You include some poems in the novel. Have you written poetry from an early age?

I have always 'attempted' to write poetry, but whether any of it was any good is open to debate. I loved reading Keats in school, and I loved the poetry section of the Leaving Cert. My dad used to read a lot of poetry, and loved Seamus Heaney and his earthiness, and there were always poetry books and literature lying around my house. I never had an idea of style and would copy the most recent poet I had read. I then found Charles Bukowski and loved how he observed life and the people around him. Then I began writing my poetry more as observations of life. I would see people on the train, or at a bus stop or walking in front of me and I would watch them and imagine a scenario, and take in the details of their character. I originally had more poetry in *Kingdom of Scars* than there is now, but not all of it was entirely appropriate and having poetry in the middle broke up the flow of the book. I would love to write poetry good enough to be published as a poetry book but I'm not sure if I'm that skilled.

The detail and immediacy of the story make it feel so authentic that some of the episodes feel like memories. Have you ever kept a diary? Do you now?

Well, some of them are based on memories, or events that did happen to me, or happened to people around me, but they are not the same as in the book. Like when I write films I use some memories of things that have happened to me and then I change them. There is a very personal feel to this book and that would be correct because it is about the area that I grew up in and the school I went to and a lot of the characters are based on real people, but they may be two or three people compressed into one, or the events didn't quite happen how they're written, or some are entirely figments of my imagination. But what I found fascinating and enjoyable about writing this book was how the truth can change in your head. I mentioned the story of one of these events recently to a friend that I grew up with and he told me that what I remembered was completely different to what he remembered! I also didn't even realize he was there! Then it clicked with me that, on the occasions I had been creating the stories based loosely on real memories, I had then completely changed the real memory in my head to that in the book! So sometimes I'm not sure what could be real or false anymore.

I have never kept a diary because it felt like a violation of my own thoughts. I wrote down some feelings on a few occasions but then when I read back on them I was disgusted with how I had apparently felt, mainly because I had only written when I was upset not when I was content. So no, I never did, and never would. I like remembering things and forcing myself to try hard to recall the feelings, and also I don't mind if the reality was actually different. Who is to know except myself?

* * *

Topics for Book Clubs

1. Do you think the title *Kingdom of Scars* is appropriate?

2. By the end of the book, has Sam left the Kingdom of Scars behind or is he still embroiled in it?

4. Can the book be described as a 'coming of age' novel?

5. Do you think this book is unique in any way? Is it groundbreaking?

6. Did the book give you fresh insights into the world of teenage boys?

7. Do you think it provides an authentic picture of the male teenage world? Or are episodes exaggerated for dramatic effect?

8. Which, for you, was the most striking episode in the book? And for what reasons?

9. To what extent is the level of violence in the book a modern phenomenon?

10. Is Sam different from his peers? If so, what makes him different?

11. What is it about Sam that makes him a typical victim for bullies?

12. Several times Sam mentions that he would be willing to bully others or at least be a supporter of bullying if not a participant. Why is this?

13. Is there a class element involved in the victimization of Sam by the local gang?

14. The sessions with Don are obviously a lifeline for Sam. Why is that so? Discuss the relationship between Don and Sam.

15. How can Sam simultaneously accept the values of both Don and those of the local gang?

16. What impression does the book give about the educational system?

17. Apart from Sam, which is the most interesting character in the book?

18. Besides Sam, do you feel empathy with any other characters in the book? Which ones?

19. What is your opinion about the depiction of girls in the book?

20. Discuss the character of Antoinette.

21. What do you think about the book's treatment of sex?

22. What do you think of the inter-generational relationships in the book?

23. Do you think this book can appeal equally to adults and teenagers?

24. Do you feel this book is largely autobiographical?

25. What is your reaction to the poems included in the book?